THE DYNAMICS OF SPACE
Mallarmé's *Un Coup de dés jamais n'abolira le hasard*

FRENCH FORUM MONOGRAPHS

67

Editors R.C. LA CHARITÉ and V.A. LA CHARITÉ

THE DYNAMICS OF SPACE
MALLARMÉ'S *UN COUP DE DÉS JAMAIS N'ABOLIRA LE HASARD*

VIRGINIA A. LA CHARITÉ

FRENCH FORUM, PUBLISHERS
LEXINGTON, KENTUCKY

The volumes in this series are printed on acid-free, long-life paper and meet the requirements of the American National Standard for Permanence of Paper for Printed Materials
Z 39.48-1984.

Copyright © 1987 by French Forum, Publishers, Incorporated, P.O. Box 5108, Lexington, Kentucky 40505.

All rights reserved, including the right to reproduce this book, or parts thereof, in any form, except for the inclusion of brief quotations in reviews.

Library of Congress Catalog Card Number 86-82794.

ISBN 0-917058-68-2

Printed in the United States of America

For Carlos

and in memory of C.E.A., Jr.

CONTENTS

	INTRODUCTION	9
I.	THE PROBLEM OF SPACE	13
II.	THE SPACE OF THE TEXT	39
III.	CONFIGURATION OF SPACE	83
IV.	ASSEMBLY BY SPACE	107
V.	TEXT AS SPACE	145
	NOTES	177
	SELECTED BIBLIOGRAPHY	189

INTRODUCTION

Ever since Paul Valéry first saw the manuscript of Mallarmé's *Un Coup de dés*, readers of the text have been struck by the use of space, and every critic has acknowledged that space has an important role in the poem. It is space which isolates verse fragments, disperses and distorts relationships, creates groupings which attract the eye, and makes the black type dramatic, intense, and challenging. The whiteness of the page magnifies the black matter of the printed text. In his "Préface," Mallarmé exhorts a "Lecteur habile" to read the "blancs" or white spaces of the text and to pay close attention to the "espacement de la lecture" (455).[1]

Space is decidedly one of the three major components of *Un Coup de dés*, the other two being the page itself and the type or printed words. Space dominates the text and determines the validity of the black type. As the element of design, space is actually the control factor in the construct of the work, for it makes the form of the text possible and visible. Space provides the primary field for the poetic encounter and directs the reading process.

Space so determines the reading of the text that indeed *Un Coup de dés* may be read on various levels. The white blanks multiply the possibilities of interpretation, as each reader attempts to penetrate its meaning. Space is effective in that numerous critically viable responses to the reading of *Un Coup de dés* abound, yet, the diversity of these readings and their inherent contradictions and basic disagreements also suggest that space is not instructive because it heightens the impenetrability of the text through an arbitrary placement of words and groupings which disorient the reader. The range of critical interpretations of *Un Coup de dés* suggests agreement with Yves Bonnefoy when he avers that the text is not to be read or understood,[2] for all readings are negated by the denial of reader freedom to circulate within and determine the restraints and limits of the reading. The text is, consequently, not "readable" because of the loss of the reader function; the reader cannot deduce or build a new frame which will permit him the act of the discovery of meaning. Space makes too many demands at once on the reader and proposes too many ways to "read" the printed words.

By reversing reader expectations, space denies reader-author conjunction in the poem. The center is consistently and constantly dispersed and displaced by space, which does not stabilize the message. There is no address, no exchange, no entry, no exit, no fixity, no agreed upon contextuality, no model, no frame, no identifiable convention, no message. The reader is so directed by space that multiple readings and messages are possible and permissible. It is the space that gives rise to the present scope of critical readings of *Un Coup de dés*. And, indeed, each reading to date has contributed in some way to our appreciation of the text.

However, each reading concentrates on the printed words or written text, an examination of the verbal blocks, despite awareness that space is an essential element of the design and Mallarmé's own dictum to read the "blancs." Reading the space has received little attention in Mallarmé studies; in fact, space as part of the text is by and large completely ignored. As a matter of fact, space is generally mentioned only in reference to its role as a constraint of the print. While readers are aware of the importance of space and spacing in the construction of the text and in the reading process, space is not commonly viewed as one of the main components of the text. In order to refocus attention on the role of space in *Un Coup de dés*, it is necessary to establish the form, substance, and function of space in the text.

Because space directs the reading process, examination of it as a major textual component in *Un Coup de dés* calls into question Mallarmé's poetic theory and practice, as well as his actual composition of the poem: the nature of his esthetics of space; how that esthetic evolves and develops in his work; how attention to space distinguishes *Un Coup de dés* from his other writings; the nature of his use of space in both quantitative and qualitative terms; and, finally, how a reader may undertake the process of "reading" the blanks and intervals, that is, the non-printed element. By no means definitive, the aim of the present study is to expand critical appreciation for Mallarmé's poetic act of construction and assembly and how his conscious manipulation of space affects the interpretation of the text.

Mallarmé is the undisputed "Maître" of French poetry, and the considerable body of criticism devoted to close readings of his work has been enhanced by allusions and references to him in the writings of contemporary poets. It would seem that Mallarmé, especially in *Un Coup de dés*, appeals to scholars and literary writers of all persuasions, from thematic and teleological efforts, to structuralist, Marxist, semiotic, generative grammar, psychological, and deconstructionist endeavors, while among his literary heirs are such diverse figures as Paul Valéry, André Gide, Paul Claudel, Guillaume Apollinaire, André Breton, Francis Ponge, Jean-Paul Sartre, Raymond Queneau, René Char, Yves Bonnefoy, Denis Roche, Jacques Roubaud. Mallarmé's own quest for a pure poetry has given rise to a vast and divergent corpus of readings and each view is convincing on its own terms. The Mallarmé text is, indeed, plural: "le Texte . . . parlant de lui-même" (663); neither open nor closed, it receives an impression, turns it into a form, and then returns it to the pure realm of poetry, revealing a permanence beyond words, authentic silence.

Fascination with the mystery of the pure realm of authentic silence has prompted this study of space, but then, as Mallarmé knew, "une approche contient un hommage" (406). The field of Mallarmé readers and admirers offers many "variations" and "divagations," but, regardless of approach adopted, all seem to agree that it is the privileged space of the page of *Un Coup de dés* which allows Mallarmé to transform the real by overcoming the material limits of print and communicate the absolute, poetic essence. Hence, the "fil conducteur" is a dynamics of space, a veritable esthetic science for producing change and variation: the poem of poetry.

Chapter I

THE PROBLEM OF SPACE

The very concept of *space* is a problem, for it is a polyvalent term which includes the expanse of the universe, a lapse of time, an area set aside for a specific reason, an unobstructed area, an empty place, room, blank interval to separate characters and words. Space is the abstract which cannot be explained, the pure which cannot be experienced, the authentic which cannot be derived: it is formless, not enclosed, colorless, being the spectrum which makes color possible, sterile, unlimited, original and complete within itself. Space is asymmetrical, having no form, a-logical, having no explanation, and a-temporal, having no beginning or end. Moreover, space is visual, never oral; it is silent in the sense that it is non-verbal and self-sufficient. Space has no direction; it is anti-linear and open or free. Space is not background, but the primary field against which form, shape, color, dimensions gain delineation and definition. Space is undeniable, irrefutable, and all-inclusive.

Mallarmé's writings reveal that he is fully cognizant of the polyvalence of space. He uses a carefully selected vocabulary to evoke it, struggles thematically with and against it, repeatedly refers to it in his theoretical and critical writings, challenges it in his verse and prose poems. His correspondence reveals a preoccupation with space, especially his letters to printers, in which he debates word placement and textual appearance. The word as it actually appears in the space of the page in its final form marks all of his writing. His demonstrated interest in theater and painting, as well as his studies of poster art and newspapers, testify to a lifelong preoccupation with space: arrangement, grouping, assembly; how to use space nearly obsesses him.

Space is viewed early by Mallarmé as the white page, the poet's canvas on which a textual work takes form. A word is an object which can be arranged and rearranged; its meaning often depends on its setting and its grouping or association with other words/objects; topography can alter definition and customary usage. The paginal appearance of the written word determines the reading of the text and its credibility. The white page is the basic circumstance of the poem. The moment a word or line is placed on that page, the page is transformed into a place of confrontation; moreover, the page fixes the word and compromises the autonomy of the word. The word, especially when arranged with other words into a line, imposes a given sense of order to both the row of words (line) and the page on which it appears. The line structures the space of the page, just as the placement or spacing of the line on the page structures the page. The white space gives shape and receives form. The page is indeed a spectacle, with a defined size and shape, which resists change and mobility. Once written upon the page, the line constricts the page by displacing part of its space.

The black ink imposes limits upon the white space or page and in turn is fixed by it. The potential of the original white space is modified; the space takes shape by its contrast with the black row of words, which appears linear, straight, united by a singleness of purpose. The space is now seen as the factor which imposes the ordering; the unprinted is an element of the printed and has power to determine the point of convergence. Adding a second line reinforces the power of the white page to direct convergence, as well as divergence, and to dictate relationships, associations, meaning. The idea or meaning emerges from the space of the white page by a marking off of the limitations; a figure of relations (words arranged into lines) is now a block of meaning and may be decoded. As each character of black ink combines into a word and the words in turn combine into a line of words, a message appears in the medium that the poet must use: ink: "l'homme poursuit noir sur blanc" (370).

Ink or print immobilizes the message, fixes the communication, and changes the circumstance of the page. The conjunction of the print on the page makes the white space linear and intensifies its whiteness; the immediate result is a plane surface, a two-dimensional effect by which the black print attracts attention by its very contrast with the white page. The text base is set lexically, semantically, and syntactically by its placement on the page.

But Mallarmé's concept of poetry is in direct opposition to the medium of its expression. For Mallarmé, the poet has the power to create with words, to go beyond the object by making an absolute out of language. The object is a word which dissolves its material reference points and reveals a permanence beyond words, an authentic silence which communicates "la certitude parfaite" (446). The pure realm of poetry gives expression to "les gestes de l'Idée" (854), for the text is a creative structure. The very act of writing on the page ordains the credibility of the text.

The problem then is that of space. How to overcome the confines of the printed page? The unit of the printed page is a utilitarian form which makes the word visible through a given assembly of words into lines and lines into stanzas or paragraphs. Rules dictate how the parts (words, lines, paragraphs) fit together and deny authorial freedom. Certain two-dimensional limits are imposed on the text by the medium of its communication. The formal order of the medium directs the reader: sequential pagination, a certain balance of type and space. Yet, paradoxically, the form of the text is possible only through its relationship to space. To reassert the original freedom of the language as an initiating experience, Mallarmé turns his attention to an art of space and the role of the reader. The poem cannot move from appearance as a concrete element to an absolute essence unless the mobility of the text ("mobiles variations de l'Idée que l'écrit revendique de fixer," 648) is captured in the medium itself.

Mallarmé's first works, *Entre quatre murs* and *Poëmes d'enfance et de jeunesse*, are marked by standard traditional verse forms and rime schemas. While he experiments with the pliancy of language, his early poems are marked by spatial localization.

Animation of words on the page ("des places variables," 455) evolves as a major evolutionary theme and technique in his work; he develops chronologically from the fixity of the texts in *Entre quatre murs* to a veritable mobilization of the writing-reading process in *Un Coup de dés*.

The first step towards ceding the initiative to the words is the reliance on a vocabulary of motion, as though the word choices themselves can unblock the immobility of the writing. The second step is an investigation into the punctuation as a means to vibrate the text. The dash, ellipses, parentheses, exclamation point (described as a "plumet," 168) attest to Mallarmé's interest in the visual power of the word in its printed form on the page. Ultimately, he finds that punctuation is artificial (407), a hindrance to textual mobility, a discovery which leads him in studied attempts to eliminate the artifice which he finds that punctuation imposes. A third undertaking involves experiments with writing on objects other than a sheet of paper, a textual gamesmanship which Mallarmé displays through the 471 poems of *Vers de circonstance*. His preferred substitute for the white page is the fan, and he wrote 21 "fan" poems.

A fan is basically a segment of a circle which is constructed with thin rods which move on a pivot; made out of silk, feathers, paper, it opens and closes, mystifies and reveals, in a simulation of movement which is neither dynamic nor static, but vibrant. Fans commonly produce air currents and promote a cooling, refreshing sensation. But fans are not limited to their use by people; they are also connected to leaves, bird wings, bird tails, cards, book pages, garden trellises, marine construction, painting. Structured on the principle of folding and unfolding, a fan always recovers its size and shape regardless of its effects and affects of deformation. Never rigid, a fan maintains a measure of control which permits resistance to change and mobility, and its elasticity is inherent to its fundamental intactness. While a fan may suggest formation through color, shape, or movement, it never abandons its original source of form or balance. Yet, a fan is not mobile in that it can change its condition; rather, a fan transforms the perspective and angles of the condition.[1]

The fan is not only linked with a given vocabulary cluster in

Mallarmé's work (wing, pen, feather, foam, fold); it is also one of his preferred intertextual structures. The fan as form permits words and phrases to move literally on the page, free from the limitations of time and space, free from material referentials. Portions of a text appear and disappear as the reader folds and unfolds the words and lines. The Mallarmé fan structure offers a text of verbal displacement and syntactical dislocation, as his later texts in *Poésies* reflect the increasing liberation of the written word from its positioning on the page.

Adoption of a basic vocabulary of motion, attention to the artifices of punctuation, and experimentation with the fan structure are by no means the only techniques which Mallarmé uses and develops in order to overcome the fixity of print and create an esthetic of space, but they do seem to be the main techniques which preoccupy both his prose commentaries on poetry and his poems. For example, in the rather early text, "Brise marine," he uses the folding-unfolding fan technique to transpose the quayside scene into an exotic dream. The final lines of the text contain the evocation of the voyage and the longing of the poet for adventure: ". . . sans mâts, sans mâts, ni fertiles ilôts . . . / Mais, ô mon cœur, entends le chant des matelots!" (38). By folding the words *mâts* and *ilôts* into *matelots*, Mallarmé creates a mobile image of the sailors and reduces the entire text to an evocation of departure.

Linguistic constriction and expansion is, in fact, present in all of Mallarmé's poetry and the examples in *Poésies* are numerous: "de la cendre/descendre" (54), "un frisson/unisson" (49), "la flamme/l'âme" (52-53), "le plumage est pris/mépris" (68), "le vide nénie/dénie" (76), "vole-t-il/vil" (73). At times, Mallarmé reverses the process and unfolds, expands a given word or phrase ("las/les lilas," 34), while on other occasions he merely alters one letter or syllable ("glacier/l'acier," 43; "lune/l'une," 42). His "Prose (pour des Esseintes)" (55-57) is rich in examples of a linguistic fan structure: "de visions/dévisions," "se para/sépara," "désir Idées/iridées," "devoir/de voir," "par chemins/parchemins," "sépulcre ne rit/Pulchérie." But then, hyperbole is a figure of rhetoric which either greatly augments or diminishes the expression; it is the extravagant exaggeration of something as much greater or considerably less. In Mallarmé's universe, hyperbole enables the poet to avoid narrative in an acceleration and retardation of movement.

The structure of the fan is not limited to linguistic contraction and expansion, however, for it also accounts for a predominant interplay of light and dark in Mallarmé's work. The use of shadows cast by the folds of things, the opening and closing of a book, a fan, a spectacle of any sort, what Mallarmé describes as suspense in the "Scolies" to *Igitur* (450), is basic to his art of space. "L'Après-midi d'un faune" is particularly rich in its reliance upon recreative fading light, as the nymphs are metamorphosized at the end into a shadow which perpetuates the fawn's dream of them (53). The scintillations of the constellation in the mirror at the end of "Ses purs ongles très haut dédiant leur onyx" (68-69) are glimpsed through the shadows cast by the lampbearer at midnight; the effect of shimmering (motion) in a fixed mode (stasis) is dependent upon a simultaneous opening and closing of the decor. The in-out and out-in juxtaposition of the mirror and the constellation is reworked into an ascending-descending motif in Mallarmé's 1891 fan poem to his wife, a text in which the setting ("logis") reflects "un battement aux cieux" (57-58).

The structuration which Mallarmé uses in his fan texts characterizes "A la nue accablante tu," which is considered one of his most hermetic and purest poems before *Un Coup de dés*. As a text of verbal displacement, "A la nue accablante tu" (76) destroys the word as concept and offers the word as object and the text as process.[2] The text is dispersed among the rods of the fan, but a fan which has been shattered; only the parentheses remain as a means to mobilize the occasion. As a fan is a curved structure which negates the dimension of linearity, parentheses serve the same function in punctuation. The words and line fold and unfold, appear and disappear. Although it is a text in which the referentials may be recovered (the floating debris of a shipwreck or Berthe Morisot's fanciful rendering of it as a bath),[3] it is the unstated which draws the reader's attention; the details of the expressed create a text of release which engenders reader desire to write on the missing rods, to fill in the space. The fan structure results in the creation of the fragment, what Mallarmé describes in a fan poem as the disengagement—liberation—of a future verse: "Le futur vers se dégage" (57)—the verse which the reader will "write" in response. The reader is supposed to be mystified in order to read the traces of the black ink in space and construct his own poem.

Mallarmé's poetry reveals a preoccupation with a stable but mobile structure, an elasticity, and this same quality characterizes his short story *Igitur*, as well as his theatrically-oriented works. His notations and articles in *Crayonné au théâtre* and *Variations sur un sujet* continually return to the problem of the elastic, as he moves in his formal poetry from fixity to displacement. In addition, in his correspondence and prose commentaries on the essence of poetry, there is a chronologically developing concern for a vocabulary and form which capture the substantive nature of a fan. In fact, one may accurately read his theoretical writings as descriptions of fans, especially his discussions of ballet and music, which he praises for their fluid, non-linear qualities which communicate an order in space despite the motion inherent to their representation. In a poem on Edouard Manet's painting of Polichinelle (161), Mallarmé views the dance in a simultaneous rise and fall motif, while his poem on Léopold Dauphin's music (161) is built around the image of a fountain. Focus on the rhythmic movements (pauses and breaks) comes about through the manipulation of space and enables the reader to grasp the relationships between things, just as the curve of a fan suggests motion and indicates the gesture of movement.

Generation without a translative intermediary is the construct of the hyperbolic fan: "Je dis: une fleur!" (368). It is little wonder, then, that in *La Dernière Mode* Mallarmé chooses as one of his pseudonyms Ixion, the tortured ancestor of the centaurs, who was condemned to a flaming wheel in the air in Hades; only when Orpheus visited was the wheel still. Like a turning sun, Mallarmé the poet seeks a textual structure which retains the mystery of its motion.

Preoccupation with elasticity is further accompanied by an investigation into the relationship between language and reality.

Mallarmé's conquest of the art of suggestion and mastery of the ambiguous are due in part to his experiments with the fan structure and in part to his attention to the reader as spectator. In *Vers de circonstance*, visual affectation, wordplay, and punning represent a verbal game in which words are the pieces to be placed in play upon the board of written expression by a masterful gamester, the poet.[4] The texts must be read with the eye in order to be understood; rime schema depend on divided syllables ("l'un," "becque-/té," 83), syntactical distortions, purposeful orthographic changes, dislocated end rimes, double entendres. Objectively, detachedly, and deliberately, Mallarmé scrutinizes words as objects; he continually moves them around to form new patterns with which to dazzle the spectator.

Throughout the brief poems of *Vers de circonstance*, which are pieces of whimsy and lightheartedness, Mallarmé is conscious of an active and educated audience. For example, "cueille" and "Eye" do not rime until the reader translates the English *eye* into the French *œil* (156). There is no logical reason to spell *gueritte* with a double t, but visually such an orthography makes a better rime with the double t in a soldier's family name, Margueritte (163). The texts must be seen to be grasped because they depend primarily on the tactile sense: "dans telle/dentelle" (177), "Cold/Hérolde" (108), "m'accommode/comme ode" (171), "rêver/ever" (170), "Commentaire/comme en terre" (179), "qu'on fit/confit" (123).

Words are objects and language is a game to be played and enjoyed. Mallarmé's interest in language manipulation is borne out by his textbooks and translations, as well as by his early poems. *Entre quatre murs*, for example, shows a Mallarmé who experiments with type size; the form of a word has a dramatic effect on the reader. In "L'Après-midi d'un faune," "Hérodiade," and *Igitur*, he pays strict attention to the setting, the space as place, and offers the reader a scenic, tactile atmosphere.

In addition to a fascination with the appearance of the written word and its possible transformations, Mallarmé was attracted to painting. His friendships with Manet, Morisot, Whistler, Chavannes,[5] Renoir, Gauguin, and others have been well-documented. His work published in his lifetime was illustrated by

Manet, Laurent, Renoir, and Regnault, and the *Chansons bas* were originally written as the legends for sketches by Jean-François Raffaëlli under the title *Les Types de Paris*. In preparation at one time was *Le Tiroir de laque* which was to have been quite ornate in appearance and accompanied by John Lewis Brown's illustrations and water colors by Morisot, Renoir, Degas, and perhaps Monet. Mallarmé even did some sketching, as his drawings of peacocks on notes to Méry Laurent show; many of his fan poems are colorful juxtapositions of the written word and the decorated object, just as his Easter egg poems are written in gold ink on red eggs.[6] The very title of *Quelques Médaillons et portraits en pied* is taken from the world of plastic art and offers verbal portraits of writers and painters alike. Mallarmé was also intensely preoccupied with "éditions de luxe," so much so that in Huysmans's *A rebours* des Esseintes is drawn to Mallarmé's poetry first by the luxuriousness of the cover and second by the aura of fantasy ("le suc concret") of the texts.[7]

The painters whom Mallarmé admired most among his contemporaries were the "Impressionists."[8] In one very real sense of the word, an Impressionist is to painting what a Symbolist is to literature. The Impressionist's work is the product of a sacrifice of detail which captures the imagination of its viewer. The lack of emotional commitment and diminished concern with the subject lead to a shifting of the viewer's optic. Space is foreshortened to convey a different sense of order, but an order nonetheless; it is a diaphanous "observational" art which lacks precise definition, hence an art of suggestion. Manet, for example, is hailed by Mallarmé for his valuation of intervals ("plein air"). Even in his reading, Mallarmé reserves praise for those who place value on space; the Goncourt Brothers are noted for their interest in Japanese art, which is based on diagonal composition and creates an artificial space, while Hugo's attitude toward poetry is marked by its reliance on verse for its identity as literary form.[9] Hence, Hugo's poems are one-dimensional (linear in construct and personal in optic); Japanese art and Impressionist painters, especially Manet, are two-dimensional and rely on the viewer's response for their interpretation. Mallarmé's admiration for Berthe Morisot, Manet's sister-in-law, is based on his observance of mobility and spatial illusion in her work: "Poétiser, par art plastique" (536). Gradually evolving an esthetic of space, Mallarmé recognizes Richard Wagner for his "figuration plastique" (541), an approach to opera which synthesizes the theater arts: poetry, music, acting, scenery, and drama. Attempting to make the written text and musical score inseparable, Wagner omits superfluous elements, ends the distinction between a formal recitative and the aria, and attempts to create a work which reflects a continuous flow of the theme and its leitmotifs. Wagner gives to music the new dimension of uninterrupted musical space, what Mallarmé describes as the "principe littéraire même . . . de tous les arts" (542). For Mallarmé, music is a plastic art, which may well account for the numerous musical metaphors which occur throughout his work, especially in his theoretical writings.

By his interest in combining the plastic and the written, Mallarmé demonstrates that he is not seeking an absolute realm beyond man's reach, but one which is within the very grasp of man. Hence, picture words abound in the texts of *Poésies*: *écume, nuage, plume, astre, soleil, fleur, faune, cygne, joyau, pli, aile*. His word choices are drawn heavily from the classical animal, vegetable, and mineral kingdoms; ephemeral terms are rare, for even *ciel* is always used in conjunction with *soleil*, *nuage, étoile*, etc. Every part of the human body is evoked directly, and the psyche figures equally, as emotional terms occur in amazing frequency: *heureux, cruel, triste, las, sourire*. His texts are also rather noisy poems (*cloche, angélus, sonneur, glas, fanfare, voix, rire, chant, appel, cri, tonnerre*), and musical instruments are used throughout his work (*flûte, cymbale, viole, clavecin*). There are very few silences in a Mallarmé poem. It is as though the reader must first be subjected to a sensory display.

Further evidence of Mallarmé's emphasis on the visual in his work is found in his constant return to and reliance upon the familiar world of myth: "Mythe, l'éternel: la communion par le livre. A chacun part totale" (656). Myth is man's attempt to personify, make concrete or plasticize those things which otherwise he does not understand. Roland Barthes could easily have been writing about Mallarmé when he said: "Ce que le monde fournit au mythe, c'est un réel historique . . . et ce que le mythe restitue c'est une image *naturelle* de ce réel."[10] Mallarmé's *Les Dieux antiques* presents myth in terms of Barthes's definition: deformation of the meaning, but not destruction and disappearance of meaning.

Myth occurs and recurs frequently in Mallarmé's work. The nymphs and fawn of "L'Après-midi d'un faune" surface first in "Pan" in *Entre quatre murs*; Venus is another mythical figure whose manifestations continue from this earliest work to his last one. Other mythological references include Syrinx, Phoenix, Chimera, Paphos, Styx, Prometheus, Hebe; there are allusions to biblical legends (angels, demons, Lucifer, Idumea), historical tales (Anastasius, Cecilia), literary creations (Hamlet); fairies, sirens, and heroes populate all decades of his writing. The constant reference to constellations is basically mythological: Big Dipper, Little Dipper, Berenice's Hair, Swan, Clock, Unicorn, Peacock, Phoenix. Above all, constellations are what the viewer groups together in celestial space. The spectator finds that stars form figures in a silent universe in much the same way that the reader of the fan poem folds and unfolds the meaning of the text: the pattern of shape does not change, but the position of viewing the object—the optic—does change. The effect becomes an affect, as things (stars, words) are mutated into emblems (constellations, poems), reading activities.

Just as star clusters are seen or read—visually interpreted—as celestial scenes, so many of Mallarmé's poems have a pictorial quality. For example, the last seven lines of "Las de l'amer repos" actually paint a landscape on a cup: the moon sinking into the waters of a lake; "Brise marine" paints a quayside scene; "Sainte" draws its inspiration from a stained-glass window; "Quand l'ombre menaça" is dependent upon the view of the constellation in the black night; "Le Vierge, le vivace et le bel aujourd'hui" is what Carol Clark describes as an emblem poem;[11] "Victorieusement fui le suicide beau" is based on a sunset; "Surgi de la croupe" describes a vase; "Une dentelle s'abolit" refers to a piece of lace; "Toute l'âme résumée" is vividly related to the smoking of a cigar, and "Salut" is a toast, inspired by the bubbles in a glass of champagne, a description found earlier in the same context in *Entre quatre murs*.

The plastic points of departure in the Mallarmé poem multiply the possibilities of their interpretation. Robert Cohn, for example, poses five different logical, concrete referentials for "dentelle" (*Poems of Mallarmé* 207-08), while in his study of "Don du poème" Michael Riffaterre asserts that Mallarmé's poetry depends on the reader's determination and ability to decipher the verbal referentials.[12] His poems are replete with unembellished concrete referentials which have a priori significance. Each object in its unadorned state of appearance invites the viewer to reestablish the adornment which identifies it. Hence, Mallarmé reworks the same objects or the same words over and over again in his texts.[13] By moving objects and words around, by placing them in different, unfamiliar settings, he alters their designated or utilitarian function. The word ceases to be a sign of cognition, derivation, or reproduction, something which imitates appearance and reflects experience; on the contrary, the word becomes the object, essential matter; it initiates experience and expresses essence. Mallarmé's demonstrated plastic sense of reality demands reader response: "Représentation = Interprétation" (L178A).[14] It is not rupture, pause, and break which give visual shape to the words on the page, but the arrangement of those words. The object is always there, as word, in the same way that the Impressionist "œil véridique" (53) focuses on filtered coloration rather than motif.

The use of objects asserts the basic dimensions of reality, time and space, and confers upon the Mallarmé text a sense of spectacle in which the word is supreme, free to determine its own characteristics, its own phenomenological details. Mallarmé's picture words create an effect of actuality, for they are trustworthy terms in accordance with the facts of existence, known through the senses (experience) and through the intelligence (idea). They conjure up visual images in space. A typical Mallarmé picture word is *fleur*. *Fleur* is genuine, having a substantial objective existence; it is a phenomenon which relates man directly to his world. In one sense, *fleur* always suggests a plant or part of a plant; its very tactility betrays its sensory power and leads intellectually to an unending range of associations. *Fleur* is a known figure in the mind of the poet and a figure chosen by the reader by force of its reality and his experience. Consequently, *fleur* evokes first a sensation and second a meaning, if not variations of meaning which are dependent upon the viewer's optic and point of view. It is, then, a dynamic term, which cannot be isolated from either writer or reader sensitivity and experience. Nevertheless, *fleur* is not an absolute which is non-derivative although it is free from the prosaic ordinary limits of experience. It is more real than the real because of its demands upon the reader's capacity to feel and therefore to respond to its actuality. *Fleur* is a maximum psychological term, a figure which the reader particularizes. The power of the word depends on its encounter with the reader, and the medium of expression is one of association which takes place in the poet-reader encounter in the space of the text.[15] The circumstances of the text are objectively identifiable and the referentials have subjective psychological values, captured in the ingenious rime play of "Salut" between "tantage" and "engage" (27).

Hence, Mallarmé uses a plastic art frame to express his method of writing a poem: "Peindre non la chose mais l'effet qu'elle produit" (1440). He purposefully eliminates certain details, but he never denies the actuality of the object. The text gains its authenticity from its emotivity or effectiveness. It does not matter which flower the poet evokes and the reader sees, but it will be some form of flower; it does not matter which constellation is glimpsed, but a constellation will be conjured up if only in the figure of the poet's words. What concerns Mallarmé is encounter: encounter on the page between the poet and his words, their shared spectacle, and, consequently, reader reaction to that spectacle. When Mallarmé makes an authoritative decision to eliminate a given detail or to detach one part from its whole as in "Une dentelle s'abolit," he is communicating through textual structure an order in life and celebrating poetry as the creative act. As the flower or fan or volume of poems opens and closes, actively bringing about an equilibrium which is at once free from exactitude but bound to its basic notion as object, the text has indeed a corpus and a meaning. And the text is "mobile mais cependant stable" (1050). The reader will always "read" some kind of flower in electing his figure of interpretation; even if the reader elects to read "a woman" in place of a "flower," his choice remains dependent upon the picture word/object of the poet's code of communication, *fleur*; the poet's code in this instance would prevent a reading of *fleur* as an oak tree or a man. The "nénuphar," for example, may be "read" as a water lily, as a reflection of a white dress in the water, or as the unknown woman of the text; it is what the reader feels it to be and decides that it is in its relation to other word-objects in the text. The reader as spectator acts on the object, "nénuphar," with the immunity of his personal sphere and sends back a figuration which is formed first by his intuition, his psychological mode, in a personal attempt to repeat the creative act.[16] The event of the text takes place in the poet-reader encounter on the page.

As the act of writing assembles the words and lines, physically organizing them in an act of demarcation which fixes appearance and order, the act of reading becomes a mobile spatial act in which the eye and mind move; the reader reads down and across in space and forward in time, as he determines the restraints and the figure of relations.[17] The act of writing is a scriptural and verbal mode of presentation, retraced by the reader; the reader performs the writing act by "acting out" the words and lines; hence, for Mallarmé, both writing and reading occupy space: "l'artiste est né pour en sortir, et choisir, et grouper" (573), and the reader "pour signification" (380). The reader "proves" the text, authenticates it by his act of reading ("prouver en lisant," L189A). Language is then an encounter between the poet and the reader; the arrangement confirms the fiction. Mallarmé makes language the impeccable source (or hyperbolic witness) of a generative grammatology in which the point of departure (text base) is "la lettre" and the point of arrival ("le signifiant") is the work through the process of the "fiction" ("le signifié"). The locutionary intent of the argument is the idea of differentiation, "expansion totale de la lettre" (380). The writing process is expansion and the reading process is correspondence.[18]

Hence, how the reader's mind operates is of vital concern to Mallarmé, for the making of the argument in terms of the act of writing determines the credibility of the text. The writing confirms the fiction and the reading affirms the real; the language makes it so by its very occupation of space on the page. Accordingly, Mallarmé concentrates on the word as it actually appears to the reader on the page in its final fixed form.

His earliest texts in *Entre quatre murs* reveal his first experiments with the visual effect possible by the opposition of upper and lower case letters, as well as the mixing of type faces. Throughout *Poésies*, he pays careful attention to word placement (*"Je suis hanté.* L'Azur! L'Azur! L'Azur! L'Azur!" 38) and to spacing (how to use it and how to overcome it is exemplified in the ingenious end rime plays of "L'Après-midi d'un faune"), as he moves towards an increasing emphasis on the role of syntax to confirm the fiction in "A la nue accablante tu." His prose commentaries are heavily marked by musings on writing and reading as spatial form: punctuation (374-75), words as stratification (901), words as pivots (1047), the artifice of typography (408), italics (1400), the limits of orthography (902), how writing fixes thought on the page (313, 573), the role of the reader (262, 363, 373, 382), the reading process (374). Spacing between paragraphs is studied as a creative separation, while rhetoric in terms of discourse, rime, and hyperbata or word order nearly becomes an obsession.

Fascination with the possibilities of language in all forms of expression is evidenced in his verse, prose poems, "vers de circonstance," translations, philological studies, and Tuesday evening gatherings. It is language which attracts him to the allied arts, theater, painting, and music in particular, for they share the problem of communication through a spatial structure. The canvas is to the painter and the stage is to the dramatist what the tone scale is to the musician and the blank page is to the writer: a problem of arrangement, of grouping, of assembly, what Mallarmé calls "Science" (573). For the poet, each "pendentif" (573) must be placed just so in order to create a new alliance (306), a "convergence de fragments" (329) which expands the writing and corresponds to the reading. The "fragment ordinaire" (368) is to be isolated so as to suggest an order which is free from the limits of experience: "Je dis: une fleur!" (368); "La Pénultième est morte" (272). Isolation and liberation of the fragment are what Mallarmé calls purity ("la notion pure," 368).

Purity depends on the effect, as creation imposes order. If there is no possibility of changing the effect, then the text succeeds (the famous "ptyx" of "Ses purs ongles très haut dédiant leur onyx"). The language initiates experience in a liberating act of discovery, as the *bloc* or original arrangement of fragments forces the reader to read in metaphors, as in "Le Nénuphar blanc." But purity of language is limited by the confines of the printed page, for the reader is attuned to a formal order: sequential pagination, top to bottom, left to right, rules of punctuation, a certain balance of type, space, and paper which direct the reader and convey a message. The page makes the word visible ("Crise de vers," 360-68).

Ironically, however, the poet's work is subject to the work of someone else before it is placed in the reader's hands—the composer or typesetter, and, in turn, his work is determined by someone else (the type face manufacturer, the paper manufacturer, etc.). Depersonalization is a condition of the printing process, which denies authorial freedom and independence and imposes on the author certain two-dimensional limits and certain rules for the construct of the text—rules which dictate how the parts (words, lines, paragraphs/stanzas) will fit together, page size, type face, margins. Paradoxically, the process of the printing transformation makes possible the form of the text through its relationship to space, an element of design. Thus, the distance between the poet's actually written work and its emergence into print enhances form by bringing attention to the element of the unprinted and creates an art of space which multiplies the possible combinations of the printed language in the transition from written word to readable format. The address in final form is solely to the reader. Hence, the arts of typography and topography are so concerned with directing the reading process that they can change the original expansion-correspondence processes generated by the poet's "lettre."

Mallarmé is considered the first to recognize the dangers of textual alteration endemic to the printing process, but, at the same time he is acknowledged as the first to realize the poetic possibilities of this process and incorporate it into his poetics. According to Jacques Damase, Mallarmé was "le premier boulet de canon qui réveilla l'esprit du livre moderne" and launched "un certain graphisme" in poetry,[19] while Claude Minère is convinced that *Un Coup de dés* is "une histoire *d'imprimerie.*"[20] In his study of printing and close examination of the poster art of his time, Mallarmé discovered the conjunction between the inner space of the writing and the outer space of the reading in typographical variations which generate their own rhythm and essence. Mallarmé's written record is an "instrument spirituel" because the printed page is symbolic of speech, language, which is, for him, "l'objet de L'Esprit" (840). It is "architectural et prémédité" (663), planned to its smallest detail and executed in the most controlled and scientific manner so that the fiction is communicated by the printed word (656).

An examination of the unedited fragments of "Hérodiade" and *Le Livre* shows that Mallarmé was concerned with printing and publication problems. Nearly every "feuille" is replete with possible reading directions, mathematical solutions to *em* and *en* spacings, signature sheet variations (sections of four versus eight versus 16 pages), verso-recto considerations, and the whole range of problems which are part and parcel of the printing trade and business. Other than a few drafts of letters and articles, Mallarmé's unedited material reveals that he is not as concerned with esthetic problems in these "feuilles," as with technical problems of his technique in order to demonstrate language not as "verbe" (act) but as the development of the "verbe" (process or activity) (853-54).

In a very real sense, Mallarmé is a metaphorical thinker on poiesis, which includes the arts of topography and typography. Throughout, he freely uses the terms *œuvre* and *livre*, and he does not restrict these terms to poetry, much less to his own writing (318, 662). In "Autobiographie" (661-65) and "Quant au Livre" (369-87), he uses both terms as metaphors for the literary process, a process which includes the creation of a specific artistic piece from its basic trace of delineation across the white sheet of paper to its final emergence in the fixity of ultimate appearance, the printed form.[21] The World-as-Written-Book image characterizes all of his work: "le monde est fait pour aboutir à un beau livre" (872).

The challenge which Mallarmé took up and indeed his legacy to all those who would write after him was to overcome the limits of the printed text. The problem is one of space: how to transpose the language of a text from confirmation in a formal sense to a rhetorically sensitive level of meaning and finally to actual essence. His experiment of *Un Coup de dés* is a poetic investigation into a poiesis which is literally and figuratively the production of things with the poet as both creator and manufacturer. The very "Préface" emphasizes his interest in the printed form of the text, which he openly admits is a "tentative" which is going against standard form and appearance. Moreover, it is this new form "pour ouvrir les yeux" which he says enables him to initiate a new genre which joins "le vers libre et le poème en prose." The technical design as part of the construct of the text makes it possible esthetically to present the work "à l'état élémentaire." His printed fragments which crisscross the white pages of the work communicate an order in which the co-references of the writing-reading process are engendered by the inclusion of an art of space and spacing in the expansion-correspondence process: "un espacement de la lecture," which calls for a "Lecteur habile . . . ingénu." In one of the fragments of *Le Livre*, he reemphasizes his need for an active reader: "Toute la modernité est fournie par la lecture" (L148A). And, indeed, Mallarmé asked Valéry if the physical layout of the text might be considered "un acte de démence" (1582).

The light-hearted tone of "acte de démence" is typical of a rarely discussed aspect of Mallarmé's attitude and esthetics. He had a sense of humor, had a reputation among the "Mardistes" as an entertainer, enjoyed playing at theatrical undertakings, and understood textual gamesmanship. His Easter-egg poems and *Vers de circonstance* show a certain humoristic, ironic, satirical, even scatological bent, a penchant which surfaces as early as his youthful texts in *Entre quatre murs*.[22] Linguistic and visual tricks fascinate him; his witty fashion journal, *La Dernière Mode*, contains clever and amusing descriptions of Parisian cultural life. Even his philological work, *Les Mots anglais*, is written in a chatty tone, which makes jokes out of linguistic inconsistencies. Verses which mock his own "L'Après-midi d'un faune" as well as those written for a friend who disliked rimes in -or (a criticism of his own highly hermetic "Ses purs ongles très haut dédiant leur onyx") are not far afield from the text which Mallarmé chose as the lead poem for his volume, *Poésies*: "Salut," inspired by the bubbles in a glass of champagne.

Ursula Franklin describes Mallarmé as a "Montreur," a showman,[23] and no reader denies the recurrence of terms of play in his work, especially the use of the word *jeu*. Play is viewpoint or attitude, as well as poetic vision and style. The nature of game and player requires detachment, objectivity, intellectualism, and imagination. In addition, gamesmanship requires the transformation of familiar everyday objects and/or experiences. The showman is not one who turns away from actuality, but rather one who knows how to dazzle and baffle his spectator. Hence, the Mallarmé text demands visual skill on the part of the poet and on the part of the reader; words are the pieces placed in play upon the board of written expression by the poet.

Reader awareness is a primary factor in the Mallarmé esthetic universe. He himself reacts as reader or viewer-spectator to other poets, artists, theater events, the 1871 and 1872 International Expositions in London, as evidenced by his translations, articles, and correspondence. Mallarmé is consistently aware of an audience: his Tuesday evening gatherings, summer theatricals at Valvins, his desire to become the "Prince des poètes," his lectures, his seeking reactions from Mendès, Valéry, Gide, and others to drafts of his work. The construct of the Mallarmé text is an invitation to the reader to participate actively in the interpretation (reading-playing) of the written representation. Reader reconstruction concerns him as much as poetic construction. Hence, he does indeed write in parentheses;[24] deleting his own personality, he increases the possibilities of reader response. He reworks the same words, same objects, over and over in his work. And his work evolves chronologically from straightforward message texts to highly hermetic, elliptical poems, but the vocabulary and general referentials remain constant, almost standard. Mallarmé draws consistently on the familiar world of people, places, and things, myth and legend; ephemeral, erudite, and esoteric terms are rare. Mallarmé favors simple everyday things. "Le Tombeau d'Edgar Poe" actually describes the granite frieze which decorates Poe's tomb, and "Prose (pour des Esseintes)" has two historical events at its base: Huysmans's *A rebours* and the Byzantine rulers. However, it is not so much the discovery and identification of the departure points for these poems which determine their reading as it is Mallarmé's treatment of them, his poetic "jeu."

By taking a known object or theme and moving it to a different, unfamiliar setting, Mallarmé "evacuates the real" (Barthes, *Mythologies* 251), transposes effect into affect, and permits each object to appear before the reader in an unadorned state. Mallarmé does not abolish matter from his work. Rather, he eliminates the particular modification which identifies his object, but the object itself is always there: "Il doit y avoir toujours énigme en poésie, et c'est le but de la littérature . . . d'évoquer les objets" (869). Granted, this is the art of suggestion, but it is also gamesmanship, which requires a skillful and intuitive reader. The Mallarmé verse and prose poem are verbal challenges, which invite the reader to play a literary game of interpretation. As Barthes says: "Le vrai jeu n'est pas de masquer le sujet mais de masquer le jeu lui-même."[25]

Poetic gamesmanship is an important part of Mallarmé's esthetic of space, for it is in space that he moves the words/pieces and it is in space that meaning occurs. The reader must determine or "plasticize" the referentials in order to restore their identity and so establish their significance. In the prose text, "Le Démon de l'analogie," Mallarmé's spatial sense of gamesmanship is evident in at least two ways. First, he deforms the meaning of his own title by positing what is at first glance a nonsense phrase, "La Pénultième est morte." Repeating it over and over, each time changing the emphasis, the poet savors the non-derivative nature of the sentence. It has no model, no Platonic noumen which fixes its meaning, gives it physical stability, determines its contours and limits, its shape. Hence, analogy is not possible, there is no operating principle of solidarity, the words are not fixed points which hold the phrase together in a logical relationship. In fact, the response value is seemingly denied, for debate is closed on lexical grounds in a betrayal by the language and a distortion of the experience. "La Pénultième est morte" exists simply because the writer speaks; the language does not order contact or accord; rather, it denies authorial responsibility and therefore reader determination. Still, the statement is one in which the words have power; they may be free from logic and rational cause and effect, but they nonetheless perform if only in their interrogation into form. Once, the poet (and his reader) concur that the phrase is performative in that it evokes a meaning (but not necessarily *the* meaning), then there is contact and therefore the possibility of identification. Meaning is deformed to be reformed; it is not destroyed: "la réminiscence de l'objet nommé baigne dans une neuve atmosphère" (368).[26]

Having established the non-rationality of meaningfulness based on analogy, Mallarmé proceeds to provide access to meaning through encounter with the phrase on the page, and it is this encounter which affirms the existence of the phrase and in turn the reading experience that contact is itself identity, a pulling together of writing (or spoken) and reading experiences. Of course, the penult is dead; it died when it was dropped in the development of the French language.

But we know what the penult was because we have the remaining syllables on each side, the parentheses which indicate its form and identity. Reader activity (and in this particular text we see Mallarmé as both writer and reader or speaker and audience) provides access to meaning; the language is differential and so it confers meaning. The words and their ordering may alter creation, but they still order a direction for establishing possible and acceptable referentials. The impersonal style of "La Pénultième est morte" demands a personal response. While the phrase may indeed pose the problem of the authority of the referents, it does evoke an authentic response and in that response asserts a value.

Once the reader reacts and responds to the meaning of "La Pénultième est morte," despite possible limitations to its significance, the phrase becomes all the more performative when he grasps the naturalness of the referents for Mallarmé. Mallarmé was a philology teacher who wrote a study on the subject (*Les Mots anglais*); he was certainly aware of linguistic changes and incongruities—perhaps more so than most writers. Just as he builds "Toute l'âme résumée" from the smoke rings of a lighted cigar and "Surgi de la croupe" from a vase on the mantle of his drawing room, he constructs the "Démon de l'analogie" from the world of experience. Proceeding not from meaning but to meaning leads Mallarmé to an esthetics in which creation replaces both derivation and description and ultimately takes place in the space of the page: "Lire—cette Pratique—Appuyer, selon la page, au blanc, qui l'inaugure son ingénuité. . . . L'air ou chant sous le texte, conduisant la devination d'ici là, y applique son motif en fleuron et cul-de-lampe invisibles" (386-87).

Hence, Mallarmé's poetry does not reveal a system; in fact, the variations of his prose commentaries on poetry emphasize his lack of a system, if not his rejection of one. Rather, his one and only subject, "fil conducteur," is the self-reflexive text which calls attention to its own composition in the space of the page; the text proclaims with authority both the moment of experience and the moment of expression in the notion of an object: "Je dis: une fleur!" "La Pénultième est morte"; "nul ptyx, / Aboli bibelot d'inanité sonore." The reader, like Igitur, arrives "in these circumstances" "au fond des choses: en 'absolu' qu'il est" (434). In reducing the complex to its most elemental yet self-contained substance, such as *une fleur* or *ptyx*, Mallarmé celebrates poetry as the creative act. As the flower opens and closes, actively bringing about an equilibrium which is at once free from exactitude but bound to its basic notion as object, the repository of "Le Nénuphar blanc" contains its own evidence of existence, and the reader discovers that the interior poem (*Je dis*) has indeed corpus and meaning (*une fleur*).

While events of the corpus of the text may not coincide with the order of their appearance ("A la nue accablante tu"), the events still occur in the poet-reader encounter. As spectator, the reader in turn acts in a personal attempt to repeat the one poetic act which is the Mallarmé universe: "Je dis: une fleur!" The reader's flower encloses him in a declarative framework which is free from external compulsion and dictation. It is "le texte véridique" (367), in which experience and expression are simultaneous and successive at the same time in the encounter between the poet and reader before the dynamic spectacle of a familiar reality. Such a text circulates in the space of its own composition and reading. The act of writing generates its own accomplishment in the act of reading. The text is its own guarantee to being "véridique" in a liberating act of discovery for both the poet and the reader.

The poem does not imitate Nature: "La Nature a lieu, on n'y ajoutera pas; que des cités, les voies ferrées et plusieurs inventions formant notre matériel" (647). Rather, it is a human creation which converts the external "real" into an intelligible reality through confrontation with legitimate knowledge, on the one hand, and intuitive poetic act, on the other. The space of the encounter leads from the eye (the visual) to the thought (organization). Space, then, is a non-determined void which permits the ultimate limit of the poetic imagination to build layers of meaning. The metaphor of the flower, for example, brings together these separate horizons; the word choice acts as filter in the process of becomingness (thing seen to thing expressed). The geometric dimensions of space are to the practitioner of plasticity what grammar is to the writer: coordination of the pieces into an organic structure. Writing is the disposition of space. Art is neither equal to the medium, which would imply adaptation, nor inferior to it, which would imply reproduction; rather, art is superior to the imagination, for it elevates the object (a flower, a fan) from the realm of the realistic and naturalistic into the sphere of the human. Recognizing the value of the visual, Mallarmé evolves to an esthetic which abolishes ornamentation, rejects the elements of traditional poetry (rime, rhythm), and suppresses syntactical transitions, especially punctuation; the image becomes the object and leads the reader, first, to the situation and, then, to the concept. The text does not proceed from a concept, but from a primordial element or fragment, which draws upon all the arts and then subordinates them to the poetic activity of written composition: "Séparés, on est ensemble" (285). By using white space as a major element of his text, Mallarmé creates the text piece by piece with the maximum degree of objective calculation possible; he lucidly and actively constructs an optic which respects cosmic reality but only to focus on human creation: "Je dis: une fleur!" The poet's act makes it so and implies control. It is not the flower or object which is interested in man, but man who is interested in the flower. The poet's pen emerges as the structuring principle of the world: "Ecrire c'est . . . dévoiler le monde et le proposer."[27] Hence, the written convention on white space directs the reading operation in white space and expands, rather than reduces, the use of spacing.

The unprinted is not background but the primary field; it is space which has power and is an element of the printed; space is the undeniable constant, which alone cannot be experienced or explained. Although space is anti-linear, it must be crossed in order to make form possible. Space does not record experience; it expands it and in expansion it hints at all-inclusiveness. By itself, space is a-temporal, a-logical, a-symmetrical, abstract. It is free. Moreover, space is always visual; it is never oral; hence, it is silence because no more is needed; it is self-sufficient, pure, authentic. Space, then, is Mallarmé's working place, "le vide papier que la blancheur défend" (38). But, instead of working against space by filling up the empty paper with words, combinations of words, and all manner of syntactical constructions, Mallarmé, like the swan, struggles against the hard plane of placement (linear line) to unblock the word as designator of appearance in order to let it stand as an expression of essence, essential matter, which initiates experience: "Le Vierge, le vivace, et le bel aujourd'hui" (67-68). Freeing the word by placement or by drawing on space as a multiple structuring element (white page, variety of spacing, interword space), Mallarmé learns to alter groupings in his fan poems and in the use of objects as writing fields in *Vers de circonstance*. He works with space as the effect of form: the arrangement confers different values: "A la nue accablante tu." Space has the power to compromise the autonomy of words as well as to demonstrate their potential possibilities of meaning ("une dentelle," "une fleur," "salut," "vague").

Poetic manipulation of space determines the reading of the text, for it is the use of space as the element of design which determines the image: where the image begins, where it stops and returns. Space controls the combinations of meaning through groupings, dispersion, and isolation, and at the same time it multiplies their possible combinations. The eye and mind move together. As the poet changes the unprinted, space, he introduces variations in the optic. The poet's "œil nu" is transferred to the viewer-reader to arbitrate meaning. Language becomes the maximum sign of corroboration, correspondence, between the poet and his reader. Using space as the primary element of composition, Mallarmé "cède l'initiative aux mots" (366).

Nowhere in Mallarmé's work is his esthetic of space more developed, yet more problematic than in *Un Coup de dés*. To come to grips with Mallarmé as poet and *Un Coup de dés* as his maximum poetic sign is to understand space as poetic substance. All of Mallarmé's writing shows a concern for and a fascination with the problem of space. Turning his back on centuries of tradition and on his own contemporaries, Mallarmé investigates the process of the text in the creation of a poem and a poetry which are beyond esthetics. Space has value in the text production, as poetry makes it the procedure and the fundamental structure. *Un Coup de dés* is both object and subject, as the reader confronts the problem of meaning (interpretation) in the space of the poem.

Chapter II

THE SPACE OF THE TEXT

No two pages of *Un Coup de dés* are visually alike. The presentation forces every reader to take into account in some way the printed appearance of the text and to note the dispersion of the black type across the white space of the pages. Combinations of words—groupings, isolation, regroupings—occur only by their placement, as the space of the page controls the reading. Spatial determination of the text, what Mallarmé calls an " 'état' . . . pour ouvrir des yeux" (456) is seen as the element which validates the printed elements, actual text to be read or the written record. The arrangement—layout—of the print determines reader reconstruction of the visual unity supplied by the white page or space.

For Valéry, *Un Coup de dés* is "la figure d'une pensée dans notre espace" (1582), the construction or "le dispositif" is what matters. The reader "sees" the unity of the text and notes lexical, semantic, and syntactical relationships among the printed elements. The physical arrangement may disrupt the ease of the reading, but it permits the reader to confer value and meaning upon the text. The field of space becomes an effect of the black form of the written communication. Space is concretized by the printed text; the flat, one-dimensional surface of the white page becomes two-dimensional when it is set in relief and intensified by the blackness of the type. The effect of contrast achieved by the visual power of type is all the more enhanced by the sizes and weights of the type, which attract attention through their ornamental power. Bold, medium, and light weights (character thickness) give rise to shades of gray, which make the white space linear and set the black letters in motion, or at least into a sense of rhythm through balance and contrast.

The printed element is, then, a limit to the white page. It is not natural, much less realistic; rather, it is stylized to sustain and direct attention, to convey a message. Type sizes (character height) are graded from large to small; they may be increased or decreased, loosened or compacted in order to vary the components of the message; moreover, type sizes may be mixed to emphasize contrast and balance. Large or display type (15-point type and above) usually dominates composition type (sizes up to and including 14-point type); it has the greatest impact on the eye and, consequently, takes on the quality of superiority. Display type heightens legibility or readability, divides a text into parts, and creates patterns in the mind's eye. Similarly, upper-case letters are more dynamic than lower-case ones; words printed completely in upper-case characters have more authority than those printed totally in lower-case letters; in addition, the reader reads lower-case words (and lines) more rapidly than he reads those in upper case. When upper- and lower-case letters are mixed, the effect on the reader is one of contrastive movement: the lower-case letters tend to reflect stability, while the upper-case ones indicate dynamism or instability.

A sense of movement in contrast with stasis also occurs within words and lines printed entirely in either upper- or lower-case characters. Kerns, those parts of a word which are printed beyond the basic rectangular body of the letter, move the eye, first, from top to bottom, then, from left to right: b, d, f, h, k, l, t ascend above the body of the letter, while g, j, p, q, y descend below it. Within upper-case letters, A, H, M, O, and T are considered static, and B, C, D, E, F, K, L generally convey movement. Hence, the choice of letters or characters may determine both the physical design of the page and the psychological value of that design: active or passive, stable or unstable.

Weight (bold, medium, light) and point size (gradations from large to small, upper and lower cases) are only two of the fundamental decisions involved in type selection. A third involves the choice of two basic faces: roman and italic.[1] The roman face is straight; it is upright, vertical, and impersonal; psychologically, it carries the value of stability. On the other hand, the italic face is oblique; it is curved, sloped, and, consequently, less stable or more animated; the italic face resembles script ("trop près de l'écriture," 1400) and so is more personal than the roman face: "Le vers n'est très beau que dans un caractère impersonnel, c'est-à-dire typographique" (1399).

Hence, the most authoritative and eye-catching line in print is one which is printed in **LARGE BOLD ROMAN** letters; the line read the most rapidly will be in *light lower-case italics*; the greatest contrast in print occurs when large bold roman letters appear on the same page with light lower-case italics. Variations between these two poles of type and mixtures of weight, point size, and type face affect the sense of proportion of the text, generate the concretization process (thought into its communication), provide the text base, and create the recognition of patterns (letters, words, groups of words, paginal divisions, design). As the word is set in type, fixed on the page, the construct of the text begins to emerge verbally and visually, in terms of both the utilitarian and the artistic. The page takes on form.

Basically, a page is a flat, unidimensional rectangle or parallelogram. Technically, it is one side of a leaf or sheet. A page is printed in signature sheets, the most common one being in multiples of four; signatures are then folded to page size, the largest signature being a folio. Pages appear as verso (left for even numbers) and recto (right for odd numbers). Hence, a page is a fixed framework which delimits the amount of words and lines which it can support. A page may be said to represent a unity of space, the place for the confrontation of printed elements, but the writer does not own at any time a whole page because of the dictum of printer space. Printer space is space owned by the printer, not the writer, to wit the first verso after a title is generally unprinted (printer space) and each page is surrounded by dead, unusable space or printer's margin. The margin frames or encloses the printed elements. Moreover, a margin (head, tail, back, foredge or top, bottom, left/inside, right/outside) cannot be altered, moved, transferred, or explained. A margin is simply there, but its presence compromises the autonomy of the page and the print on the page. Center margins or gutters (righthand margin of a verso and lefthand margin of a recto) further compromise the integrity of the page and create a columnar effect; as a result, the vertical always dominates the horizontal although the horizontal does not actually oppose the vertical, but is harmonious in its subordination to it. The restraints of the page (geometrical shape, signature form, margins) impose spatial ordering. Every page in a given printed work begins and ends with a predetermined line length (number of character or letter spaces), a length further dictated by type selection (point size) and margin space, which is a function of line length. Hence, it is little wonder that Mallarmé was fascinated by poster art and newspapers and undertook such meticulous research into all aspects of the printing process for the publication of *Un Coup de dés*.

With Mallarmé, the tools of the printing trade become the tools of the writer. His correspondence and theoretical essays show his relentless interest in the technical problems of printing, as well as in the visual effect of the page on the reader. From his earliest texts in *Entre quatre murs* and *Glanes* to one of his last poems, "A la nue accablante tu," he experiments with type sizes and layout: the printed paginal appearance of the text. And, indeed, André Gide's 1913 lecture on Mallarmé's *Un Coup de dés* confirms the importance of the role that printing considerations played in the writing of the text. According to Gide, who had been one of the "Mardistes," Mallarmé wrote to him that the layout was an important part of the text: "la pagination, où est tout l'effet. Tel mot en gros caractères a lui seul demandé toute une page de blanc. . . . La constellation y affectera" (1582).

Just as the physical presentation is not fortuitous, the artistic arrangement of the words and their groupings (lines or verses) must itself draw upon and use the medium of print. However, the actual writing also carries its own restraints lexically, semantically, and syntactically. The challenge, then, becomes one of correlation: the writing process as design, as the angle of union between the medium and the message. As the print manipulates the space of the page, the writing must in turn incorporate the print and the space of the page. Therefore, for Mallarmé, "les 'blancs' . . . assument l'importance" (455). Only through the disposition of the words and lines is it possible to free the text from the confines of the page.

Consequently, layout becomes a major Mallarmé focal point, what he described to Valéry as "le dispositif": "[Mallarmé]a essayé . . . *d'élever enfin une page à la puissance du ciel étoilé*" (1582). Space and type which delimit form become the same means for unlimiting form: a re-formation. Placement on the page is disciplined, word choices are scientific, precise, deliberate, and the ordered assembly is a skillful construction. Minute attention to the details of the surface appearance of the text legitimizes the intellectuality of the work. *Un Coup de dés* has such an imposed, immutable order which cannot be changed, anymore than a spectator can change the order of the stars in the sky. Mallarmé's work is linear in that each grouping or line is arranged in a single row, suggesting a singleness of purpose, a unity of concept, a physical figure of relations. Each word is a delineator, a "pivot" which indicates a stratification ("pendentif") of meaning. What appears on the page is real; it exists; it is both trustworthy and credible because it is so deliberately set, displayed, and constructed. Visually, the space of the page is performative because it leads the eye from unit to unit, page to page, even event to event. But the order of appearance and the order of sequence do not coincide. The differentiality of the physical appearance (the validation of the black type) is not stable evidence of order. On the contrary, the space is not instructive; the black type or text does not stabilize space nor does it negate its formlessness. Rather, the space heightens the impenetrability of the text by interrupting groupings, multiplying the possibilities of convergence and divergence, aborting events, undermining units. The space negates differentiality, as it destroys associations, interrogates lexical and semantic meaning, places syntactical principles in doubt, and reverses all expectations of the printed page or written text. Space distracts, disrupts, interrupts, distorts, destabilizes, and invalidates the fixity of the form or design which it alone can make possible. The immediate effect is displacement, confusion, disorder, and detachment. Space destructures what the printed units compose. It is unreliable, uninstructive, non-performative space in *Un Coup de dés* which determines the reading process. In his "Préface," Mallarmé refers over and over again to the "espacement de la lecture. . . . Le papier intervient" (455). Because space is the primary element of the text, it is by, in, with, and through space that the reader must pursue relationships and seek to establish points of contact which confer meaning upon the units of the text. Space is the authorial controlling factor which directs the reader and orders the accumulation of data which may be read and interpreted. Space encodes the form, substance, and links of the communication. It is the polyvalent structure of the only text Mallarmé calls "poème." To read *Un Coup de dés* demands a reading of the space which supplies its order and confers on the text its ultimate form.

But a reading of the space of *Un Coup de dés* presupposes space to be read, an edition which establishes the space of the text, or at the very least a workable description of the space. *Un Coup de dés* was first published in 1897 in *Cosmopolis*, the only edition which appeared in Mallarmé's lifetime, and it was solely for this publication that Mallarmé wrote the "Préface," in which he acknowledges the problems of having a magazine undertake such a venture: "mais il ne m'appartient pas, hormis une pagination spéciale ou de volume à moi, dans un Périodique, même valeureux, gracieux et invitant qu'il se montre aux belles libertés, d'agir par trop contrairement à l'usage" (456). One of the major problems with the *Cosmopolis* edition was that it condensed the text to ten pages, considerably reducing, if not altering, the space of the text, leading Mallarmé to write the "Préface," which he did not wish to have republished with subsequent editions. Hence, his "Préface" focuses on the role of space in the text because of the form of the *Cosmopolis* printing.

At the time of his death in 1898, Mallarmé was correcting proofs for an "édition de luxe" in-folio. A set of these proofs was reproduced in 1966 by Robert Cohn in his *Mallarmé's Masterwork: New Findings*.[2] Called the Lahure proofs, they are

The Space of the Text 45

quite close in appearance to the 1914 NRF edition, which was supervised into print by Mallarmé's son-in-law, Edmond Bonniot. The 1914 Gallimard edition is still the one considered "ne varietur" in page size and textual disposition, and, indeed, it is the edition reproduced by Gallimard in 1931 and again by Daisy Aldan in 1965 and by Malcolm Bowie in 1978. In fact, most critics use some reproduction of the 1914 edition, which is itself out of print.[3]

The Lahure proofs reproduced by Cohn are not the only set of extant proofs, but at least they are available and are in Mallarmé's own hand. The proofs demonstrate how Mallarmé wanted the different units of the text grouped: word alignment, right- and lefthand margins, top and bottom margins, actual disposition on the page, even which lines on the verso and recto pages must be in agreement. The proofs show ruled lines to indicate the flushness of margins, to measure margins accurately and to guarantee alignment across the center margin: "faire concorder . . . sur une page et l'autre, les deux fragments de la même ligne"; "faut placer sur des lignes absolument droites . . . sans baisser ni monter"; "en cas que l'intercalation de la majuscule A doive chasser un peu, faire que ce soit à gauche, le mot devant finir exactement où il finit ici"; "reculer jusqu'à ce trait la fin du mot"; "veiller à ce que cette marge n'ait pas plus de quatre centimètres juste comme partout"; "avancer jusqu'à ce trait la fin du mot"; "commencer la ligne à ce trait"; "en égaliser la fin du mot à celles des deux autres." In addition to this sort of meticulous attention to the details of placement, the Lahure proofs reveal a Mallarmé who was acutely conscious of the actual type weights being used, for he continually asks the printer to verify certain letters: "vérifier," "vérifier ces lettres," "lettres à vérifier." *Vérifier* is not a request to change a letter, but a direction to the printer to check on the weight of the letter in order to make sure that a "bad" letter is imprinted in its entirety. Kerns are frequently subject to these problems; the part of the letter below or above the body of the letter often breaks off or the metal wears down. And, in the Lahure proofs, it is the letter f which does not print out completely; the bottom or the top part is weak and Mallarmé points it out on nearly every page. Mallarmé is not seeking a more fluid, flowery, flowing letter f; he merely wants the full letter struck properly. Elsewhere, he criticizes the bold roman type; it is too light and must be "plus fort." Bold italics also need to be "plus fortes" and he adds impatiently "comme je l'ai précédémment demandé." Textually, there are relatively few corrections or changes; "abîme" is to begin with a capital A and "fiançailles" with an initial capital letter. Only two lines show any change in order: "le Nombre unique" is to become "l'unique Nombre" and "la mer tentant par l'aïeul ou contre la mer" is changed to "la mer par l'aïeul tentant ou l'aïeul contre la mer," but interestingly "évènement" remains untouched. Unlike any other document, the Lahure proofs show incontestably just how layout was of overriding importance to Mallarmé in the construct of his text. Without a doubt, he drew upon his knowledge of the print medium to create *Un Coup de dés*.

The 1914 Gallimard edition and its subsequent reprintings correct "évènement" to "événement" and include all the textual changes indicated by the Lahure proofs, but the edition does not follow strictly the alignments (words, lines, margins) as scrupulously as Mallarmé demanded. However, there are other sets of proofs, also in Mallarmé's hand, prepared by the Didot printing firm, but to this day no one knows exactly how many sets were produced and corrected. According to Danielle Mihram, there are at least seven authentic sets and study of them shows that "on the whole, the NRF edition did not violate Mallarmé's intentions."[4] Mihram's examination of the available sets of proofs also points out Mallarmé's concern with the typography and topography of his work.

The 1945 Pléiade edition by Henri Mondor and G. Jean-Aubry draws upon the 1914 Gallimard edition, but the small paper size and the binding misrepresent the text on every page. The alignment is faulty throughout, making the disposition of the text completely erroneous. Moreover, margins are only erratically observed, over half the pages end too low on the page, and numbering the pages interferes dramatically with paginal appearance. Space is so restricted and so misrepresented that this edition is literally unusable for a close study of the poem.[5]

The best edition to date is by Mitsou Ronat (published in 1980 by the Groupe d'Atelier), for this edition preserves almost to the letter Mallarmé's sense of space. Where the Lahure proofs measure 15 1/2 inches, the Ronat edition insists on 15 1/8 inches, and the gutters or center margins are carefully maintained at the four centimeters prescribed by Mallarmé. Textually, all corrections to the *Cosmopolis* edition of 1897 have been incorporated and "évènement" has been kept intact. In fact, because of the unavailability of a readable and accurate edition of *Un Coup de dés*, Ronat undertook a reproduction of the corrected *Cosmopolis* version, and, by and large, her work is remarkably free from error; several pages end perhaps too low and there are nine minor alignment problems (for example, "Fiançailles" is not isolated enough and should not be placed under "probabilité"). However, it remains the most accurate edition in terms of its presentation of the space of *Un Coup de dés*, for it follows rigorously the known dimensions desired by Mallarmé.

The Ronat edition not only takes great care to present the page size which Mallarmé demanded and preserve its form infolio, but it also makes a highly respectable effort to reproduce the Didot typography, "une édition en tous points conforme aux vœux du poète."[6] Unfortunately, the Ronat edition was printed in limited numbers and now it too is unavailable.

Because there is no readily available accurate edition of *Un Coup de dés*, the modern-day reader must undertake the layout of the text in order to establish it. Since the text is demonstrably a construction, a deliberate and premeditated arrangement of the parts or units, the first step in the reading process must include a confrontation with its formal presentation, a literal re-creation of the patterns in order to begin any decoding of its communication. In fact, the communication cannot be separated from the calculated, fixed form of the layout of the text. The disposition of the words is crucial, as Mallarmé demonstrates in the extant proofs.

Un Coup de dés consists of 21 pages: one single page and ten double pages (doublets) or 11 rectos and 10 versos.[7] The text properly begins on the first recto and ends on a recto (11r or page 21). Throughout, printer margins and gutters (top, bottom, inside, outside, center) are scrupulously observed. Printer space also accounts for the other three pages of the six signatures necessary to print a 21-page text: the title page, a recto; its verso; the verso of the last recto page.[8] Mallarmé desired a folio edition, that is, the largest page size possible, which meant that each page would measure 27 x 36 centimeters and that each page would be a double, the doublet being standard for such an edition. The center margin or gutter was specified as four centimeters. In order to reconstruct the arrangement of the text within the type area, that part of the page that receives print, the next step, based on Mallarmé's page-size specifications, is to establish a standard line length in picas, thereby delimiting the total number of characters any one point size of type can print per line. Provided the line length is maintained, with the attendant number of characters per pica, analysis of the type area can be based on any composition size. In *Un Coup de dés*, approximately 80% of the type size is uniform. Hence, working within the page dimensions specified by Mallarmé and choosing 8-point type for a 22-pica line length, the reader may establish as a viable working base a 38-line type area with 72.6 characters per line. As a result, there are a possible 836 lines in the 21-page text; of this total, 224 are printed and 574 are unprinted.[9] Space, then, occupies 72% of the text and print a mere 28%. In other words, there is 2 1/2 times more space than printed text. Quantitatively, space is the predominant structuring component.

Since nearly 80% of *Un Coup de dés*'s printed units conform to the composition size outlined above, only 20% of the printed lines appear in different sizes, faces, and weights. Examination of the type shows that there are seven different type sizes (including the standard or basic 8-point) and three type faces (medium, bold, and italic). If we eliminate the standard 8-point type size or the print norm, there are only nine actual variations in the type itself. There are two mixed type faces (bold italic and medium italic). It is possible to establish 12 type variations, but, just as the standard composition size is used 80% of the time, so its medium type face dominates: fully 51 1/2 % of the lines are in 8-point medium type and 28 1/2 % in 8-point italic.

Looking at each single page, one (2v)[10] is all space; eight show one type face and size only (1r, 3r, 5v, 5r, 7v, 7r, 8v); 11 pages mix two type faces and sizes (2r, 3v, 4v, 6v, 6r, 8r, 9v, 10v, 10r, 11v, 11r); no pages mix three or four types; only one page, 9r, mixes five type faces. Such a count shows that only 57% of the pages mix type faces and sizes and, of these, only five double pages are printed in a mixture of type faces and sizes: 5, 6, 7, 10, 11. Five double pages are the same, verso and recto, while just three doublets show a mixture on the facing page (3, 4, 8). There is only one significantly unusual double page, 9, in its mixture of two type faces and sizes on the verso and five on the recto. Fifty percent of the double pages are typographically harmonious, while only 10% may be said to be striking in the mixtures of type faces and sizes.

The regularity of the type is also seen in the type faces and weights. Two single pages are in all bold (1r, 5r), nine in all medium (3v, 3r, 4v, 4r, 5v, 10v, 10r, 11v, 11r), and five in all italic (6v, 6r, 7v, 7r, 8v); of these, six double pages are in one type face and weight only (3, 4, 6, 7, 10, 11). One page (2r) mixes medium and bold, two pages mix italic and bold (8r, 9v), and only one page, 9r, mixes all three (bold, medium, italic). Eighty-one percent of the single pages and 60% of the double pages do not mix type faces and weights and can be considered "regular."

The same sense of uniformity is found in the mixture of lower- and upper-case letters in that no double pages contrast all upper-case letters on one side with all lower-case letters on the other. There is only one double (5) on which the recto is in all upper-case letters and the verso is in a mixture of the two. Fully 37% of the pages are in one case only, while only 10% show degrees of variation.

The variations in type weights, sizes, and faces are not quite as extraordinary as they might seem although they remain a factor in the physical disposition of the text. Where then do the striking variations in the layout of *Un Coup de dés* abound if not in the typography? In the number of printed lines per page and their arrangement. No single page is fully occupied by print, and no double pages have the same number of lines; only eight single pages have the same number of lines, and only two pages (1r, 5r) have the same number of lines in the same type face. Out of a maximum of 38 possible lines per page, the lines per page vary from two to 27 (the largest type size occupies two printed lines). Four pages begin on the first line of the page and another four on the second line. The remaining 13 pages all begin on a different line with no repetitions, for example, 8r begins on line 4, 10v on line 13, and 5r on line 36. Hence, only 20% of the pages begin on line 1. Ten pages end on different lines, another two consist of only one line, eight end on the same line, but only one, the last one, 11r, ends on the last possible line, 38. The maximum number of printed lines on any page is 27 (5v), while the least number is two (1r, 5r) although it should be remembered that 2r is completely blank, having no printed lines.

However, the numerous variations, which examination of the number and placement of the printed lines reveals, occur primarily on single pages only. Crossover lines, those lines which are so placed that the double page is in effect a single unit, occur less than one percent of the time. In the entire text, only 19 lines cross from the verso to the recto. Three double pages (2, 10, 11) have no lines which continue across the gutter or center margin. The other seven double pages or 70% of the doublets do cross the center margin but not with any measure of frequency or regularity. Double pages 3, 5, and 7 have one crossover line only; page 9 contains two, page 8 has three, and page 6 has four. Page 4 has the most crossover lines, nine. Crossover lines which eliminate the central margins are few indeed and must give rise to questions concerning the reading of the double page (verso-recto) as single units.

Central margins or gutters are also part of the layout and their preservation as columnar internal divisions by Mallarmé is conspicuous in the construct of the text.[11] Verso and recto pages retain their integrity as separate units 99% of the time. The simultaneous reading of the verso and recto is not borne out by the arrangement of the text. If crossover lines are so few and if their infrequent use does not destroy the distinction between the verso and recto pages and the center margin is rigorously safeguarded, then contrast between verso and recto pages must be more important than their conjunction.

The recto pages contain considerably more printed lines than the versos; in fact, 64%. Moreover, the only blank page is a verso, which is literally ignored as unused space and therefore useless. Only 4r and 4v match in the number of lines on the page. Most recto pages begin and end lower on the page than the versos; for example, the first recto page begins on line 15, while the first verso begins on line 1. In fact, all versos begin in the top half of the page and none begin lower than line 20, whereas four recto pages begin with line 20 or below it. End lines follow similar patterns of arrangement: ten out of 11 rectos end between lines 20 and 38, while only four of the nine printed versos end before line 20. In the top fourth of the page, only four rectos begin, while ten end in the bottom fourth. A nearly opposite placement occurs on the versos: eight begin in the top fourth of the page and only two end in the bottom fourth. The recto pages begin and end lower than the versos and contain twice the number of lines. Hence, the recto pages bear twice as much type or print as their versos and, accordingly, they continually pull the eye to the right and invite the reader to turn the page. The recto pages, in comparison with their verso opposites, are quantitatively heavy and attract the most attention.

In addition, the rectos have longer lines of print than the versos. Using a 72.6 character line length as the maximum norm, 76% of the text is seen to be written in varying character counts. The only maximum character line appears on a recto (2), while the shortest count of 30 characters appears on a verso (10). Ten percent of the printed lines use a character count between 65.2 and 72.6; this long measured line appears on six rectos but only on three versos. Twenty-five percent of the printed lines measure 54.4 or more characters, and these lines appear on nine rectos and on only six versos. The character count reinforces the importance of the number of printed lines on the recto pages.

Weighting the rectos is further achieved through indentation, the space in which the first character of the first line begins. The greatest occurrences of use of the first indented space are for such determinations may be used, such as the 8-point type size elected for this study, just as long as the amount of space is maintained and the sense of proportion is preserved.[12] Because an examination of the mechanical decisions involved in the arrangement of the text reveals more differences between recto and verso pages than similarities and consequently fewer genuine double pages or doublets than suspected, it is logical to recreate the text single page by single page before undertaking the reading.[13]

The first page is the title page; while it is a part of the preliminary matter and not a counted text page, it is part of the signature, and its layout actually announces the text. Mitsou Ronat is correct in her insistence on the importance of the title page to any reading of the text.[14] After all, Mallarmé did not plan to include the "Préface" with any post-*Cosmopolis* editions and, indeed, the "Préface" is not included in any extant proofs of *Un Coup de dés*. Mallarmé envisaged a recto title page, followed by a blank verso, in turn followed by page one (a recto) of the text. As Ronat points out: "[Mallarmé] rectifie explicitement une erreur, significative puisqu'elle a été réitérée par la suite: l'imprimeur [Didot] avait imprimé le 'titre' sur un papier épais et bleu de couverture, tandis que le reste du poème était imprimé sur un papier blanc ordinaire. Mallarmé indique que la première page doit être imprimée sur le même papier que l'ensemble." While one may not agree with Ronat's conclusion that "la page du titre doit être considérée comme une partie du poème" (3), one cannot argue against the evident significance of the title page and the dismissal of the importance of the "Préface." The title page desired by Mallarmé introduces the reader to the text in two primary ways. First, it announces that the ensuing text is a poem and the title of the poem is a complete sentence: "**POÈME** / *Un coup de Dés jamais n'abolira le Hasard.*" The text is fully identified and the opening dispersed line of the poem will always be read in its entirety by the reader; the dispersed opening line and its interspersed digressions will not completely surprise the reader, who expects the title to appear eventually in its preannounced completeness. From the outset, the reader knows he is going to read a poem whose title is a complete sentence, which contains the subject/theme/topic of that poem.

The second important piece of information imparted by the title page concerns the layout of the text. The title page is virtually a typographic and topographic demonstration of the technical aspects of the text. In the four basic lines of the title page, one discovers four of the seven type sizes used in the text, all three basic type faces (bold, medium, italic), lines completely in upper-case letters and others completely in lower-case ones, even one line in type mixtures of lower- and upper-case letters. The first line is "**POÈME**," printed in 15-point bold upper-case letters. The second line is the actual title in 9-point italic; three letters are in upper case: U,D, H. The line is not centered; rather, it begins in the first possible character space. The third line, "par," is in lower case and appears in 8-point medium or in the standard ("normal") form of the printed line. The fourth line resembles the first in that it uses only upper-case letters: "STÉPHANE MALLARMÉ." Appearing in 12-point medium, the visual printed form of the author's name returns the reader's eye to the first line, "**POÈME**." Association by the typography and topography is first detected on the title page.

Noting that the actual title is not centered in the space or type area of the page but begins flush against the center margin initiates a closer look at the page. The title is not centered at all, and the spacing between the lines, as well as the indentation, is irregular. In fact, the spacing assumes equal importance with the two typographically overpowering lines: "**POÈME**" and "STÉPHANE MALLARMÉ." The "unique" source may be "la Poésie," but the text is unequivocally by a very human poet, whose title page is dramatic in appearance, intense in its type sizes and faces, and provocative in its mixtures of type sizes, faces, and lettercases. It is the surrounding space which magnifies the drama of the layout, confirms the text as poem, and establishes the authority of the constative declaration which is the title. "*Un coup de Dés jamais n'abolira le Hasard*" is fixed by the surrounding space and will remain, for the reader, an immutable ordering for the pages of the text. The axiom of the title precedes the communication of the text; while it may not be sustained in its predictability, it will be maintained in its traceability.

Typographically, however, the title of the poem commands the least attention of the four lines of the title page. The generic designation, "**POÈME**," and the author's identification, "STÉPHANE MALLARMÉ," receive the most weight by their elevation (use of upper-case letters), while "par" stands out by its isolation. The very presentation of the title page emphasizes the lengthy title itself—a title which reads rapidly because of its appearance in the italic type face. The title literally races across the page. In contrast to the overpowering bold of the designation and capital letters of the first and last lines, as well as juxtaposition with the smallness and brevity of the "par," the title is not seized in its entirety at first glance. Its extended length in the more oblique or more dynamic italic and dominant use of lower-case letters signals a transformation of the fixity of type. Variation of the fixed elements creates chance, as the surrounding space emerges as an element of the printed which controls the ordering and multiplies the possibilities of the reading. The title page is a representation of how a page may harmonize and contrast at the same time through the use of unequal weights, various type sizes, and mixture of upper- and lower-case letters. The practicality of the title page becomes the artistic introduction to the text.

Study of Mallarmé's title on the title page which was approved by him shows how type may be effectively used to create a dividing and patterning element. The single sentence of the title draws upon three upper-case letters to indicate emphasis, rhythm, and word value: *"Un coup de Dés jamais n'abolira le Hasard."* *"Dés"* and *"Hasard"* clearly receive maximum reader attention and interest. The line is not read by its syntactical, lexical, or semantic structure, but by its own visual appearance, and it is unalterable. *"Hasard"* receives the most stress because it is placed last and begins with an elevated *H*. The adverb *"jamais"* attracts the least interest because of its placement after the first interval generated by *"Dés,"* its appearance in lower-case letters, and its use as an element of initiation to the longer part of the sentence which, in lower-case italic, draws the eye quickly to the H of "*Hasard*," the final word. "*Dés*" and "*Hasard*" are spatially placed in a clear relationship to each other. Had Mallarmé placed "*jamais*" in its usual syntactical position after the verb, he would have created another pause, "*n'abolira jamais*," which would have been all the more disruptive by its relationship with "*Dés*"; an upper-case letter on "*Hasard*" would not have been as dramatic. Instead of reading the title as a 4/9, it would have been an impair in 4/2/6/3; the first section would not have a unit of emphasis, the point of concentration.

One of the effects of the "*Dés-Hasard*" relationship is an alteration of the plane of the page itself. The flat, one-dimensional surface of the white space has been rendered two-dimensional by the impact of the bold roman large-sized upper-case "**POÈME**." The next element, "*Un coup de Dés*," evokes a familiar geometrical form, a cube, which is a three-dimensional figure; the lower-case *c* on "*coup*" and upper-case *D* on "*Dés*" stress the object, dice. The space is transformed; it now has length, breadth, and thickness, material existence and physical reality. Concretization of space by the visual arrangement of the title page is further achieved through the association between "*Dés*" and "*Hasard*." The reader literally and figuratively crosses space in bringing these two words together and annihilates the distance between them; "*Un coup de Dés*" becomes "*un coup de Hasard*," the number of points arithmetically earned when dice are thrown. The atmosphere is set; the title contains valuable information and gives a general idea of the poem to follow and its interrelationships. The design of the title page arrests the event of the poem through its layout, conveys a solid structure of thought through its patterning, and validates the white space. Single elements are enlarged, but the continuity of their constituent parts is preserved by space. Space becomes the frame of order.

Hence, the title page is important to any establishment of the text because of its placement on the white page, and the determination of the title itself is an integral part of the reader's introduction to the text. Yet, Mallarmé's title is constantly written incorrectly. The title should always be what Mallarmé said it was, but variations abound. In referring to the text as text and not to a specific edition—a problem compounded by the lack of an available definitive edition—it has become somewhat standard to shorten the title and resort to French rules of capitalization: *Un Coup de dés*, which is the practice in this study, although Gardner Davies, Robert Cohn, and Mitsou Ronat, for example, prefer to write *Un Coup de Dés*, preserving the capital D of Mallarmé's title. The complete title, however, is written correctly only by Ronat; all the rest are modifications which alter the title considerably: hence, one sees *Un coup de dés jamais n'abolira le hasard* (Gallimard, Coll. Poésie, 1976), *Un Coup de dés jamais n'abolira le hasard* (Gallimard, 1914), *Un Coup de Dés jamais n'abolira le hasard*, and *UN COUP DE DÉS JAMAIS N'ABOLIRA LE HASARD* (Pléiade). These variations are often further mutated in shortened form, *Un coup de dés*, which is the practice of the Pléiade edition, Bonnefoy, Kristeva, Rogère, and so on. But, even beyond these changes, the title is frequently written in two lines: *Un Coup de dés jamais / n'abolira le hasard* (Gallimard, 1914) and *UN COUP DE DÉS / JAMAIS N'ABOLIRA LE HASARD* (Pléiade). In addition, "**POÈME**" is frequently placed after the title and also appears with a diaeresis instead of a grave accent (*poëme*, not *poème*); in fact, *Un Coup de dés* is the only text which Mallarmé designates as a "poème" (grave accent) and not "poëme" (diaeresis). These misrepresentations of the title and of the title page destroy the integrity of the writing-reading processes which are differentiated by the typography and topography.

Because Mallarmé understood the poetic possibilities of the printing process and incorporated it into his poetics, the transition from written word to printed format is a fundamental concern in his work and part of his composition. Final emergence of his poem into the fixity of ultimate appearance, print, is a continuing concern in all Mallarmé's poems, prose commentaries, and correspondence. Assembly, what Mallarmé calls "Science" (573), communicates order and confers meaning. The very mobility of the titular phrase on the title page (*"Dés"*-*"Hasard"*) and the primary positioning of the generic designation, "**POÈME**," call into play the structure of the ensuing text, as well as its constituent elements. The first unit of the title page, "**POÈME**," dominates by its superior type; indeed, it appears as the virtual title of the text, rather than subordinate to it. In its initial position and dramatic form, "**POÈME**" is a stable, solid, immobile, determined, and authoritative sign. By contrast, the decreased size of the titular phrase and its appearance in italic face are a mobile expansion and correspondence of the opening unit or inherent subject of the work. The poem is and confirms itself through the informative and descriptive declaration of the titular phrase. The "fiction" is actualized in its subsequent constative announcement. The title page is structurally important to the text, an importance attained through its multi-dimensional surrounding space, which sets in motion the fixity of print. The medium which the poet must use—fixed print—is destroyed, the medium is not the message, for the message here is the "*Dés*"-"*Hasard*" conjunction. The layout of the title page invites reader response; art arises from a chance encounter which produces meaning; the printed fixity of the words will never abolish the chances of meaning or interpretation. Print cannot do away with reading as chance. The title page affirms itself and signals that the text is a poem.

The next page, a verso, is completely blank. It is standard printer space since the printing process dictates that this page be unused space. It is accepted in its empty whiteness and dismissed by the reader. The space is of no interest or concern in its return to the flat surface plane of normal appearance.

The text itself begins properly on the first recto of the body of the text, 1r. This page contains one line in extremely large bold roman type and it is completely in upper-case letters: "**UN COUP DE DÉS.**" The one line appears on line 15, two-fifths of the way down the page, and the first character, U, is in the first possible print space, no. 1, flush against the left margin. Having a character count of 69 (out of a possible 72.6), it visually towers over the surrounding space, a space which in turn sets the line in relief. Still, the title has already been established and the four words on 1r merely repeat the first words of the titular phrase of the title page. It is not unusual for a poem to begin by repeating its title, nor is it unusual for the title of a poem to be no more than an extrapolation of the first line of the text, and, indeed, the placement of the line confirms its relationship to the title. In point of fact, the title page begins on line 13, "POÈME," and the titular phrase on line 17; the four-word line of 2r is exactly in the space in-between, line 15. As one line, it appears to be a standard phrase, a regular form for a title. Proof of its validity as title, a validity which the large dark type receives from the possible 36 readable lines of space which surround it, is demonstrated by critical practice, the use of these four words as a substitute for the actual long title. Page 1r seems so normal, so standard, so general that it literally becomes the accepted title of the poem—more is not considered necessary.

In addition, the arbitrary dramatic appearance of the one printed line on 1r reaffirms the three-dimensionality of space. The cube of the dice is emphasized by its isolation and position. Moreover, the cube is actualized by its very typography, rendered all the more authentic by its compactness in such a large expanse of space. Space confers authority upon the line.

The authority of 1r is further confirmed by the following blank page, 2v. The completely white page seemingly agrees that the line on 1r is the title, for, after all, it is common practice to leave blank the first verso after a title page. Consequently, the reader ignores 2v, but the reader who undertakes to recreate the layout of the text must still recreate this blank page, or else ponder the need for a work with two title pages, one right after the other, there being no intervening preface. Hence, 2v is part of the text, for it indicates that space is going to have a large role in the construct of the text. The space of 2v is instructive in its non-performance.

Page 2r, opposite a completely blank page, is busier than its two preceding pages. It consists of four lines, all in upper-case letters, but in two type sizes and faces: 22-point bold and 9-point medium: "JAMAIS / QUAND BIEN MÊME LANCÉ DANS DES / CIRCONSTANCES ÉTERNELLES / DU FOND D'UN NAUFRAGE." The "smaller" type, by contrast, appears as an explanation of the larger, more authoritative type used for "JAMAIS." By its indentation (character space no. 10) and its

The Space of the Text   61

type, "JAMAIS" would seem to agree that 1r is the title and
that the poem actually begins on this page. Having four lines,
2r establishes the printer margins. The second line completely
covers the maximum printed space possible; it has a 72.6 character count; in fact, the desired single phrase is so long that it
cannot fit into one line of print and therefore it must continue
onto the next line. "ÉTERNELLES" clearly modifies "CIR-
CONSTANCES" and syntactically belongs to that noun. The
fourth and final line on the page is in the same type face as the
central two lines (lines two and three); moreover, its position
continues those two lines. "ÉTERNELLES" ends on space 15,
and "DU FOND D'UN NAUFRAGE" begins on space 17,
space 16 being the standard space between words. In other
words, the layout of 2r is rather regular despite the mixture of
two type sizes and faces, and the patterned direction is in a top
to bottom, left to right reading grid. Even though "JAMAIS"
begins on line 19, considerably "down" the page and the last
line is on line 34, almost the predetermined last line possible
(38 being the maximum number of possible printed lines), the
topography is neither startling nor even dramatic. On the contrary, it is extremely legible and readable because of its placement "down" the page opposite a blank page, a positioning
which recalls the four words or supposed title of 1r. In fact, the
type and position on the one line of 1r are maintained by the
use of the same type in a slightly lower position of "JAMAIS"
on 2r, a continuity of the constative declaration of the titular
phrase, which also prevents the positioning of the adverb
"JAMAIS" out of grammatical sequence from becoming either
puzzling or problematic to the reader; its placement before the
sign of the negative "n'" and before the verb is an accepted
grammatical structure, which does not strike the reader as unusual at all.

Page 2r contains more print and less space than its preceding
pages; in one sense, space is not an important factor on this
page because it continues its performative role already established on 1r. But, it is the aspect of space as a blank interval
which separates characters and words, the plane of organization for those characters and words, which occurs on 2r. Space

is seen as the area set aside for a given reason in the design, the place of the text, and it provides a continuum in ordering the direction of the reading. On 2r, the sense of continuity and nondisruption is created by unobstructive space, which permits logical combinations ("ÉTERNELLES" as the modifier of "CIR-CONSTANCES," "JAMAIS" in an acceptable grammatical place). Space lends constancy to the page and reinforces the completeness of the only verb form on the page, "LANCÉ." In addition, the temporal conjunction "QUAND," which begins the second line and which is only indented eight spaces (an almost standard indentation), introduces into the space of the white the fourth dimension: time. The external appearance of the layout now includes a relationship with time. The conjunction "QUAND" and past participle "LANCÉ" affirm the continuity attained through the type size and face of "JAMAIS," and the reader begins to reestablish the text through memory—he recalls the layout of 1r, as well as that of the title page. Association occurs between the title page, 1r, and 2r through the unprinted 2v and permits a topos, "NAUFRAGE," to emerge.

Topographically, 3v and 3r represent the first double page or doublet: "SOIT / que / l'Abîme penché de l'un ou l'autre bord." The print begins in the top of the verso and continues into the bottom of the recto. The one crossover line, "par avance," occurs on line 16 of both pages, and the ordinary two-word phrase is used as the connector, as "par" is flush right, ending in the last possible character space of the verso (no. 72) and "avance" is flush left, beginning in the first one on the recto. In general, the movement is top to bottom, left to right, the normal reading grid, and the vocabulary of motion reinforces the topography: "étale," "inclinaison," "plane," "aile," "vol," "penché," etc. The words also bear out the shipwreck theme introduced on the previous page: "désespérément," "voile," "furieux," "jaillissements," "bonds," "bord."

The type used is the regular 8-point medium. Although this is the first example of the type norm in the text, it is regular in appearance, just as its disposition in a usual top to bottom, left to right reading grid asserts. While each page is fully two-thirds space and line indentation is considerably varied (each line begins in a different space on the verso and nine of the ten on the recto continue this irregular indentation practice), the groupings created by the indentations and spatial intervals are by and large not illogical. The layout is poetic, and the reader knows from the outset that the text is a poem, an observation borne out by the seemingly balanced layout, a balance which the space intervals create. The 11 lines of the verso are so placed that they seem to cover nearly the top half of the page (lines 2, 4, 7-11, 13, 15-16) and the final verso line ends exactly at the center margin, while the ten lines of the recto seem to cover the bottom half of the page, beginning in the quite ordinary first character space at the left center margin. The layout actually looks poetically regular, so the print groupings do not seem illogical at all.

The initial word of the double page attracts attention by its upper-case 10-point medium type face, but it is not a dramatic variation from the 8-point which is used regularly throughout the two pages. The initial "SOIT" is unequivocally an introductory subordinate conjunction of hypothesis, and the readability of the doublet is in no way affected by its slightly larger and more elevated type. Syntactically, the function of "SOIT" is rendered intact by its printed form, and it provides continuity from the shipwreck topos previously announced. In fact, there is very little change from the "DU FOND D'UN NAUFRAGE" line to "SOIT," except that "SOIT" is in slightly larger type (10-point as opposed to the 9-point of "DU FOND D'UN NAUFRAGE") and it is also in medium. The change in the type effectively shades "SOIT" and the entire doublet 3; the entity of the double page appears subordinate to the more powerful bold upper-case 22-point and 9-point lines of 2r, but "SOIT" retains its connective function by its size and use of upper-case letters.

The 8-point medium lower case, with only one exception, "Abîme," appears as an explanation of the "SOIT," in harmony, not in juxtaposition or contrast, with it. The preservation of the normal reading grid conveys a sense of progression through the word groupings and a sense of narration. The verso describes the situation of the abyss, while the recto describes reactions to it ("dresser le vol," "cette voile alternative," "adapter / à l'envergure"). But, the predominant lower case in 8-point medium is not intense, not dramatic in comparison to the typography of the preceding pages. Despite a vocabulary, theme, and ideogrammatic appearance generated by so much indentation and the one crossover line, doublet 3 is not visually an active page. There is much more print on the recto than on the verso and the print pulls the eye from the sketched-out situation of the verso to the narrated reaction of the recto.

Nevertheless, reconstruction of the layout reveals an imbalance between the verso and the recto, a tipping, a diagonal grid, which moves from the upper-left corner of the verso to the lower-right corner of the recto. The space visually simulates a ship going down into the turbulent foam of the angry sea, the abyss. Where the print is descriptive in its summation of a situation and the reaction to it, the space contributes emotivity to the logical groupings in taking on the form of the "bâtiment penché." Doublet 3 is a calligram, created by the white space. As the psychological matrix of the doublet, space confers emotional registers upon the positioning of the fixed printed lines. Space activates summary description, as 3v and 3r introduce the reader into the layout device of the doublet or double page and prepare him for the provocative properties of space.

And, indeed, 4v and 4r ("LE MAÎTRE . . . sans nef / n'importe / où vaine") are provocative in appearance. The layout is not formally calligrammatic, the reading grid is not normal, and the fixed print seems to converge upon the center which is continually interrupted by a rigidly maintained margin. The center margin no longer serves as a reading aid, but as an obstacle, which causes full stops in the linearity of the printed doublet, which, by contrast to all preceding pages, is extremely busy, filled up with black print. Placement of the words is irregular, if not erratic, as the variety of space intervals has been considerably increased: space not only serves to isolate and construct words and lines, but it also impedes their identification. Space is dense; it has solidity, which is disruptive, obstructive, and non-informative. The frame of space is no longer found in the top, bottom, and side margins; rather, it is now central, a physi-

The Space of the Text 65

cal column which divides the doublet. But the partitioning is not equal. The indentation on the verso is far right, reinforcing the center column of space, while nearly one-third of the lines on the right begin at the center margin and extend nearly to the usual outside margin (character space no. 66), only to be dramatically pulled back as far as possible to character space no. 1 at the center.

Reconstruction of the layout confirms the problematics of the reading procedure: top to bottom, then left to right? Or left to right, then top to bottom? Or a mixture to be decided line by line, space by space? Is the "que se" of line 11, 4v, to be read across the center space margin as part of "prépare" of line 11, 4r, or has the "que se" been arbitrarily cut off in order to capture an incomplete thought? Certainly, the "prépare" of 4r is grouped with two complete verb forms, "s'agite" and "mêle," and can be read syntactically without either the conjunction "que" or the reflexive pronoun "se." Do pages 4v and 4r even form a doublet? Space is unreliable as a guide: it is no longer performative.

Study of the typography of 4v and 4r shows that it repeats exactly that used on 3v and 4v. The highest line and first unit on the verso is printed in upper-case 10-point medium; "LE MAÎTRE" is print-wise equal to the "SOIT" of 3v, and, indeed, it serves as the organizing element of the page space. The rest of the print is in the standard 8-point medium and only two words, "Nombre" and "Esprit," feature an initial upper-case letter; all the rest of the lines are in lower case. Because the space is so obstructive and non-instructional, the type becomes reliable and informational. Indeed, unstable space stabilizes and validates the black print.

Page 4v contains more space than 4r. The verso consists of 16 short lines, the longest single line contains only 37 character spaces, the longest grouping of lines covers only slightly half of its possible character space length (45 out of 72.6), and its least indentation is 27, while the verso itself begins in character space no. 47, off-center, and in such a position that it calls attention to the center which is space. Moreover, 4v is marked by considerable spacing which is achieved not only through tremendous indentation (every line is emphatically indented), but also through interline spacing. The 16 lines of 4v are 2, 5-6, 8, 11, 14, 16, 23-30, and 33.

In contrast, the 21 lines of 4r are longer, extend further across the page (as far as space no. 66), and seem to assert the normalcy of the center margin. Also, the recto does not rely on the verso; it can be read in its entirety without reference to the verso. Where the verso seems suspended, cut off, and incomplete—arrested, the recto is self-sufficient, independent, and whole.

While the recto is an entity by itself, the verso calls attention to the recto. The recto lines apparently "fill in" the spaces in-between the verso lines, for on the recto one finds lines 2-3, 6, 8-9, 11-14, 16, 18-21, 24, 30-31, 33, and 35-37. There are nine possible crossover lines since there are nine lines on both the verso and the recto which occur concomitantly and which may syntactically agree: lines 2, 6, 8, 11, 14, 16, 24, 30, and 33. In all of *Un Coup de dés*, 4v and 4r have the most number of possible crossover lines, in fact, twice as many as on any other pages in the work, or, in other words, over one-third of the entire group of crossover lines in the text. But, of the nine possible crossover lines, only one, line 11, has the potential to be an authentic crossover line on syntactical grounds: "que se prépare." The rest are syntactically, lexically, and semantically variable and open to interpretation.

The recto opposes the verso on what may be called doublet 4 (by virtue of its one credible crossover line) in terms of layout, filling in the spaces, but actually countering the recording of the verso. For every coherent group displayed on the verso, there is a negating unit on the recto: "unique"-"autre," "Nombre"-"Esprit," "ne peut pas"-"être," "inférant"-"calculs," "conflagration"-"horizon unanime," "hésite"-"détient," "naufrage"-"sans nef." The obstacle of the white center becomes the subject of the page: a struggle. The efforts of "LE MAÎTRE" described by the printed elements are crystallized by the obstruction of the rigorous center margin. The key to the layout of doublet 4 is its space.

The struggle of doublet 4 is intensified on 5v which confronts maximum unused space on 5r. Of all the pages in *Un Coup de dés*, 5r contains the least number of printed elements: only one: "N'ABOLIRA." Because the exercise of laying out the pages has already established earlier pages as doublets (3 and 4), the reader's eye automatically looks first at 5v and 5r as one unit, another doublet, only to be struck by the tremendous space on 5r, a space which is all the more enhanced by its single word in 22-point bold upper-case letters, placed on lines 36-37, nearly at the very bottom of the page. The impact of the physical appearance of "N'ABOLIRA," as well as its inscription in the future tense, figuratively repudiates the emptiness of the space which precedes it. The space of the recto is literally "read" and intellectually grasped before the reader undertakes the details of the verso. Again, as on doublet 4, the recto counters the verso, is in contrast to it, and is a complete entity by itself. However, 5v and 5r do not form an authentic doublet. The phrase on the recto also recalls the titular phrase of the title page and its first elements on 1r and 2r. It is not startling in appearance; on the contrary, its very typographical appearance recalls its own actual subject, "UN COUP DE DÉS," and its negative adverbial modifier, "JAMAIS." The great amount of space confirms its legitimacy and forges intertextual relationships.

Reading the recto before the verso alters the reading grid; instead of the pattern of top to bottom, left to right, the space on 5r requires a new procedure: right to left, bottom to top. In opposition to the vast space and highly ornamental printed unit of the recto, the verso seems quite regular in its 8-point medium, lower case, and rather well-filled with units of the printed, some 28 lines of print which are spatially subdivided fairly evenly into several viable, rational groups. Page 5v appears stable, and the impression of order is reinforced by the only word on the page which begins with an upper-case letter: "Fiançailles," a word of harmonious union. The sense of structured calmness is brought about by the six lines which begin in character space no. 1, several groups which continue almost to the center margin, several groupings which have no additional interline spacing so that they resemble deliberately composed stanzas or paragraphs, and no units so isolated that they disrupt the coherence of the page. Even the isolation of "Fiançailles," which is indented 62 character spaces and ends exactly at the center margin, is not disturbing because it follows the phrase "une chance oiseuse," in turn directly below the line which repeats twice the word "aïeul" (terms of conjunction and succession) and because it leads directly back to the left side margin where there is placed a term of continuity: "dont."

The setting off of "folie" at the end of the page is equally non-surprising, for here the surrounding space serves as a pause before the final summation of the page: "folie." "Folie" is, of course, a psychological term, which influences the second reading of the space on 5r. But, because the reading grid was altered, this space has already been repudiated by the printed unit "N'ABOLIRA." The isolated summation of "folie" further denies the futility of space. On the contrary, the space is undeniable in its own right; it has body, it has existence, it is—and it will not be abolished. The space is psychologically and literally "read."

In fact, the space of 5r is continually recalled throughout the layout of 5v. The layout of 5v maintains the normal reading grid, top to bottom, left to right, but the pull is actually to the empty space, to what is not, rather than to what is. As the lines of 5v lengthen in a movement to the right, to the space, the space increasingly becomes a structuring factor, a desired place to "read." But, as the groupings of 5v stretch right, they are suddenly returned to the extreme left, all the way to the lefthand printer margin. The space of 5r cannot be entered, cannot be penetrated, it exists without print; it is immutable, enigmatic, non-derivative, non-explicable. Moreover, it cannot be experienced. Neither hostile in its impenetrability nor welcoming in its presence, the space simply is—beyond attitudes and beyond definition.

The use of such a large amount of space and its dominating position on 5r prevent the actualization of an authentic double page. On the other hand, the display of intensified space in opposition to a page of visual orderliness and the emphasis given to the word "Fiançailles" by capital letter and placement, as well as its lexical base, do serve to create a doublet in reverse.

The Space of the Text   69

The two pages are not read as one unit, but their layout in counterpoint generates the illusion of a doublet, an illusion which is then made real by the movement of the verso toward the recto. The impenetrability of the space on the recto is magnetic in its attraction. By using so much space on the recto, the layout reveals an annihilation of the center space margin; the recto has no role in establishing a center margin, thereby destroying the rigid columnar division of the preceding doublet, 4. The crossover lines of 5v and 5r are those of space, which in reverse destroy the linearity of the verso. The space of the recto forces the geometrical straightness of the verso into a circularity. Space is irrevocably non-measurable and destructive to linearity. Space is, then, a-logical and asymmetrical.

The reversal pattern of doublet 5 is in turn effectively reversed by the next doublet, 6, on which the rapid, more animated italic face seems to penetrate the space: *"Une insinuation . . . simple."* In contrast to the 22-point bold elevation of 5r, 6v begins with a unit in 10-point upper-case italic, *"COMME SI,"* and 6r ends with the very same unit. The space of doublet 6 is framed, as the italic lines seemingly flow across the pages. The italic face of the 8-point lower case is lighter than the 10-point italic upper-case units which determine its beginning and end. But, unlike doublet 5, 6v and 6r form an authentic, straightforward doublet, confirmed by the two framing conjunctions, *"COMME SI,"* and reaffirmed by the constant movement to the right. The verso *"COMME SI"* is on line 8 and not deeply indented (it begins on character space no. 13). However, the next line is deeply indented, character space no. 58, and lowered to line 11; moreover, the first word begins with an upper-case letter, *"Une,"* which calls attention to its parenthetical nature. The left-to-right sloping, characteristic of the italic face, seems to deny the divisiveness of the center margin, as all four lines on the verso reinforce the negation of center space by operating as crossover lines: *"insinuation"-"simple," "silence"-"enroulée," "proche"-"tourbillon," "voltige"-"autour."* But syntactically, there is interruption in the *"silence"-"enroulée"* combination; *"enroulée"* must refer to the only preceding feminine singular noun on the doublet, *"insinuation,"* which is on the verso.

Hence, the back and forth movement between the verso and recto is strengthened on syntactical grounds.

However, these same syntactical grounds for setting relationships also call attention to the previously unobtrusive center margin. The verso is an independent page, which does not require the recto for a cohesive reading. It can be read top to bottom, left to right or left to the right center margin. Awareness of the layout of the center margin and of the finished appearance of the verso reestablishes the impenetrability of space. Space orders the page, establishes the units to be identified and to be read, and determines the limits of the page. Page 6v is serene, orderly, and quiet; the surrounding space is so peaceful that the great field of space on the verso is not noticed. Page 6v is self-sufficient in its silence. The indentation and position of the *"COMME SI"* is not an enclosing frame; rather, it indicates space beyond the frame or the field of space as the primary component of the page. Space on 6v is delimited, as top, bottom, and left margins are effaced by the inner frame of *"COMME SI"* and the inherent left to right tilt of the lower-case italic.

However, effacement of the top, bottom, and left margins forces 6v to 6r; not only does the first line of 6r begin in character space no. 1 on the same line as the first 8-point line of the verso, but it also ends lower down on its page and its final unit repeats exactly the first unit of the verso: *"COMME SI."* The *"COMME SI"* of the recto also ends flush left at the printer margin on character space no. 72. The topography of 6r carries the left to right movement from 6v to the farthest point possible and then reasserts space as frame, maximum solidity: *"tourbillon"* and *"gouffre."* Of the 12 lines on 6r, four begin at the center margin in character space no. 1 and extend to the left in a downward position. For example, *"hurlé"* ends on character space no. 44 and completes a group of five lines, a group created, first, by no extra interline spacing and, second, by having each unit in the spatially created group begin where the previous unit ends. The lines are so positioned on 6r that they are visually hurled back to the center margin to begin again their extension across the white page, only to end with a bracketing frame in the final unit *"COMME SI."*

The Space of the Text

As a doublet, page 6 is deceptive in its appearance. The layout clearly shows an imbalance of 5 lines on the verso to 12 on the recto, as well as an imbalance of character counts—the longer lines being on the recto. In fact, there are only ten words on 6v, while there are 29 on 6r. In addition, the main lines of 6v are orderly in their alignment with the center margin, while the main lines of 6r are disorderly in their figuration upon the page. Page 6r is more animated than 6v, and, indeed 6r features a vocabulary of action: *"enroulée," "précipité," "hurlé," "tourbillon," "joncher," "fuir," "berce"*—a lexicon which clashes with the quiet gentleness of the verso: *"insinuation," "silence," "voltige."* As the *"COMME SI"* of the recto recalls the *"COMME SI"* of the verso, the doublet is redoubled upon itself; within the circle of the frames (*"COMME SI"*), the left to right direction is maintained, but the space beyond retains its mystery of formation. Space multiplies the possible directions and combinations; it has the potential to unite opposites as well as destroy their union: *"silence"-"tourbillon."* Space has the power to create.

The omnipotent quality of space continues to be a dominant factor in the suspended layout of 7v: four words in lower-case 8-point italic on only two lines (9 and 17) in a total of 26 character spaces (31-53 and 68-71): *"plume solitaire éperdue / sauf . . . par sa petite raison virile / en foudre."* Yet, the layout of 7v is not centered in its field of space; rather, it moves continually to the right; there is no return to the left. The first printed line is simply there, surrounded by space above, below, left, and right: origin and outcome, limitlessness and definition, at the same time. The *"plume solitaire éperdue"* is dwarfed by its positioning in such isolation; it is directionless, being all directions at once (north, south, east, and west); space is open, non-measurable, multiplicitous. But, the formless void of space is the undeniable field for formation. The far right positioning of the isolated *"sauf"* leads directly to the recto, which begins on the exact same line (17) and in the first possible character space (no. 1).

On the other hand, the 15 lines in the lower-case 8-point italic of 7r differ completely from the two brief, isolated lines

72   The Dynamics of Space

of the verso. Page 7r is active in its left to right movement and, by having its longer lines placed in the lower half of the page, it carries more weight in its activity. Page 7r repudiates the void of 7v. The layout of 7r may almost be described as defiant, for it challenges the space above and the space to the left (the bottom half of the verso). A layout in opposition, introduced by the last printed unit on its verso, *"sauf,"* stratifies the void through the encounter. Line 17 is a crossover line, *"sauf / que,"* and the next element on the recto, *"la,"* functions also as a crossover line in reverse, for it must refer to the *"plume,"* the very first printed element on the verso. The double crossover not only creates an authoritative doublet, but it also requalifies the amount of space on both the verso and recto: the verso, having no margins, no end, is absorbed into the layout of the recto and receives its substance through the elongation of the recto italic lines. Space does not record (*"immobilise"*), but extends the fixity of print *"en foudre."* Space expands form; it does not reduce it.

Yet, as doublet 8 asserts, space modifies and controls flux: *"soucieux / expiatoire et pubère / muet . . . qui imposa / une borne à l'infini."* Doublet 8 concentrates on the center; the verso lines move towards this margin and are fixed by it; the recto lines move out from the center margin in a looser positioning on the page, but their outward (to the right) extension is limited. The final element on the recto ends in character space no. 40.

Page 8v begins in an orderly, logical position: line 1, character space no. 1: *"soucieux."* The entire page is in lower-case 8-point italic face, which continually slopes right to left, reinforcing the normality of the reading grid. Order is maintained by the spatial division of the page into two well-defined groups: lines 1-3 and 16-24; the second group is further subdivided by space into two sections: lines 16-21 and line 24. The first main group on 8v confirms the top and lefthand side margins or frames, while the second group (including the two subdivisions) confirms the center margin or frame, for three of the seven lines end in the last possible character space, no. 72, while the second group is delineated by a deeply indented first element (character space no. 39), which begins with a capital letter: *"La."* The expansive

The Space of the Text 73

characteristic of the first group is opposed by the more compacted nature of the second group.

The groupings on 8v create an independent page, which can be treated or read by itself. Only the last line is an incontestable crossover line *("ultimes"-"bifurquées")* which extends the quality of the description but does not vitally contribute to it. In fact, *"bifurquées"* seems superfluous; a siren or lorelei's final scaly appendage is generally accepted as being forked. Indeed, *"bifurquées"* is placed so that its semantic and syntactical base make line 24 an undeniable crossover line, and the layout of 8v does not need to cross until the end. Furthermore, it automatically crosses at the end because the page does not continue to the bottom margin; it stops short with line 24, while the recto is the most occupied by print from line 24 to 33. The final printed element of the last line of 8v, *"ultimes,"* also ends in the last possible character space for that line, no. 72, and *"bifurquées"* begins in the first possible space on its line, no. 1.

One result is that the bottom of the recto receives attention before its first half. After all, the first group of the verso ends in character space no. 54, considerably short of the center margin; it is not a line which crosses this margin. In fact, there is no printed line 3 of the recto—crossover is denied and the integrity of 8v as an independent page, not part of a doublet, is established, and the indented, capitalized *"La"* confirms it.

The layout of 8r is a layout of space. Where space seems to be a patterning device which creates a sense of order on the verso, it disorders on the recto. Page 8r begins on line 4 in lower-case 8-point italic at an indented character space (no. 15) and consists of a very short four-letter unit: *"rire."* Line 5 is space. Line 6 consists of an even shorter unit, *"que,"* and is indented to character space no. 21 (*"rire"* having ended on no. 18). Lines 7 and 8 are space. Line 9 is disruptively different; the two-letter unit, *"SI,"* appears in all upper-case letters and in 15-point bold italic face; its two letters cover six character spaces (nos. 24-30), and, as a unit, it is then followed by six lines of space. The concomitant lines on the verso are also space. Space crosses to space; space is flux. The italic face which has an inherent built-in left to right motion is stabilized, as the space itself becomes the active element. To attain stability and restore fixity to the black print, 8r must relate to 8v. Syntactically, it is logical to lay out 8v and 8r as a doublet, for the masculine singular adjectives on 8v agree with the masculine singular noun *"rire"* on 8r, if indeed *"rire"* is a noun as Gardner Davies asserts and not an infinitive.[15] Space interrogates form and places its identity in doubt.

Space continues to be the main feature of the layout of 8r. The remaining 11 lines are short and draw upon interline spacings, which disrupt rather than cohere the groupings. Lines 16-33, the block of the printing in the rest of the recto, contain seven lines of space (17-19, 21, 25, 27, 31) and the longest line of the 11 printed lines covers only 20 character spaces (line 33). Three lines begin in character space no. 1; of the three, *"bifurquées"* does not "fit" and forces a crossover to the verso for identification. The interrogation by space established by the layout of the top half of the recto is continued in the bottom half, for the page "reads" until the unit, *"bifurquées,"* is set out. The cue, *"bifurquées,"* establishes 8 as a doublet, but, what is more important, it identifies the forked crossover pattern of the doublet itself. Line 3 of 8v (the end of the first group on the verso) crosses into the space of line 3 of 8r and moves down to line 4 of 8r; the top to bottom direction continues on the recto, down to line 9, *"SI,"* and then the space of the recto returns to the space of the verso—space is the continuum of the doublet. Lines 16 and 20 of the verso and recto become printed crossovers, *"aigrette de vertige," "sirène debout."* But crossover by space predominates: the space of lines 17-19 on 8r crosses to the print of those same lines on 8v, and the patterning with space, in space, continues in a back and forth manner until the verso ends in space and the recto continues to complete what the verso began. The center margin of space, while maintained almost rigidly on both the verso and recto pages, ceases to divide the verso from the recto by entering the space of the doublet as a whole. Only space is self-sufficient, can penetrate itself and experience itself.

Where space dominates doublet 8, the black print seems to take over on 9v and 9r, which are pages of considerable typo-

The Space of the Text

graphic and topographic variation. The print is literally out of control, as the eye races from type change to type change, up and down, left to right, right to left, down and up. The 22-point upper-case bold of "LE HASARD" attracts by size and position, as well as by association to the titular phrase, which this unit completes. Not only does "LE HASARD" dominate, but it describes the disorderliness of both the verso and recto and indicates that print, not space, is the patterning component, a reversal of doublet 8. The print asserts that 9 is a doublet, as well as the organizing principle.

Layout of 9v reveals only two mixed type faces: the 12-point bold italic upper case of *"C'ÉTAIT"* and *"CE SERAIT"* appear in dramatic contrast to the 3-point italic lower case of the units, which are also placed so close to the considerably elevated units that the difference between the two is exaggerated. *"C'ÉTAIT"* and *"CE SERAIT"* define the side margins; *"C'ÉTAIT"* is placed on line 2, flush against the right margin and ends in character space no. 72, while *"CE SERAIT"* on line 21 begins at the left margin in character space no. 1. The intervening 20 lines of space serve to create a right to left movement and negate the usual reading grid of left to right, as well as the left to right tilt of the italic face. Three-point is the smallest type size used in *Un Coup de dés*. Its appearance in italic face lightens its darkness (gray, not black), while its placement in contrast to one of the three larger type sizes used serves to diminish it even more. The gray shadings achieved by the 3-point italic face also contrast with the bold weight of the 12-point italic type face. Hence, the units in the lower-case 3-point italic are not only the smallest in *Un Coup de dés*, but they are also the lightest in shade and so have the least weight in the entire text. Only by their positioning in direct relationship with the larger, darker 12-point upper-case units do they gain distinction as printed units. Each 3-point character occupies a half character space, a typographic means for presenting the maximum in minimum space. While *"issu stellaire"* consists of 14 letters, it only occupies seven character spaces and, therefore, can be centered exactly under the seven-letter unit *"C'ÉTAIT,"* which in 12-point requires one character space per letter. Because the 3-point is

76   The Dynamics of Space

also only a half space in height, its positioning under *"C'ÉTAIT"* creates an interline space; *"issu stellaire"* is on line 3 but technically on only the lower half of that line, bringing about an extra one-half interline space. The unit is slightly more isolated in layout than it first appears to be, still grouped with *"C'É-TAIT"* but not quite as dependent upon it as it would have been had it been placed in the upper half of the line. Its centered position creates a grouping, in which no print unit is more distinctive than the other, regardless of size and weight.

The other 9v grouping bears the same contrast in size and weight, but the placement differs. The four units in 3-point italic lower case resume the left to right motion on lines 25-27. The first, *"pire,"* occupies character spaces no. 11 and no. 12; while it is not centered under the full larger unit, *"CE SERAIT,"* which covers 19 character spaces (nos. 1-18), it is centered under the verb itself, *"SERAIT,"* which provides the starting point for the four small print units which complete 9v. These units extend nearly to the center margin at the right, as the interspacing (character space and interline space) increase the magnitude of the surrounding space.

While 9v mixes two faces, weights, and sizes, 9r mixes five and represents the only page in *Un Coup de dés* which uses more than two different type faces, weight, and sizes. Such a mixing of types is extravagant, to the point that the page is choppy and does not sustain interest. It is neither a typographical nor topographical unit but several units in one, multiplied by the spatial components. The five different type sizes and faces are in order of appearance on the page: 12-point uppercase bold italic (*"LE NOMBRE"*); 8-point upper-case medium ("EXISTÂT-IL," "COMMENÇÂT-IL ET CESSÂT-IL," "SE CHIFFRÂT-IL," "ILLUMINÂT-IL"); 3-point lower-case medium (lines 5, 8-9, 12) placed in alignment with the 8-point medium upper-case units); 22-point bold upper case ("**LE HASARD**"), 8-point italic lower case (lines 29-36), with one upper-case initial letter (*"Choit"*). The spacing creates four distinct blocks: line 1 (*"LE NOMBRE"*); lines 4-13 (the 8-point upper-case medium and the 3-point lower-case medium); lines 23-24 ("**LE HASARD**"); and lines 29-36 (8-point italic lower case). The page is more highly disciplined in layout than its appearance indicates. The spatial blockings create unrelated areas, which the type sizes and faces of each print area confirm since the typography is not overly mixed. There are no crossover lines of print; offsetting by space prevents interaction by type. The space blocks out the figure of the page, gives the page its identity and unity as a page; the print is secondary despite its topographical and typographical variety.

With no authentic printed crossover lines, the layout of the doublet is denied. However, there are numerous crossovers of the space, and the overpowering use of the 22-point upper-case bold of the recto dominates both the verso and recto—the recto by print contrast, the verso by its placement opposite the larger block of space (lines 4-24). In addition, the recto has no discernible center. The most dramatic printed unit, "**LE HASARD**," covers lines 23 and 24 and character spaces nos. 18-62. The center of both the verso and recto is the same: space. While the verso identifies the lefthand side margin and the center margin, the recto identifies only the top margin. Having no side margins, especially having no center left margin, and having no bottom margin, the recto draws into its space the verso page and then is in turn extended into space. The recto, for all its studied finality of mixed type sizes and faces, has no limit, no beginning, and no final resting place: *"gouffre."* Hence, 9v and 9r form a doublet; the type does not provide the system of the double page, but, instead, the space supplies the left to right, top to bottom directional grid. The unsystematic layout is organized by space. Doublet 9 is between chaos (a non-system of print) and the possibility of system through its space.

Organization by space continues on 10v, which begins with space and which is characterized by the use of a large amount of space. Page 10v contains four lines, divided into two groups, which are separated first by space and second by type. Beginning on line 13 in character space no. 42, "RIEN" is in 10-point upper-case medium. The second group is in the regular 8-point lower-case medium, covers lines 17-19, and is indented to character space no. 50, ending at the center margin in character space no. 72. Page 10v is a return to linearity in the straightness of the medium type face, and the lines move in the standard left to right order until the center space poses an end to the direction. However, the linearity of the apparent horizontals of the printed lines—the topography—is actually one of verticals by the typography. The upper-case 10-point medium type for a four-letter (short) word is more vertical because of the large amount of space which surrounds it. In the second paginal print group, the 8-point lower-case medium block, there is considerable verticality attained by the ascending kerns, especially d, l, b. The unit begins with "de la mémorable," and the ascending kerns point upward. Moreover, the layout demands that this group be placed so that the b of "mémorable" be over the f of "fût" and that f be over the l of "l'évènement." The t of the last print element of the page is also vertical. The top to bottom reading of the print group is not so much reversed as it is neutralized. The f of the intervening word "fût" is an ascending kern in print—its descending kern in script is eliminated by type.[16] The vertical kerns and the capital letters stabilize the space of 10v; contrary to the lexical meaning of the unit "RIEN" which dominates by size, it has identity. Space is not a meaningless void.

Page 10r uses the same two type faces and sizes as 10v: 10-point upper-case medium and 8-point lower-case medium. But, more important, it begins where the verso ends, not on the same line (19) but on the next line, 20: "accompli en vue. . . ." Page 10r, then, resumes the top to bottom direction neutralized by the verticals of 10v, which the observance of the center margin reinforces. All three groups of print on the page begin scrupulously on character space no. 1 (lines 20, 27, and 33). Two of the three groups contain both kinds of type, but the 10-point upper-case medium units do not create the groups, which are formed by interline spacing and indentation. Space has greater power than print; space actually dissolves differences. The units "N'AURA EU LIEU" and "QUE LE LIEU" attract attention but do not pattern the topography. Space is, indeed, place.

Not a true doublet, 10v and 10r are, however, complimentary; 10r finishes 10v. Moreover, the layouts of 10v and 10r show that once the two type sizes are examined and demonstrated to be non-patterning devices, each page can stand alone; there is even a possible negative noun subject for the "N'AURA EU LIEU" phrase in the preceding "nul / humain" on the recto. As compliments, 10r continues the metamorphosis of "RIEN" into "LIEU," and the past participle, "accompli," extends the event of the verso into the recto. Even the verticality of the verso is maintained on the recto through the capital letters of the 10-point units and the frequency of ascending kerns, especially in the keywords of the 8-point units: "accompli," "résultat," "élévation," "l'absence," "clapotis," "disperser," "l'acte," "fonde," "perdition," and even more so in the final phrase: "toute réalité se dissout." As a plane of organization, space extends upward as well as outward and effaces vertical and horizontal directional grids. Space even denies that capital letters actually are initiatory signals, much less indicators of the parts of a whole.

The type faces and sizes of 10v and 10r are used on 11v, which contains the same type mixtures: a 10-point upper-case medium unit on line 2 is followed by an 8-point lower-case medium on line 3, another 10-point upper-case unit on line 4, followed by a final 8-point lower-case medium phrase on line 5. Moreover, the interval spacing from print line to print line is maintained in a regular manner. As the print lines descend the page, indentation is maintained at one interval from the end of each preceding line. The neutralization of the descending pattern is also continued through the capital letters and the ascending kerns: "à l'altitude," "aussi loin qu'un endroit." Interestingly, the only print group extends across the page, from its first character space, 9 1/2, to the center margin, character space no. 72, effectively introducing the first printed line on 11r.

The first line of the recto begins, or continues, on line 7 in the no. 1 character space. Page 11r, in contrast, is a full page, having 24 lines of print and being the only page in *Un Coup de dés* to end on the last possible print line, 38. Page 11r has a finished topography; even the first six lines of space do not lend the page an incomplete quality, rather, this top space permits the recto to continue and complete the verso. The space creates a doublet where print does not, and it does so at the beginning of the layout of the page. Pages 11v and 11r contain no topographical surprises; they are remarkably harmonious, as the space of the pages integrates the four lines of the verso into the 24 lines of the recto. The recto is the natural successor to its verso and the space on the verso envelops the product of the recto.

The recto is almost a perfect integration of space and print, as the only non-standard print line, "UNE CONSTELLATION," appears on line 19, exactly halfway down the page. This print line also balances the 10-point upper-case medium units of the verso, a second reintegration of the verso into the recto. Moreover, "UNE CONSTELLATION" establishes a new inner frame; it is the first line on the page which ends in character space no. 64, the exact space on which lines 24, 26, 35, and 38, the last line, end. No line extends beyond character space no. 64. The symmetry of the right margin is also observable on the left: lines 7, 12, and 29 all begin in character space no. 1. The topography aligns the page vertically in establishing left and right margins, while the final line identifies and sets the bottom margin, yet the variety of line indentation moves the printed lines horizontally from left to right. Respect for printer margins and the standard type base, as well as the establishment of a paginal center and the recto as the natural successor to the verso, reveal the all-inclusiveness of space. All is possible because of space.

The two 8-point upper-case letters ("Septentrion" and "Nord") do not even draw attention. They are standard, used because they begin proper names. The apparent fixity of "UNE CONSTELLATION" in upper-case 10-point is overcome by the return to the standard 8-point for the rest of the page, a page which moves quickly downward, left to right through indentation and interline spacing. The direction too is usual, regular, standard. Doublet 11, especially its recto, reasserts paginal familiarity in its very normalcy. Space is a comfortable, almost comforting, facilitator to permanence; moreover, openness and freedom are intelligible (if not intellectual), readable (if not decipherable). Space provides access to creation and to the communication of creation.

The final line of *Un Coup de dés* is a lexical, syntactical, and semantic affirmation of infinite, abstract, pure, creative, authentic space. Placed on the last line of the page and indented to character space no. 33, that is, indented deeply to the right, and following a double interline space, its very position announces its importance and independence.[17] The typography is equally emphasized by the four upper-case letters ("Toute Pensée émet un Coup de Dés"), which further finalize the page and the text. Topography and typography combine to complete the work. However, the last part of the line repeats the first four units of the titular phrase and the first page of the text itself, returning 11r full-circle to the title page and to the beginning of the text. But, of even more significance, the typography of the last line is not the same as that of the titular phrase: *Un coup de Dés* of the title is now "un Coup de Dés." The change from product or effective outcome (*"Dés"* of the title page) to the activity which causes it makes possible the existence of the object ("Coup de Dés"). The context of the present (and all verbs on 11r are either in the present tense or the present participial form) is then linked to the future tense of the title (*"abolira"*) and to the completed immediate past evoked by the past participle "LANCÉ," the first verb form in the text, which qualifies the temporal adverb of the title, *"jamais."* The fourth dimension of space, time (and *Un Coup de dés* is a text replete with adverbs and conjunctions of time) is transmuted into all time ("Toute Pensée émet"). Space is not only immeasurable, but also a-temporal: all-inclusive. As the last line of the text returns to the title page, the text itself has no beginning and no end, no established system of procedure. The space of the text is the fundamental structure and procedure, both subject and object, a Sartrian *en-soi-pour-soi*, "une incorruptible unité."[18]

Establishment of the layout of *Un Coup de dés* from the actual title page to the final recto reveals that the text has ultimate form; it is "**POÈME**," presented in such a contrived and studiously artificial layout in its typography and topography that it must return to its only source—itself, Poetry. Hence, there are no rational divisions but polyvalent deviations and variations. Differentiation becomes expansion, the last word is first, and analysis is a synonym of synthesis. The form is its own function in the continual adjustment—layout—of the substance of space.

Chapter III

CONFIGURATION OF SPACE

Space is indisputably the predominant element of Mallarmé's *Un Coup de dés*, occupying as it does 72% of the text. Examination of the layout reveals an orchestrated typography, a set calibration of each word, line, and page, and an arbitrary placement of each unit on the page. No two pages are alike: type sizes and faces, alignment, indentation, margins, beginning and end lines, groupings and interline spacing so vary in general appearance and in the details that the composition itself emerges as the focal point of the reader's attention.

To a printer, *Un Coup de dés* is an outrageous waste of space, and, indeed, as Danielle Mihram reports, the printer Didot allegedly refused to print the work, saying "c'est un fou qui a écrit ça" (43). Even in today's highly technological and sophisticated world, the cost of printing *Un Coup de dés* according to Mallarmé's wishes and including the Redon illustrations is almost prohibitive, which may explain why we do not have a readily available, affordable, accurate edition. Nothing in *Un Coup de dés* lines up; the embedded codes of the printing trade (font style, type size, column measure, interline spacing) are not respected; if anything, they are violated on every page. But, even more "scandalous" to a printer's eye is Mallarmé's denial of the printer's goal, namely the reduction of wasted space. It must also be noted that a printer prints in a completely different order than the writer writes or the reader reads. A printer does one page at a time, and the order of the printing is dictated by the folding and cutting processes of the signature of four pages. The first printer decision is the basic type style; once it is determined, all pages are then based on that style, which determines the basic type size; the page size (exterior size) dictates the type area and its line length, and every page conforms to the chosen line length. Printing is an exact technology, based on an intentional, utilitarian process, as well as a commercial industry. Print makes the page intelligible and legible.

Certainly, Mallarmé understood the basics of the printing process. But, he saw beyond the set tabulation of print as a practical, functional, and strictly mechanical arrangement. In what could well be described as an act of deliberate mayhem, he consciously destroys the pragmatics of printer space and replaces it with literary or esthetic space. The space makes the text; the space elevates print to the level of art. Print, then, by itself is at best only quasi-esthetic as in newspaper layout, but, for Mallarmé, print is an element of space if not an actual art of space in *Un Coup de dés*. Hence, Mallarmé views the function of print only in terms of its surrounding space. The greater the surrounding space, the less utilitarian and the more artistic the print. On this point, one need only look at the Pléiade edition in comparison to the 1914 Gallimard edition or the Ronat 1980 reproduction; the reduced format of the Pléiade printing makes *Un Coup de dés* more legible, more organized, more orderly, more fixed in its compactness, and, therefore, more rational. In contrast, the considerable expanse of the white space of the folio-sized pages desired by Mallarmé disorders the printed units of the text and emphasizes their irregularity and discontinuity. The appearance is bizarre, the design is untrustworthy, and the format is so stylized that its very artificiality is set in relief. The sense of a rational arrangement layout in a compact format becomes in the full-scale format an arrangement of deliberate confusion. Print is not meaningful, for relationships are grasped through the use of space, which annuls the normal patterns established by print.[1]

Basically, print is static, inert, concrete, impersonal, and utilitarian. Print is what the reader reads; it bestows order in its linearity, sets points of convergence and divergence, establishes sequence and stratification (subordination), fixes the fiction by controlling groupings of words which in turn offer precision and concision in the determination of the restraints which bring about meaning and the communication of that meaning through the assembly of the words into lines. Print is a psychological framework for the reader, who goes forward, word by word, line by line, page by page, identifying figures and their relations, or he goes backward in order to reconstruct the events of the forward-motion of the narrative. As Marshall McLuhan states, the medium of print modifies human sensibility by arresting thought and speech; print is, then, a mental state because it manipulates space.[2]

The dynamics of space in Mallarmé's text are comparable to the challenge which the sculptor faces before a mass of uncut, unpolished stone: how to impart vitality to the inert, a problem which Mallarmé poses in his "Le Tombeau d'Edgar Poe." Of all the commentaries on *Un Coup de dés*, those offered by Robert Cohn unerringly initiate readings which include the "added dimensions of 'polypolarity.'" For Cohn, the space of the white page is the "lucidity" of the multidimensional or sculptural poem.[3] Despite these perceptive remarks on space,[4] readers still accept Valéry's observation that Mallarmé combines "la vision avec la parole" in an effort to "fixer le dessin [de la pensée],"[5] as well as Teodor de Wyzewa's early division of all of Mallarmé's poetry into "Prose" for the ideas and "Dessin" for the sensations.[6] Beginning with, first, Albert Thibaudet, and, second, Henri Mondor, and continuing with the Groupe d'Atelier, the type choices and their placement constitute the essential part of critical commentaries. As a result, readers concentrate on the type as a pictorial device for the ordering of the text and subordinate space to a purely supportive role. At best, space promises a pattern in its invitation to pause and develop another reading (Bowie 123), while the type variations permit different readings, what Tibor Papp terms the "outil" which dictates the "icône" or reading through its "ordonnance graphique."[7] Space is a "sur-signifié . . . un vide structurant"[8] which so affects the print that the construction by type permits language to incorporate and express silence. Space simply replaces punctuation and, in so doing, offers configurations upon the page.

Certainly, the type in *Un Coup de dés* is important, but the basic problem in a text which consists of 2 1/2 times more space than print is perforce not affected by the type on the page (patterning), but by the effect of the space on the type. Contrary to a prevailing iconographic view of the type in *Un Coup de dés*, it is space which manipulates the type and makes the inert, immovably fixed print dynamic. It is not a question of configuration but of defiguration; the space surrounding the type is in Mallarmé's own words "où se trouve armature intellectuelle" (P207).[9]

What then is the role of type? For Mallarmé, type is "l'état de communication matérielle avec le lecteur."[10] Type is matter and, as matter, it is measurable in its physical appearance; it has dimensions, and it has specific qualities for the purposes of identification. Moreover, type choices are restricted; there are only so many kinds of type sizes and faces available. The problem, then, is not to reproduce these choices and possibilities, but to transform them in the same way that the sculptor transforms the inert mass of stone before him into vigorously expressive art. While Mallarmé recognizes print as matter, his space does not emphasize the physical quality of type; on the contrary, it dematerializes it in an act of expansion. Not only do the words and lines become mobile, dynamic, and free, as the page replaces the verse, but the very text itself becomes its own process and procedure. Space abolishes the medium that the poet must use: print.

Even more important, Mallarmé's esthetics include the conquest of the fixity of print. He understands just how the medium of print determines the text itself, is a constraint imposed on the writer, and is an undeniable limitation to the reading experience. Hence, he deliberately and meticulously experiments with type in order to free the text from its preordained, determining function. In *Un Coup de dés*, Mallarmé literally and figuratively draws upon the immutable fixed order—the highly disciplined layout—so that neither the printer nor the reader is free to determine the restraints of the text. The poet manipulates the medium of print to such an extent that it ceases to make the words and lines speak for themselves. The response to the text—and therefore the communication—lies in the dynamics of the space, not in the print.

To the plastician's eye, the general layout of *Un Coup de dés* greatly resembles poster art: a certain regularity in the positioning of the various elements, the lack of a defined center, typographic gradations and variations, a sense of order but a lack of emotional commitment, a shifted optic, value given to intervals, and a sense of a unified continuous flow as opposed to formal demarcations. Poster art is the art of illusion; it is visual in its reliance upon observation and verbal in its suggestion of a situation or idea. Poster art is synthetic and analytical at the same time, but it is, above all, artificial, belonging neither to the world of formal plastic art nor to the world of the formally written text. In many ways, poster art is to Mallarmé what the mannequin is to the Surrealists: ambiguous, being neither human nor formally artistic, yet sharing both realms of identity and depending upon viewer response for meaning. Hence, Mallarmé writes that Victor Hugo's verse takes the verbal form only of "les cris d'*une* orchestration" (361). What Hugo's verse form lacks is "les cris de *l'*orchestration" because Hugo's verse has delineated demarcations, demonstrated concern with *a* subject, a sense of authorial involvement, a delineated focus, and is based on a symmetrical use of space (regular stanzas).

Turning from poetic models, Mallarmé finds appropriate counterparts in Impressionist art, especially in Manet's work, and in the composer Wagner. Even the Goncourt brothers are kindred creators because of their interest in oriental art, which creates artificial space. For Mallarmé, the Impressionist painters practice asymmetry, convey a sense of organization but not a formal sense of order. While there is a contact with nature, nature is not reproduced in its details which impose a given identity and definition. Impressionist painting is fundamentally unnatural (anti-realist) and therefore based on association and not on narration. Similarly, Wagner's operas are synthetic; the text and the score are inseparable, as his leitmotif is a phrase associated with a character, situation, and idea; it is orchestration of all the parts, not an orchestration of each part. Mallarmé, the Impressionist painters, and Wagner share the same artistic concept, expressed by Mallarmé as "musique dans le sens grec: idée . . . entre" (ibid.).

The concept of being *entre* (ambiguous or a-linear) demands an artistic order which cannot be changed, an author who multiplicitously directs and controls the reading-viewing by a procedure which is undeniably contrived, made-up, unnatural, unreal, and non-stratified. The formalities of the work affirm its design and the discipline of its author, but these same formalities are so obviously artificial that they annul relationships and deny access to referents in the work. The only response possible to such works is reaction (intuition) and then action (intelligence). In the case of the Mallarmé text, the reader is the one directed—not a doer ("faiseur") but a thinker who must ponder the composition before him.[11] He must analyze and synthesize at the same time.

The medium of print may then be described as the fixed points of the text, points which the space of the layout determines. Hence, the text is an object of analysis and the print serves as a system in the space of the page. On the other hand, as examination of the layout shows, space is not just an object in *Un Coup de dés*, for it is so flexible that it changes, page by page, and affects the fixity of the print. In its flux, space may be said to be in a state of becoming, so it is not a system and not just an object (something to be viewed), but also the actual subject of the text. Hence, space hints at systems or all-inclusiveness in being both object and subject, synthetic and analytical. Writing on Edgar Allan Poe, Mallarmé reveals that one of the esthetic affinities between the two of them is the use of space: "Eviter quelque réalité d'échafaudage demeuré autour de cette architecture spontanée et magique, n'y implique pas le manque de puissants calculs et subtils, mais on les ignore; . . . quelle foudre d'instinct renfermer, simplement la vie, vierge, en sa synthèse et loin illuminant tout. . . . le blanc du papier: significatif silence qu'il n'est pas moins beau de composer, que les vers" (872).[12] Space is the procedure and the fundamental structure, which initiates and maintains reader inquiry into the text.

Looking strictly at the print of *Un Coup de dés*, it has become standard to read the work by type similarities, and, accordingly, tradition breaks the text cleanly into four general and very regular divisions:

1. The large bold upper-case units: **UN COUP DE DÉS JAMAIS N'ABOLIRA LE HASARD**. Because this line is also the title, it is read as both the main idea and primary subject or theme of the work.

2. The secondary theme is read variously as consisting of those words which appear in all upper-case letters and appear in a type size smaller than the largest display size used: QUAND BIEN MÊME LANCÉ DANS DES CIRCONSTANCES ÉTERNELLES DU FOND D'UN NAUFRAGE SOIT LE MAÎTRE EXISTÂT-IL COMMENÇÂT-IL ET CESSÂT-IL SE CHIFFRÂT-IL ILLUMINÂT-IL RIEN N'AURA EU LIEU QUE LE LIEU EXCEPTÉ PEUT-ÊTRE UNE CONSTELLATION.

3. The "aside" or hypothesis of the text appears in upper-case italic letters: *COMME SI COMME SI C'ÉTAIT LE NOMBRE CE SERAIT*. Those lines in the smallest italic size and in all lower-case letters are "extenders," modifiers, qualifiers: *"issu stellaire pire non davantage ni moins indifféremment mais autant,"* etc.

4. The "episode" of the text—the explanation, description, recitative body of the poem—is identified as those units which appear in the standard type size and face (8-point medium); the capital letters indicate various adjacent themes, subdivisions, and the general development of the main theme and secondary theme. The eight key words and pragmatic breaks are indicated by capital letters: "l'Abîme," "Nombre," "Esprit," "Fiançailles," "*Une insinuation*," "*La lucide*," "*Choit*," "Septentrion . . . Nord." The four upper-case letters in the last line indicate the conclusion of the text: "Toute Pensée émet un Coup de Dés."

Admittedly, there is logic in the above reader organization of the text by these four typographic groupings, but they are at best a creative interpretation of the ordering of the text. These four standard groupings by type ignore the actual type sizes and faces used and assume that the seven other type sizes and faces are unimportant. Groups 2, 3, and 4 are replete with mixtures in size, face, weight, and letter case. Group 2, for example, contains 12-point bold roman and italic, 10-point medium, and 9-point medium. Group 3 mixes 10-point italic,

8-point medium upper case, with 3-point medium and italic lower case. Group 4 consists of 8-point medium and italic lower case and upper case. Organization and reading strictly by type size and face should be at the very least consistent; moreover, the type variations are either important, change by change, or the type is purely ornamental and not a major construct of the text.

There are three possible ways of organizing by type: A) descending order of sizes; B) type faces in order of appearance; and C) variety of type faces in order of appearance in the text.

A. Reading by descending order of size:
1. 22-point bold upper-case roman: **UN COUP DE DÉS JAMAIS N'ABOLIRA LE HASARD**
2. 12-point bold upper-case italic: ***C'ÉTAIT CE SERAIT LE NOMBRE***
3. 10-point medium upper case: SOIT LE MAÎTRE RIEN N'AURA EU LIEU QUE LE LIEU EXCEPTÉ PEUT-ÊTRE UNE CONSTELLATION
4. 10-point italic upper case: *COMME SI COMME SI*
5. 9-point medium upper case: QUAND BIEN MÊME LANCÉ DANS DES CIRCONSTANCES ÉTERNELLES DU FOND D'UN NAUFRAGE
6. 8-point medium lower case: "que" (3v on) which represents the majority of the text, for this is the predominant type size and face (50%)
7. 8-point medium upper case: Abîme, Nombre, Esprit, Fiançailles, EXISTÂT-IL COMMENÇÂT-IL ET CESSÂT-IL SE CHIFFRÂT-IL ILLUMINÂT-IL Septentrion Nord Toute Pensée Coup Dés
8. 8-point italic lower case: 28% of the text
9. 8-point italic upper case: *Une, La, SI, Choit*
10. 3-point italic lower case: *issu stellaire pire non davantage ni moins indifféremment mais autant*
11. 3-point medium lower case: autrement qu'hallucination éparse d'agonie sourdant que nié et clos quand apparu enfin par quelque profusion répandu en rareté évidence de la somme pour peu qu'une.

Configuration of Space

B. Reading by type faces in order of appearance:
1. **UN COUP DE DÉS JAMAIS N'ABOLIRA LE HASARD**
2. QUAND BIEN MÊME LANCÉ DANS DES CIRCONSTANCES ÉTERNELLES DU FOND D'UN NAUFRAGE
3. SOIT LE MAÎTRE RIEN N'AURA EU LIEU QUE LE LIEU EXCEPTÉ PEUT-ÊTRE UNE CONSTELLATION
4. "que" and all regular 8-point type
5. Abîme Nombre Esprit Fiançailles EXISTÂT-IL COMMENÇÂT-IL ET CESSÂT-IL SE CHIFFRÂT-IL ILLUMINÂT-IL Septentrion Nord Toute Pensée Coup Dés
6. *COMME SI COMME SI*
7. *Une, La, SI, Choit . . .*
8. *Une insinuation . . .*
9. *C'ÉTAIT CE SERAIT LE NOMBRE*
10. *issu stellaire . . .*
11. autrement qu'hallucination. . . .

C. Reading by variety of type faces in order of appearance in the text:
UN COUP DE DÉS JAMAIS QUAND BIEN MÊME LANCÉ DANS DES CIRCONSTANCES ÉTERNELLES DU FOND D'UN NAUFRAGE SOIT Abîme LE MAÎTRE Nombre Esprit Fiançailles **N'ABOLIRA** *COMME SI Une insinuation COMME SI La SI C'ÉTAIT issu stellaire CE SERAIT LE NOMBRE* EXISTÂT-IL autrement COMMENÇÂT-IL ET CESSÂT-IL SE CHIFFRÂT-IL ILLUMINÂT-IL **LE HASARD** *Choit* RIEN N'AURA EU LIEU QUE LE LIEU EXCEPTÉ PEUT-ÊTRE Septentrion Nord UNE CONSTELLATION Toute Pensée Coup Dés.

None of the groupings by type is fully acceptable, for not one offers a single lucid organizing principle. But, what is even more important and perhaps more interesting is the fact that any grouping by type size denies the notion of a layout of the text on double pages or doublets. In fact, organization by type size and face not only negates the doublet of the page, but it also refutes all concept of reading grids (top to bottom, left to right), as well as the effect of contrast achieved by mixing sizes and faces on the same page.

In addition, any attempt to organize by type sizes and faces alone negates the importance which Mallarmé gave to the paginal layout of each page. The corrections he made to the 1897 *Cosmopolis* edition and those which appear on the Lahure proofs are primarily changes which affect the visual appearance of the text, rather than actual changes in the text. Text changes are rare, and they have been well noted by Roulet,[13], Davies, Cohn, Ronat, et al.[14] The 1914 Gallimard edition, now considered *ne varietur*, made the textual changes (shown below in italics) in the 13 lines which Mallarmé called for in his revisions and corrections:

1. *a*bîme: *A*bîme (3v)
2. le *n*ombre *unique* qui ne peut pas en être un autre: l'*unique Nombre* qui ne peut pas être un autre (4v)
3. hésite *tout* chenu plutôt que de jouer la partie: hésite plutôt que de jouer *en manique* chenu la partie (4v)
4. *e*sprit: *E*sprit (4r)
5. l'*âpre* division: la division (4r)
6. assouplie par *les ondes*: assouplie par *la vague* (5v)
7. la mer *tentant* par l'aïeul ou *lui* contre la mer une chance oiseuse: la mer par l'aïeul tentant ou *l'aïeul* contre la mer une chance oiseuse (5v)
8. *f*iançailles: *F*iançailles (5v)
9. Une *simple insinuation d*'ironie enroulée *à tout ce* silence ou précipité hurlé: Une *insinuation simple au* silence enroulée *avec* ironie ou *le mystère* précipité hurlé (6v, 6r)
10. La lucide seigneuriale aigrette: La lucide *et* seigneuriale aigrette (8v)
11. davantage ni moins *mais autant* indifféremment: davantage ni moins indifféremment *mais autant* (9v)
12. flétrie *en* la neutralité identique: flétrie *par* la neutralité identique (9r)
13. *où* toute réalité se dissout: *en quoi* toute réalité se dissout (10r).

In these 13 lines, the changes are mainly those of syntax or order; one finds only one word deleted ("âpre"), one word added ("le mystère"), one lexical change ("la vague"), two syntactical substitutions, and three actual grammatical changes. On the other hand, four lower-case nouns are changed to begin with an upper-case letter: "Abîme," "Nombre," "Esprit," and "Fiançailles"; hence, four of the standard eight key organizing words are changed after the first printing and only two of these, "Abîme" and "Fiançailles," are not changed until the text reaches galley proof stage. There are no other typographical changes. Of the changes made by Mallarmé to the text as it appeared in *Cosmopolis*, most were made by him for a reprinting in an "édition de luxe," and only four changes are made on the proofs themselves: 1) "Abîme"; 2) "le Nombre unique" (order, not capital N); 3) substitution of "l'aïeul" for "lui"; and 4), in the same line, change of position from "tentant par l'aïeul" to "par l'aïeul tentant."

Certainly, Mallarmé did not in the revision and proof stages suddenly decide to make "Abîme," "Nombre," "Esprit," and "Fiançailles" key terms or indicators of subthemes or even counterpoint movements. The revisions to the text are relatively minor and, in fact, indicate concern with the layout itself, rather than the text. The printed lines of the text, as they appeared in 1897 in *Cosmopolis*, are established in its first printing; it is the arrangement on the page which Mallarmé's revisions and proof corrections address. As noted earlier, there is a considerable visual difference between *Un Coup de dés* as published in a compact or reduced format (*Cosmopolis* and Pléiade editions) and as it appears in a larger size (1914 Gallimard edition and the 1980 Ronat folio edition). The large format is distinctive in the increase of the amount of space which surrounds the print; the more space that is used the more the topographic concerns become important. The changes demanded by Mallarmé are topographic—not really typographic, for he never changes a type face in the revisions or on the proofs, nor are they significant textual modifications. As the technician of his own manuscript, Mallarmé knows exactly how to render his text into serving as its own procedure and fundamental structure. He is highly conscious that the use of more space in the folio format will have the surface effect of increasing the disorganization of his work. As a result, his very few revisions and then corrections on the proofs attest to his concern with a textual construct based on space.

The changes in only 13 of the 220 text lines are modifications which facilitate the reading on a field of space. They are alterations which clarify—alterations which are not important in a compacted format, changes which decrease the role of the print and increase the dynamics of the space. Each line revision intensifies the surrounding space. The line is so straightened out lexically and syntactically that it does not call attention to itself as a linear communication, but it does focus attention on the space the reader must fill and cross in viewing and then reading the line. The most important change is actually no. 9, a change made in the revision stage, for it ensures that 7v and 7r form a doublet (*"Une simple insinuation"* becomes *"Une insinuation,"* 6v, *"simple,"* 6r). Changing four lower-case letters to upper case is not thematic since these words are already there in the original; the initial upper-case letter on these words draws attention to their position, not to their meaning, attention to their interplay with the surrounding space and their isolation: "Abîme," "Esprit," "Fiançailles." The modification on "nombre" is a change which maintains textual consistency; first of all, it is one of the few terms repeated in the text and, when it is repeated, it is in all upper-case letters; it is natural to prefigure *"LE NOMBRE"* by "le Nombre" (the first change made in this line and made in the revision stage). Second, at proof stage, "le Nombre unique" is no longer syntactically viable with the upper case N; logic dictates that the phrase now be changed to the more dramatic and actually more precise "l'unique Nombre."

Every single textual change between the *Cosmopolis* printing and the correction of the proofs for a definitive luxurious in-folio edition testifies to a Mallarmé who revels in the role of layout artist and who appreciates all forms of esthetic structuring: poster art, Impressionist painting, Poe's poetry, and Wagnerian opera.[15] The intriguing changes sought by Mallarmé are those which address letter weight (shadings) and word alignment. On every page of the proofs, he meticulously notes letter verification, margins, verso-recto agreements, indentation. The proofs are considerably marked by his use of a ruler. Space and spacing change the relationships established by the typed elements and unstructure the restraints of meaning which the groupings by type faces construct. Hence, the textual changes are actually those which make the line more comprehensible and more lucid. By its space, not its words, their groupings, or their typographic strata, *Un Coup de dés* is a text of instrumentation, not inscription, of expansion, not differentiation, literally an extratext. The text itself is its very production.

As its own production, *Un Coup de dés* must be read as one complete work; the only subdivisions or strata possible are its own paginal components. Unlike the fan poems, *Un Coup de dés* is not a mobile work in that the pages are not interchangeable and "pliage" is not a determining factor. The printed order of the text—its layout—is determined by Mallarmé, just as he includes marginal center space in his topographic design. Instead of reversing the technicalities demanded by the printing trade through the use of fan techniques, writing on various objects, wordplay, or even distorted syntax as in "A la nue accablante tu," he incorporates specialized printing requirements into the construct and structure of his text. The eye-catching type variations, which account for only 22% of the text, actually receive their dramatic effect by their placement in contrast to each other and in contrast to the stable and standard 8-point medium size and type face. This may well be why Mallarmé opts for the extremely clear and legible Didot type style and not a more decorative style such as the Garamond type style popular at the time: "traits of [the Didot style] are the capitals H and M (narrower than in other contemporary styles) and R (typified by a vertical tail). In addition, the complementary italic font . . . blends harmoniously with the roman font. Such a particularity resolved an old problem in typography: the creation of compatible italic and roman fonts" (Mirham 44). The 8-point medium and italic faces, for example, are usually grouped together as one face, and, indeed, they constitute, together, 78% of *Un Coup de dés*. Similarly, the two 3-point faces (medium and italic) are usually seen as one, and it is common practice to detect seven faces instead of the actual 12 different type fonts required by Mallarmé: "L'imprimerie n'est pas un paradis artificiel. En y allant, Mallarmé n'a pas été guidé par les sensations de l'homme, mais par les préoccupations de l'écrivain: il avait besoin des *outils appropriés* pour parachever son texte" (Papp 24).

The selection of the conservative Didot type style and the rejection of a more elegant, ornamental style (the Garamond or a smaller style such as the Elzevir style used in the 1914 Gallimard edition) reinforces the observation that Mallarmé's primary preoccupation in *Un Coup de dés* is one of poetic composition.[16] The text is to be seen, rather than read, and the skill of its construction is to be admired, appreciated, and contemplated by its viewer-reader. The construction is based on strict rules and an intricate system of formal constraints; the poet is the "ordonnateur de fêtes" (330), and his work is "une jonglerie (tout l'Art en est là!)" (341). According to Tibor Papp, the Didot style selected by Mallarmé was at the time the official style of France: "Tandis que le fondement élémentaire de la visualité de son texte illustrait son nonconformisme, le choix du caractère Didot représentait son rapport à la loi." The type style, then, is standard in 1898 for the publication of official documents. In his selection of the Didot style, "Mallarmé ne s'est pas arrêté à transgresser la lecture classique, il a créé un nouveau code par la mise en jeu" (25). Analysis and synthesis occur simultaneously, as creation and production merge in *Un Coup de dés* and the reader assumes the stance of contemplative thinker.

Setting the type in play through space reinforces the notion of gamesmanship in Mallarmé's esthetics. After all, dice are the initial object named in *Un Coup de dés*, and his "Préface" invokes "un Lecteur habile." One of his more hermetic sonnets, "Une dentelle s'abolit," evokes the "Jeu suprême" although a persisting subject of debate remains on the interpretation of the image: poetry or daybreak.[17] Certainly, Mallarmé's writings in *La Dernière Mode* and *Vers de circonstance* belie a sense of humor, wordplay, and visual deceits,[18] and his flair for theatrical showmanship was admired by friends at Valvins, as well as by the "Mardistes," who were so spellbound by his Tuesday

Configuration of Space 97

evening gatherings that they forgot to write anything down although all agreed with Valéry that Mallarmé had a definite gift for oral mesmerization: "Personne n'a parlé comme lui" (xxvi).

Indeed, Mallarmé sets the text in play, not unlike a master strategist or chess master. His converging-diverging techniques of structure, ingenious rime schema ("Hérodiade," for example), constant attention to the visual appearance of the text (capitalization, punctuation, word placement), as well as sonority itself (the famous "ptyx" of the sonnet "Ses purs ongles très haut dédiant leur onyx"), and the penchant for studied ambiguity (the "fumer"-"fumée" and "Ta vague littérature" of "Toute l'âme résumée") demonstrate just how his poems are constructed along the lines of purely intellectual craftsmanship.[19] Above all, Mallarmé is aware in every line (verse and prose) that he is constructing a literary game, an invitation to an "other."

Because the disciplined layout of *Un Coup de dés* imposes order on the reader and the appearance of the text is one of artifice in which all is contrived, deliberately confused and approximate, normal reading grids are negated. Moreover, no rectos or versos are alike; some pages are undeniable doubles, while others do not bring into play at all the design of the page as a doublet. The vast amount of paginal space and the fragmented positioning of the lines of print bring about a loss of reader contact with the text, rather than a mode of reader entry into the text. Stratification—normal textual division and subdivisions—is absent. The layout does not confirm relationships between the printed units, but prevents them and posits a problem of referents and authority. Moreover, the fixed type is not trustworthy. Space generates a crisis for the reader; it denies all reader expectations and contradicts access into the text. The reader is figuratively, if not actually, lost at sea, a navigator on an unknown ocean of white space in a textual vessel which pitches and tosses, having no specified direction, no known purpose for the voyage, no familiar navigational guides. He can only respond to the situation, gamble that he can work out some way of charting a course through his skillful reading of the elements around him, identify enough fixed points which permit him to enact and understand the drama even though he cannot alter its circumstances.

The reader's effort to get his bearings inevitably increases his disorientation, the sense of shipwreck. The center is constantly dispersed, as the reader discovers that he cannot enact the text, cannot identify with the continual frame-breaking of the referents nor participate in the unreliable structure of dislocation. The only "pattern" is chaos: distortion, dispersion, decontextualization. The reader can neither deduce nor induce a connective thread, much less build a new frame. The text cannot be "read," and the reader loses his function and identity; he has too many things to do and too many ways in which to do them. The dynamics of space prevent the accumulation of stable reading data.

The reader must, then, accept the impossibility of conjunction with the author and become an admirer of the skill of the textual constructor, an appreciator of the challenges to penetrate the black and white display, to play the game. Accepting the challenge changes the role of the reader to that of the viewer, player, and thinker. The reader must undertake the text, fill in space, cross space, and organize the text by riveting attention on an interrogation into the text and its immutable composition. The reader must analyze and synthesize at the same time in order to detect and establish possible communication. The text is both object and subject, and the reader must read in all directions and on all planes simultaneously.

Unless the reader consciously changes his function and procedures, he will remain on one textual plane only. Moving first to the role of viewer or observer, he adds a second dimension to the text. Next, recognizing that he is also a game player, he recognizes the challenge inherent in the very opening words of the title: dice. By accepting to play the poet's game, initiated by the idea of dice, he grasps a third dimension and expands his reading role to include the thinking process. The reader no longer seeks to enact the text, for he agrees that he cannot change its order nor determine its restraints; he must respond to the challenge set forth by the author. He has the possibility of reacting to the text, becoming a textual organizer, but never the possibility of becoming its co-author. He rejects the quest for authorial conjunction in agreeing to focus on the composition of the work before him. Hence, *Un Coup de dés* is a multilinear or multidimensional text. The "fil conducteur" is both the author's challenge and the reader's response: an inquiry into "poème" and ultimately into poetry itself.

No one disputes that *Un Coup de dés* is a poem, but its canonical classification remains problematic. Is it a free verse poem as its display indicates or a prose poem in a dispersed form? The most recent point of view is one which relies on Mallarmé's description in the "Préface": "la tentative participe, avec imprévu, de poursuites particulières et chères à notre temps, le vers libre et le poëme en prose. Leur réunion s'accomplit sous une influence, je sais, étrangère, celle de la Musique entendue au concert. . . . Le genre . . . laisse intact l'antique vers" (456). The layout tends to confirm its display as a free verse poem, while the absence of clearcut non-metric divisions mark it as prose. Its initial appearance in a mimetic ideogram and use of varying type faces and sizes establish an allegorical framework, a myth, as well as a monodramatic ballet ("forme théâtrale de poésie," 308). The space intervals evoke various registers, intonation patterns, rests and pauses, which permit word associations and create resonances through accords and discords, echos ("Nombre"/"ombre"/"sombre"). Ronat, for example, detects 19 "positions métriques (dans la définition traditionnelle)." Based on her detection of regular meters throughout the text, she finds that a great deal of *Un Coup de dés* is written in free verse, while Mallarmé's construct of the entire text out of two "longues phrases, complexes, structurées, et articulées" mark the text as a prose poem.[20]

However, the layout shows that there is a deliberate avoidance of internal rhythm and meter. Verso by verso, recto by recto, doublet by doublet, resonance is eliminated. The only regular verse line is the final one, which is a perfect decasyllable: "Toute Pensée émet un Coup de Dés" (4/2/4), while the title, *Un coup de Dés jamais n'abolira le Hasard*, is at best an "impair" of 13 syllables. It may well be that Mallarmé converts an impair into a decasyllable because poetry is the order of the text and there may well be as many as 19 traces of regular metric forms in the text, but these observations still do not validate the generic definition of the text as either a free verse or prose poem. After all, a free verse text does not depend on its use of metrics and a prose poem does not rely upon long, complex, structured sentences. Mallarmé is, of course, a practitioner of the prose poem, but he is not on record as being a proponent of free verse, and he did not write in the form.[21] Even "A la nue accablante tu" is a sonnet.

Nevertheless, Mallarmé's commentaries, especially *Variations sur un sujet* and *La Musique et les lettres*, as well as his *Réponses à des enquêtes*, reveal a man of letters who finds poetry in all forms of expression, not in one genre. In fact, he effaces all efforts to identify a poem by rules of versification: "Dans le genre appelé prose, il y a des vers, quelquefois admirables, de tous rythmes. Mais, en vérité, il n'y a pas de prose: il y a l'alphabet et puis des vers plus ou moins serrés: plus ou moins diffus. Toutes les fois qu'il y a effort au style, il y a versification" (867). At best, a verse is a "dispensateur, ordonnateur du jeu des pages," while prose is found "parmi les marges et du blanc; ou qu'il [le langage] se dissimule, nommez-le Prose" (375).

However, from another point of view, only the paginal arrangement distinguishes the prose poem from the free verse poem. Neither form is divided into a set number of syllables, nor arranged by fixed divisions (stanzas or paragraphs), while both draw upon rhythmic units and are marked at times by internal rime and assonance (sound echos). In a sense, the successful inauguration of the free verse text by first Jules Laforgue and then Gustave Kahn is a natural outcome of the development of the prose poem and freeing of the constraints of the verse poem throughout the nineteenth century.[22] Always interested in the esthetics of the poem and poetic creation, Mallarmé continually experimented with the formalities of prose and verse, and, although he preferred to work within and upon the technical restraints of versification, he was consistently fascinated by the new or modern in all aspects of art. In his response to Jules Huret in "Sur l'évolution littéraire" (866-72), he praises "les récentes innovations" which permit "chaque poëte . . . dans son coin . . . les airs qu'il lui plaît; pour la première fois . . . les poëtes ne chantent plus au lutrin . . . je me suis toujours intéressé aux idées de jeunes gens." Even the scandalous Eiffel Tower found favor in his eyes: "La Tour Eiffel dépasse mes espérances" (xxv).

Poetry for Mallarmé is any human creation ("la seule création humaine possible," 870), while a poem is an act which "consiste à voir soudain qu'une idée se fractionne en un nombre de motifs égaux par valeur et à les grouper: ils riment: pour un sceau extérieur, leur commune mesure qu'apparente le coup final" (365). Nowhere does Mallarmé write that the poetic art is identifiable by generic descriptions or classifications. In fact, he praises its end ("Sur l'évolution littéraire"). He writes on poetry in terms of orchestral music, theater, dance, opera, painting, sculpture; he describes painters in terms of verse, musicians in terms of painting, novelists in terms of music or plastic art: "l'artiste et lettré . . . sous l'unique vocable du 'poëte'" (401). He "reads" a painting, "listens to" a written text, and "looks at" a symphony. Some of his more illuminating writings on poetry are found in his notes entitled *Crayonné au théâtre*. Hence, his reflections on human creation are poetic, non-generic, and polyvalent in their referents. Indeed, his own literary production is equally eclectic, for he tries his hand at diverse forms of written expression (tale, verse, prose poem, philology, translation, journalism, criticism), writes on and about whatever strikes him at the moment and for all sorts of occasions, and thoroughly enjoyed a wide circle of friends which was as cosmopolitan in character as it was stimulating in artistic creation: "Nous naviguons, ô mes divers / Amis . . . Une ivresse belle m'engage" ("Salut").

It is not surprising then that his last work, *Un Coup de dés*,[23] is in the form of what Mallarmé calls a "réunion," for in this text one discerns reflections of everything he ever wrote, contemplated, and appreciated about poetry. In a very real sense, *Un Coup de dés* draws upon all forms, or more accurately, upon all expressions of Poetry. It is the *nec plus ultra* Poem. It is, even for him, "différent," expresses his life-long interest in esthetics, and crystallizes all of his own work, what Valéry has described as "la figure d'une pensée, pour la première fois placée dans notre espace:. . . Mallarmé percevait sans doute l'Impératif d'une poésie, une Poétique" (1582).[24] Moreover, it was not to be performed in the sense of theater as he wished his "Aprèsmidi d'un faune" to be performed; rather, it was written for a thinking, contemplative reader. The reader is not the place of the communication; that remains on the page; on the contrary, the reader is invited to undertake the text and play the poetic game. Consequently, the poet-author deliberately sets relationships which cannot be enacted; they can only be encountered in reader reaction. The fiction of the text is not real; the reading of the fiction is real. It is not a question of historical reality but rather of artistic reality. The text is what it says it is: a shipwreck without a ship, not rational but still lucid in points of identification. There is no theme, no thesis, no unifying myth; there is only "POÈME." The text is tentative; there is no cluster of sustaining metaphors, only the reader's pursuit (cataphor) of points of contact, for the circular construct impedes a sequential ordering by a reader. Response may recover parts of the text, but not *the* text, for the text is always emerging into the reading reader's memory and experience. In this respect, *Un Coup de dés* is historically a work of literary evolution in the scientific or even biological sense. It is not a text which derives from poetic tradition, nor one which follows established paradigms; it has no model.[25] Technically, it may perhaps be best described as a hybrid, the "Anastase"-"Pulchérie" of "Prose (pour des Esseintes)," which purifies and redefines the very meaning of the term *poem*.[26] Hence, Mallarmé labels *Un Coup de dés* "poème" and not "poëme"; the orthographic change also modifies slightly the pronunciation of the word, as "poëme" becomes a mark of tradition (virtual and actual definition and meaning), and "poème" becomes the written sign of possible meaning, if not a veritable symbol between what happens or occurs as a poetic fiction and what is absolute, pure, and eternal: Poetry.

Non-derivative, non-rational, non-restrictive, *Un Coup de dés* as "POÈME" is an authentic object which is at the same time its own subject (an alpha-omega). It is an exterior representation of the poetic article of faith, which needs no intermediary—the

"Hyperbole!" of "Prose (pour des Esseintes)" and the refutation of allegory in "Le Démon de l'analogie." The word *poème* has power beyond its written form, its concrete identity, as it opens to something beyond personal myth and opinion: Poetry. Hence, Mallarmé's text draws upon those attributes which are particular to the poetic genre in both prose and verse form, but which also mutate the whole assemblage of arbitrary decisions on what defines and identifies a poem. He takes his text from the realm of the poetic figure (the allegory of "poem-ness") and transforms it into a symbol of creation. The idea of Poetry is born from the poem: "Car j'installe, par la science, / L'hymne des cœurs spirituels / En l'œuvre de ma patience, / . . . / Gloire du long désir, Idées" ["Prose (pour des Esseintes)"].[27]

With *Un Coup de dés*, Mallarmé creates a new form of poetry and a new esthetic of poetry, in which creation itself has value. The text is not to be "read," but to be felt and contemplated, to be fully experienced. The layout design prevents one element from being substituted for another; the reader cannot enact the text because it is unchangeable in its order and the language is provocative in its shipwrecked form, not evocative in a logical sequence of appearance and placement. The space destroys linearity, reinforces separation of the printed units, engenders interaction in its negation of relationships, and permits recovery of fragments only, not the whole. The reader is a viewer, player, and thinker on poetry, not the co-poet of a text. Prose is verse; the signified is the signifier. Through the dynamics of space, Mallarmé forces the reader to reconstruct the text itself, deform it in order to reform it in a never-ending procedure or circle, which prevents both forward and retrograded movement. There is only the act of re-reading in an eternal textual circumstance of destructuring-restructuring; each "reading discredits rather than confirms the one that went before" (Bowie 117).

As reading signs, grids, and conventions are deliberately and arbitrarily destroyed, the only definite ordering or stable element of the text becomes its space. Yet, as examination of the layout shows, the space of the text is not stable, not reliable, and not instructive. Space annuls relationships, unstructures meaning by groupings which at times limit meaning and at other times deny access to meaning because the groupings permit too many codes of meaning. Linguistically, the text cannot be read aloud, for the spaces halt the reading process, parallel the process in the creation of multiple grids simultaneously, and negate resonance in an erratic movement from register to register. There is not ever agreement on the points of contact. While there is an appeal to nostalgia as place condenses memory (word repetition, parallel structures, sound association), space does not permit the reader to preserve memory of all points of agreement, as in the text "A la nue accablante tu," which, at least, permits the reader to cling to certain syllables through resonance. Space is a constant frame-breaking structure, which prevents the building of a new frame because it is unalterable and defies reader deduction.

Un Coup de dés is a text which depends on its unity, on its meditated composition and construction, much as a painting which the viewer approaches first as a whole and then studies the details of that whole. To read *Un Coup de dés* aloud demands, first, familiarity with the complete text and, second, a selection of the parts to read aloud; reading aloud may indeed animate the text through varying intonation patterns, but to perform the parts is to reconstruct a verbal system only and to dismiss in its entirety the visual system. It also demands selectivity and interpretation on the part of the oral performer: "une partition" (455). Mallarmé carefully bases his text on space so that his reader reads into the text, uses his intuition before his intelligence. Part of deconventionalizing or even decontextualizing *Un Coup de dés* through space is the ideogrammatic form that every reader "sees" in the typographic and topographic variations and changes of the layout and in the format of the double page (a recto and a verso together). Another is the omission of all punctuation ("écrire sans accessoires," 363).

The absence of punctuation and its replacement by space create in the reader a desire to unify the dispersed units of print through some means of condensation. The space expands by forcing the eye (and the mind) to move from printed element to printed element. Usually, punctuation has the role of setting relationships and providing access to the layers of meaning. But, in *Un Coup de dés,* the reader cannot assume that an upper-case letter begins a sentence, much less a coherent paragraph or strata of groupings or indications of meaning. The use of capitalization throughout the text is artificial, illogical, and unintelligible. Each time a point of convergence is detected, it is interrupted by space and is transformed into a point of divergence. Moreover, the reader cannot punctuate the text, for there are too many simultaneous possibilities of conjunction and too many potential associations and relationships. Space destroys reading decisions by pointing to multiple reading directions.

Not only is the reader unable to punctuate the text, but he is also unable to make it syntactically correct. He can make some decisions, but he cannot make all decisions. Nevertheless, because the reader can make some decisions, even if that decision is to read in more than one direction or grid, he accepts his role as viewer, thinker, even player; he gives up his conventional role as reader and takes on that of organizer. Where the syntax is concerned, the reader works within the ambiguities and incompatibilities rather than against them. The reading situation becomes that of reassembly, as the reader puts coherence into the chaos of the distorted lines. Recognizing that the text cannot be performed, linguistically read aloud, nor made syntactically correct, he begins to admire space as a positive component of reading freedom. Syntactical distortions (is "étale" an adjective or verb, is "vers" a preposition or noun?) open the text by going beyond what is printed. The printed units circulate through the white space of the page, giving rise to hidden relationships in the pursuit of meanings. Replacing punctuation by space and creating syntactical confusion by spacing so alter logical categories that the reader as viewer-thinker-player is provoked into reacting to the text before him. The author could have built into the text more accords and a rational pattern of oppositions, but Mallarmé's decision to eliminate the details of a unifying anecdote ("on évite le récit," 455) in favor of minute attention to the details of the visual surface appearance of the page itself is one of dispassion, scientific objectivity, and impersonality. The author is the director of a project and the dispenser of a product; his very detachment in his focus on construction legitimizes the text as text. The author disappears from the text; he figuratively and literally vacates the print. There is no argument, no point of view, no opinion to accept or reject, no message to be decoded, no experience to share, and no exchange to enjoy.[28] The only traces that remain of the author are the spaces—his personal signature as "le Dieu de la page blanche" (Hinostroza 18-19). Hence, there is only space in which to maneuver, space to cross and fill in with the "accessoires" of re-readings which endlessly contradict each other; space is the *"vierge indice"* of the fiction. Space creates reader desire for union between the reader and the text and initiates re-readings. It is in the flexible expanse of the white space that the reader's investigation takes place over and over again; he deconstructs, reconstructs, responds, reacts, revises. The reader retranslates in a conscious, lucid, intellectual act of adjustment and readjustment. In his linking of form and function in the non-linear whiteness of the page, he discovers through space the substance of the text: "Poème" = "Poésie": *Un Coup de dés*.

Space permits the reader the freedom to pursue meaning and meanings. The layout subverts the conventional reality of order, sequence, and solidity, while at the same time it is so disciplined that its space conveys a sense of form, not a sense of loss. Space persists from page to page in the manipulation of the printed elements. The very free play of the traditionally fixed printed units which only the tremendous amount of space makes possible invites the reader to undertake the composition of the text. The reality of the text is then a construction of the mind. The words or the language do not lead to the discovery of coherence, a pattern, an image—substance; the trigger is thought itself: "Toute Pensée émet un Coup de Dés." Art and life (reader memory in the readjustment of the form and function of the units) correspond in the ideal plane of space, where all things meet, converge, overlap, and cohere: "RIEN N'AURA EU LIEU QUE LE LIEU." Space is place—it is where creation occurs.

Chapter IV

ASSEMBLY BY SPACE

Despite a layout which denies a systematic linear procedure in *Un Coup de dés* and an unusual amount of unaccounted for space on each page of the text, the Mallarmé reader invariably tends to view the white paginal areas as measures of decorative unity in which the type differentiates various strata of relationships. The gradations in type sizes and mixing of several type faces lend it the dimension of solidity by dramatically weighting individual groups of printed elements into focal points in space. Strong value contrasts between each strata of the type faces and sizes compress the spatial surface into a composite scene which is viewed by the reader as an arrangement of both economy in the elimination of unnecessary details and harmony in the reappearance of type faces.

Reading by typography confers upon *Un Coup de dés* what Valéry termed a "sens presque de l'algèbre" (17). Type as a geometrical or mathematical form maintains a distance between the text and its reader. Words are what they are on the surface plane of the page—the reading is a construction in space, as the reader determines syntactical, semantic, and lexical patterns and registers of contact. The deliberate, calibrated ordering of the type emphasizes the fixity of each word and each grouping of words. It invites the reader to produce meaning by making decisions on the basis of points of agreement, parellelisms, word differentiation and repetition, rhythmic demarcations (assonance, alliteration, homographic and homophonous effects, identification of figures, and the conferring of value on reading blocks. The reader makes contact by the space which isolates combinations, organizes areas of groupings, measures the particular set of circumstances of each page, sustains attention through divisions and subdivisions, provides balance and contrast, and permits each letter to expand into a word or "bloc" in lexical, semantic, and syntactical terms which occasion word recognition and reader confrontation. The typical reader follows the type. In his determination and decision to decode or read the text, reading attention passes from space as the controlling element of the structure to type as the visible form which permits encounter with meaning. In this approach, space limits what is printed, functions as a reading guide, and enhances the legibility of the page by bringing attention to embedded codes of type: font style, size, column measure, and interline spacing. Viewing space as the frame for the construct of *Un Coup de dés* stimulates the reader to respond by positing his own sense of organization upon each page (870); the sense of order grasped by the layout involves the reader in conjuring up possibilities of meaning.

One of the more frequent readings of *Un Coup de dés* is an ideogrammatic act of discovery. The dispersion of the words on the page is undeniably visual and may be seen as an emblematic spatialization, even a symbolic one, what Ernest Fraenkel and Etienne Souriau term "l'art *présentatif.*"[1] The essentialist view offered by Fraenkel and Souriau is basically one of analogy: "**LE MAÎTRE**" is the poet and man, "**LE HASARD**" is the source of his anguish over being in a universe devoid of meaning, and the "CONSTELLATION" symbolizes his desire for order ("Valeur," "Beauté," "Harmonie") (34). Hence, the design is useful because it delineates the essence (not the appearance) of the subject of the work. On a psychological level, the configuration of the layout reveals Mallarmé's impotence before "le vide papier," his struggle to demonstrate the relationship between the finite or concrete and the abstract or infinite, and his communication in *Un Coup de dés* of how language denies chance and orders chaos. The constellation is the Little Dipper which contains the fixed North or Pole Star, the only star which never goes below the horizon and can be seen from every point on the globe and consequently the major navigational aid for the reader.

Thus, the printed language and its arrangement are elements of certainty. The writing composition of the text and its reading occupy space, as the exactitude of layout is in direct conjunction with the non-rational chaos of the page: a constellation of type is detected by word clusters in the same way that celestial constellations are "seen." The viewer-reader selects his pattern and transforms it into a meaningful authority. The "Septentrion aussi Nord" is both the Little Dipper and Ursa minor, depending on the viewer. Meaning is in the eye of the beholder, determined first by optic and second by imagination. The constellation has multiple meanings and forms, but it is always recognized as an element of orientation, order, and symbolic condition. Like the print on the page, a constellation is known through its isolated focal points in space, a grouping which compacts the vastness of the cosmic into a human recording of experience. The very act of recognizing (seeing or reading) a constellation is an act of interpretive creation which manipulates the chaos of the unlimited into a coherent assembly or visible form. Admitted by the imagination and by the mind, a constellation in the sky or on the page remains an arbitrary representation and human invention: an allegory.

And indeed the allegorical and the ideogrammatic possibilities of *Un Coup de dés* are inseparable. The "MAÎTRE" becomes a metaphor for the ship captain (or poet or Man) who is at sea during a raging storm (life) which causes his vessel to founder; he is literally and figuratively in the throes of a shipwreck. The dispersed lines evoke the tumultuous waves, the layout further reinforces the rising and falling motion of the stormy sea; both the "MAÎTRE" and the reader have navigational problems and both take chances in their efforts to bring order into disorder, meaning into the threatened loss of meaning. The rolling dice emphasize risks and perils, the need for a decision, the desire for an answer not to sink into nothingness, not to go below the horizon but instead to leave at least a visible trace of one's unpredictable voyage in life. The throw of the dice does not abolish chance, for it is an act of chance which confirms chance.

Still, there is always a result from the act, something comes up; the result is not predictable, but it is visible and traceable. Like a constellation, dice have fixed points; each pattern is not predetermined by the throw, just as each constellation is not fixed (the stars are fixed, not the figure itself). The dice, then, are a human terrestrial rendering of the celestial, just as the print may be seen as the verbal expression of an idea or absolute. As constellations are "born" from the fixed elements of stars, so meaning is generated by the materiality of words. The observable elements are real, undeniable in their actual existence, valid in their combinations, and unlimited in their possibilities. While a single throw of the dice means only one possible combination will result, it nonetheless contains a design and affirms contact by its visual result. Reading of the points on the dice unites them into a meaningful relationship, just as detecting a constellation through the reading of the stars establishes a pictorial unity. Flux or chaos is fixed in a moment of observation and interpretation. While access to the cause of the design may be denied, the design itself is an authentic non-stratified figure.

Both the constellation and the dice are pictorial. However, the pluri-dimensional dice are compacted into the unidimensional stellar figure of a constellation, which is in turn expanded into the multi-faceted and very solid human cube. If indeed the words are points on the page in the same way that stars are points in the sky and the circles on the dice are points on the cube, then a roll of the dice, the rotation of the earth on its axis, and the turning of a page will send forth an observable pattern through the conjunction of the economical (minimum number of points) and the harmonious (their arrangement). Hence, the dice and the constellation meet on the plane of the page where incompatibilities are juxtaposed and differences are resolved: earth and sky, cosmic and concrete, limited and unlimited, defined and abstract. While the dice do not inscribe the constellation on the earth, they do transcribe it into an authoritative assembly of meaning. Moreover, both figures (dice and constellation) are silent—beyond words. The dice and the constellation are, then, mimetic designs which capture the bifurcation of the layout of the text: space and print, the visual and the verbal, the unsaid and the articulated. The thrown dice indicate the constellation, which first contracts the vastness of the universe and gives it form and, second, expands beyond itself into the unmeasurable formlessness of the cosmos. As the dice emerges into a sign of the human (gesture, chance, change, emotion), the constellation gives mute evidence to the absolute: pure and perfect all-inclusiveness, a-temporal, a-logical, asymmetrical, authentic, non-explicable and non-derivational. But the place of association and consequently of communication is on the page, which by its very layout is beyond words. Silence is the mark of fullness—no more is necessary: "Le silence . . . tue et . . . c'est au poëte, suscité par le défi, de traduire" (340).

Using an ideogrammatic or mimetic approach to *Un Coup de dés* reinforces the notion that the text is to be read visually, just as the dice and the constellation are "read"—interpreted—by the viewer. Both figures demand that the reader-viewer annihilate space in his reading; the throw of the dice crosses space in order to provide an answer or result, while the stars of the constellation pull space together in a crisped, identifiable form. Both figures deny chance, for both contain fixed points (dice and stars), but the pattern observed confirms chance because both rely on the optic of the viewer-reader. Both manifest a traceable pattern, but neither is predictable in its actual result. The encounter produces meaning and chance lies in the reading. Hence, the print on the page will never abolish chance in the act of interpretation, for *dés* is also a printing term: the hammering to box-in the frame of the characters (letters) which are then expanded into words. The formal layout invites a reader layout, which is incalculable, but traceable, yet unpredictable. Print is no longer fixed, as the poet abolishes the medium he must use.[2]

Writing in *Les Dieux antiques*, his translation of classical myths, Mallarmé emphasizes the role of chance in the creation of "transformations capricieuses": "le hasard qui se mêlait aux mythes . . . incita ce peuple . . . à trouver une ordonnance qui n'existait pas essentiellement" (1167). For Mallarmé, myth concretizes and plasticizes the abstract: "le récit de quelque chose qui peut avoir eu lieu, mais qu'aucune garantie ne me permet d'envisager comme un fait historique. Les noms et les incidents du mythe appartiennent au beau pays des nuages . . . dans l'orage et le calme, dans la splendeur et l'assombrissement, le long des mers bleues du ciel" (1272). Myth, then, manipulates the exterior world by making it familiar and recognizable through interpretation; in turn, interpretation is an optical act by means of the imagination. Because myths (classical, biblical, historical, literary) do not reproduce fact but are fictions which represent a variety of ways of "seeing" the world at large and grasping it through the imagination, myth provides both a useful and pleasure-giving pivot for the evocation of essence. Through myth, the imagination becomes a means of seeing (reading) continuity, order, and harmony, and it confers meaning upon the fiction: "les mythes, mêlés intimement à la parole, acquièrent une existence nouvelle et isolée" (1170). The primitive form of myth is evidence of the energy and creative power of the word. In *Les Dieux antiques*, as well as in *Les Mots anglais*, Mallarmé shows how a word is an object which initiates experience.

Several myths may be read as the psychological frames for *Un Coup de dés*. For example, there is in operation the Orpheus legend or Orphic explanation of the Earth, in which the earth is the shell of an egg, whose upper part is the sky and lower part is the earth; chaos is surrounded by Night, while Ether is the day or life within. Graphically, *Un Coup de dés* may be viewed as the birth of the world. But the Orphic myth is only one legend which may be detected in the Mallarmé text. Others include the fable of the Halcyon birds, Venus, Callisto, Hamlet. In his *Contes indiens*, four of the rather didactic legends by Mary Summer which Mallarmé rewrote for Méry Laurent around 1893, the tale of Nala and Damayantî (616-32) could well serve as the basic myth for *Un Coup de dés*. Nala, the king of Nichadha, gradually loses his money, chariots, jewels, and finally his kingdom, everything except his wife, Damayantî, in a dice game with his brother: "La cuirasse de vertu enveloppant Nala cache un défaut, le roi est joueur: passionnément: à tout . . . engager sur un coup de dés! Il accepte une partie. . . . La chance tourne contre le roi. . . . Les dés, en retombant, marquent . . . leur inimitié . . . son désespoir les lance dans l'espace comme on montre le poing. . . . Le joueur s'obstine . . . fiévreux . . . dardant les dés, il les invoque, les menace et, tant qu'enjeu restera, sa main crispée agite la ruine" (621). In exile, Nala learns "la science des dés" (628) and becomes a "maître dans l'art de lancer les dés" (632); regaining his kingdom in another dice game with his brother, Nala shows compassion as the victor; he is worthy to "triompher des destins contraires" (632). Additional analogies exist in the conventional topoi of the World-as-Written-Book, the Nautical-Voyage-as-Composition, and the Theater-as-World-Stage. The Book-Voyage-Theater schema is undeniable in all of Mallarmé's work and one which is especially found in Mallarmé scholarship on *Le Livre* as Mallarmé's *nec plus ultra* sign or co-referencing in order to confirm the fiction of the text as reader truth; the language makes it so.[3]

While the fragments of *Un Tombeau pour Anatole* bear some affinities with *Un Coup de dés*,[4] an observation borne out by one of Redon's illustrations for the text, that of a young man, it is doubtful that the 1879 death of his son provides Mallarmé with the actual anecdotal line of development in *Un Coup de dés*. In the first place, the 20-year-old event would most likely have surfaced in texts written during the time between the tragic event and the writing of *Un Coup de dés*; second, the death of Anatole was probably far too personal for the poetical detachment which is such an integral part of Mallarmé's esthetics and would repudiate his practice by the time of the composition of *Un Coup de dés* of having the word initiate experience. Third, *Un Coup de dés* is not a tragedy; it is dramatic, but there is no moral vision that all human efforts are futile and that the best of this world must perish. In fact, there is no moral point of view or discernible ethical code in *Un Coup de dés*, an aspect which greatly separates Mallarmé from Baudelaire, for example, and which evolves in Mallarmé's poetry during the early years of "debaudelairization." The same observation concerning Anatole Mallarmé applies to the theories which see the prince as Hamlet.

On the other hand, *Igitur*, Mallarmé's aborted tale, as a possible anecdotal frame for *Un Coup de dés*, deserves some attention.[5] Certainly, the affinities between the two texts are well-known. In *Igitur*, Mallarmé delineates a hero whose descent "au fond des choses" takes the form of a hesitation. Structured around the motif of a spiral (438-39), contradictions surface, disappear, and resurface in Igitur's desire to act and his reluctance to act (the stairs, the "will act" and the "does not act," motion and its cessation, past and future, gesture and word). Suspended between the "Folie utile" (434) of his act and its being necessary to negate "le hasard," Igitur's decision is one of "Infini"/"fixé" (442). The "double heurt" of the unfinished tale remains "le hasard infini des conjonctions," for nothing happens in *Igitur*. The divisiveness of chance remains in opposition to the "même somme," while the quest to "me dissoudre en moi" is left unresolved: "Il ferme le livre . . . l'Absolu a disparu . . . Le personnage . . . trouve l'acte inutile, car il y a et n'y a pas de hasard—il réduit le hasard à l'*Infini*—qui, dit-il doit exister quelque part" (442). Are "les dés-hasard" (443) absorbed or is it simply a trace of the possible combinations, "le souffle, fin de parole et geste unis . . . Preuve" (34), that "l'absolu existera en dehors" (433)? The effort to defy chance and assert the intelligence winds up in a stalemate, between "la négation et l'affirmation. . . . Il contient l'Absurde" (441).

Igitur is impotent, for the very act which denies chance confirms it: "cette folie, le hasard étant nié, cette folie était nécessaire" (442). As Malcolm Bowie points out, "the larger effect of these passages is muddled by much private mythology and a diffuse Gothic scenario. The main problem left unsolved by Mallarmé in *Igitur* was that of finding a concrete situation which would enforce rather than limit the generality of his theme, and a dramatic structure which would suggest the metaphysical uncertainty inherent in that theme without appearing loose and indecisive" (125). In order to resolve the problem of "decisive uncertainty" or "certain indecision," the basic theme and structure of *Un Coup de dés* must turn upon a hero who has the opportunity to make one last throw of the dice in order to conquer the nothingness of the absurd condition of life (shipwreck) in a structure which unites prose and verse in a theatrical paginal spectacle.

In some ways, *Igitur* is a theatrical piece in that it has stage directions, settings, and gesture, but Mallarmé calls it a tale or short story, and his epigraph indicates clearly that it is to be read; the reader's mind will animate the text: "Ce Conte s'adresse à l'Intelligence du lecteur qui met les choses en scène, elle-même" (433). In *Un Coup de dés*, the layout itself animates the scene and forces the reader to follow the events. The author of *Un Coup de dés* is the stage director and is in such control of his presentation and its animation that the reader's imagination precedes his reflection or intelligence—the reverse of *Igitur*. The layout of *Un Coup de dés* is one of such certainty (author) and at the same time such indecision (both "LE MAÎTRE" and the reader) that the text becomes an active work which the reader must undertake (re-layout) as opposed to *Igitur* which can be enacted by the reader because it has a definable order and an evident narrative. *Igitur* is an anecdote in time and in space, while *Un Coup de dés* replaces a single continuing storyline of development by multiple strata of analogies, anecdotes, referentials. The proposed combinations of *Igitur* are undeveloped and obscure; they take form in *Un Coup de dés*.

Another important modification which Mallarmé brings to *Un Coup de dés* is the elimination of the notion of time. *Igitur* is situated at the hour of midnight, the hour of conjunction between morning and night, between dream and clarity, light and shadow, beginning and end. Midnight is usually viewed as the number 12 (rather than its double 24), and it stands for a number of cosmic order. Because of *Igitur*, many commentators read into "l'unique Nombre" and *"LE NOMBRE"* of *Un Coup de dés* the hour of 12, the hour at which Igitur "quitte la chambre" (439), shakes the dice, throws them, and turns up the number 12: "Il jette les dés, le coup s'accomplit, douze, le temps (Minuit)" (451); the throw of 12 coincides with the striking of the clock. In these circumstances, which is the meaning in Latin of the word *igitur*, lies "la Folie d'Elbehnon," the subtitle of the text: the "rien" of "Salut" and "le néant" of Sartre, the tragedy of man ("Il est désolé de l'humanité," 442) that the very act or gesture which affirms his being is the one which also destroys him. The number 12 is a losing number in any throw of the dice: the "certitude se mire en l'évidence: en vain, réminiscence du mensonge" (437); purity, the Absolute, demands non-being.

Elimination of the time, midnight, in *Un Coup de dés* opens the circumstances of the text and permits the text to offer reader encounter, but not accomplishment. Time is the fourth dimension of space, all-time or non-measurable time. By not designating a specific hour, Mallarmé is able to group together the successive and the simultaneous; he destroys chronology and orderly sequence by affirming the potentiality of occurrence. Hence, "PEUT-ÊTRE" salvages the shipwrecked captain from the impotence of his gesture and the nothingness of the impending disaster into a surviving fixed astral victory. The trace of passage remains in the debris of the text and in its refracted dice-constellation figures. In his "Toast funèbre" to Gautier and his "tomb" poems to Poe, Baudelaire, and Verlaine, Mallarmé emphasizes the ultimate or final victory of the poetic act. In death, Poe is fixed for all time, "en Lui-même enfin l'éternité le change" (70), and Gautier's words survive him: "Le splendide génie éternel n'a pas d'ombre" (55). Similarly, the Master's gesture in *Un Coup de dés* remains; while the act may indeed not save him from death, it does go beyond mere existence in its denial of impotence and in its conjunction of the act on matter with matter. The text correlates the sky and the sea, the chaotic and the cosmic, as matter rejoins matter (dice-constellation) in the limitlessness of possibilities: Poem.

Where Igitur is limited to a situation in time and place (midnight, château), the Master is transformed from the condition of being (circumstances of the shipwreck) into the possibility of resurgence as a constellation of an idea or figuration (thought). Winning or losing is not the primary issue for either Igitur or the Master; rather, it is a question of the gesture or act: annihilation of being (finite reality) or establishment of the infinite through dispersion and dissolution into the unlimitedness of the absolute. The end (result of the throw) is the beginning for the Master but a defeat for Igitur, whose throw of the dice expresses separation (cause). On the other hand, the Master's act is one of attitude and effect; life and art coincide: "Toute Pensée émet un Coup de Dés." The pattern of the dice reflects the astral figure of a constellation, as the solidity of the cube is absorbed into the formlessness of the cosmos. The metaphysical anguish of Igitur is conquered by the Master whose act may well annihilate temporality. Only the risk taken by the Master has possible value (forming a constellation).

On the surface, there are many textual affinities between *Igitur* and *Un Coup de dés*, most notably the vocabulary. It is not surprising that there are in *Igitur* a wide range of similarities with *Un Coup de dés* and with other Mallarmé texts, such as the effort to conjoin a marine and stellar motif, the referentials of "chambre," "rideaux," "minuit," "nuit," "ombre," "ennui," "éternité," "battement," "tombeau," "glace," "science," "dentelle," "naufrage," "frisson," "livre," "page," "scintille," "science," etc. Moreover, the structure of *Igitur* is one of "pliage"—a fan expressed by a theatrical lexicon: "les parois latérales" (437), "les panneaux à la fois ouverts et fermés" (450), "l'opposition double des panneaux" (437), "intervalle" (437, 446), as well as a motif of alternation (motion-immobility, light-dark, clarity-obscurity, opening-closing, sound-silence, absence-substance). But, what does not succeed in *Igitur* is the reliance on description, narrative, chronology, even emotion. The "Argument" (434) is one of procedure by the intelligence; despite Mallarmé's parenthetical note to "Creuser tout cela," as author, he has a definite point of view, a hypothesis which he sets out to demonstrate ("Preuve") in *Igitur*, an approach which is philosophical rather than esthetic, an embracing of codes to show logical relationships between qualities and to establish contact, a structure of reflection, and a language of identification in performative sentences which progress through a set sequence of images. *Igitur* is contextual, derived, and limited in its signification. The very style preserves form through its authorial affirmation and authority. The impotence of the "scission" (429) is reaffirmed, what Sartre terms a suicide: "L'homme de Mallarmé [Igitur] . . . s'exprime en termes de drame et non en termes d'essence: . . . il se définit par son impossibilité" ("Préface," 8). In contrast, the Master of *Un Coup de dés* is defined by his possibilities, even though he risks self-annihilation in his act.

The major differences between *Igitur* and *Un Coup de dés* are more substantive than is usually thought. However, if one compares the layout of *Un Coup de dés* with the thematic structure of *Igitur*, one is struck by the fact that the themes (rather than the vocabulary and the event) are by and large eliminated in the printed vocabulary of *Un Coup de dés* in order to resurface in the vast amount of space of the text. In the space, not in the print, of *Un Coup de dés*, the reader detects the basic notions expressed in the "Argument" of *Igitur*: the descent into the self, the infinite which "sort du hasard," occurrence "dans les combinaisons de l'Infini vis-à-vis de l'Absolu," "tout a été." Where Igitur does not discover the absolute in his inner space, the Master conjoins inner and outer space in the establishment of human presence—essence. From chance is the "Don du poëme," the "Salut" of "le blanc souci de notre toile." The dualities and contradictions of *Igitur* are seemingly retained in the black print of *Un Coup de dés*, only to be dissolved in the virginal white space of the text: "RIEN N'AURA EU LIEU QUE LE LIEU."

If nothing really happens in *Igitur* except for the throwing of the dice, does anything occur in *Un Coup de dés*? Does the Master throw the dice or have they been thrown ("LANCÉ") anterior to the drama of the text? The final line of the poem, which leads back to the opening line and the title and which represents one of the two formally complete sentences in the text, suggests that thought precedes the throw. The dice reinforce the notion of chance (**"LE HASARD"**) and the problem of creation. While Sartre, for example, is convinced that Mallarmé's original impotence is theological, conquered only when he repudiates God ("Préface," 6-8), there is no hard evidence regarding Mallarmé's rejection of God or Christianity, just as there is very little documentation on his religious faith.[6] Most likely, formal religion was not a major concern to Mallarmé. Typical of his generation, he remained within the confines of established societal order, attended and, in general, acknowledged the institution of the church. Certainly, biblical allusions and themes invade all of his work, as well as familiarity with church liturgy and practices in both form and content: "Offices," "Prose (pour des Esseintes)," "Hérodiade," "Don du poëme," "Sainte," "Pour un baptême," verses "sur des livres à prière," etc. Basically, Mallarmé is an archetypal poet, drawing on all human expressions of creation, from classical myth to the Bible to plastic art, even fashion. If there is religious thinking in his work, it is not that of Pascal, the Romantics, Baudelaire, or even Verlaine; rather, he assigns to poetry the role that poets of the decades and centuries before him traditionally assigned to God. Mallarmé makes a religion out of poetry in the sense that he ascribes to it the principle of coherence, order, beauty, harmony, unity, and synthesis. He does not poeticize religion in the manner of the Romantics, nor does he wrestle with God and Christianity in the manner of Baudelaire. His dualities, especially as expressed in *Igitur*, are not theological, much less moral.

Nonetheless, it remains possible to read into *Un Coup de dés* a given affinity with the Bible, particularly Genesis and the story of creation: "la terre était vide et vague, les ténèbres couvraient l'abîme . . . un vent . . . tournoyait sur les eaux . . . des luminaires au firmament du ciel . . . qu'ils servent de signes . . . pour éclairer la terre . . . un flot montait de terre . . . et arrosait toute la surface . . . modela l'homme (les conséquences commanderont les conditions). . . ." In Psalms, one reads "il plana sur les ailes du vent / Il fit des ténèbres son voile" (no. 18), "Non point récit, non point langage / mais pour toute la terre en ressortent des lignes / et les mots jusqu'aux limites du monde" (no. 19), while in Proverbs there appears the line, "La folie fait la joie de l'homme privé de sens" (15:21). "Vieillard," "chef," "prince," "aïeul," "sépulcre," "ténèbres," "flots," "gouffre," etc. appear with frequency in the Bible along with creatures of the sea and sky, astral signs, ship travel and shipwrecks, the equation of life with light and death with darkness, and interest in written communication (page, book, rolls). However, a similarity between a biblical lexicon and the vocabulary of *Un Coup de dés* does not validate a Mallarmé as either religious or anti-God. Instead, it may well be that as an archetypal thinker, interested in the problem of creation and more specifically the how of creation, rather than the what, he combines elements of the Bible with classical myth in a quest to assert a common denominator between the experience of separation and the desire for unity. The torment of "L'Azur" (*"Je suis hanté!"*) becomes in *Un Coup de dés* a longing "qu'un endroit fusionne avec au-delà." The condition of being finite (anguish) is man's historical struggle against the unintelligibility of the circumstances of his existence.

The chances of victory are not predetermined; rather, they reside in the effort to comprehend not the condition but the circumstances of that condition. Hence, a throw of the dice is a maximum sign for any attempt to transform the fixed into the potentiality of change. And casting a lot to make a decision is uncontestably a human act, not divine in origin or inspiration. Throughout the Bible and human history, results are often reported as determined by chance, not by preordained laws; the principles at work are probability, established as a legacy of the past, and possibility, projected toward the future: "legs en la disparition . . . N'ABOLIRA JAMAIS LE HASARD." Only chance holds the opportunity to dissolve the present of impending disaster. The points on the dice have human consequences and are rolled in the context of the eternal circumstances of being man: to risk life is not to risk it, to be deceived in expectations or to arrive "à quelque point dernier qui le sacre," to acquiesce to the tragic condition or defy its circumstances, to break the limits of existence or transform them into the possibilities of essence in an act of discovery. Fifteen years later, Gide's Lafcadio in *Les Caves du Vatican* will refuse to follow the decision of the dice in order to be his own master, abstain from adopting an attitude, and live in defiance of everything, including himself. Yet, as Lafcadio learns, every act is for the self and so for everyone; hence, he gets off the train and decides that he prefers the police to Portos.

The throw of the dice is an act which invents or creates a value, and its meaning, like that of a constellation, occurs only in human terms. Where for Igitur, the contradictions only serve to reinforce his metaphysical anguish, they enrich the Master's responses to that anguish. The act affirms human will to question his destiny and perhaps even create an anti-destiny, a means of survival beyond the form of the act—its very absurdity—into the substance or essence of beingness. The Master is heroic in his affirmation of human freedom and power. In anticipation of Gide's Theseus, Mallarmé's Master claims himself and acts out of personal necessity, out of "Esprit" to create an order, no matter how foolish. Creation replaces action, as *Un Coup de dés* turns on itself in a circular structure. One could, then, argue that Igitur is conquered by the absurd, a victim of his condition, whereas the Master escapes the absurd by affirming his freedom to act and not reducing it to the historical human condition. The act is necessary to give meaning (identity), as the dice become a tool for self-discovery and a means to express life, not danger, risk, death. For Bonnefoy, Mallarmé's "poésie doit sauver l'être" and thereby save all men by opening the text to presence; words have the power to organize knowledge—they are the human act which transforms being into essence, the finite into the eternal and form into unlimited space ("L'Acte et le lieu," 185-214). Act is poetic place; presence is created by absence.

Hence, the dice may be said to represent resistance by the conscience ("Esprit"), an effort of the will to struggle against the absurd. Thought is a word, which is in turn an act, as subject and object are united in space. The past participle "LANCÉ" is incorporated into the present tense "émet," which is projected into the future, "**ABOLIRA**," as an ever-resurging axiom, a universal truth. *Un coup de Dés jamais n'abolira le Hasard* because "Toute Pensée" confers sense upon life and upon death; the possibility of transformation, changing the pattern on the dice ("compte total en formation") establishes value.[7] To initiate experience is to act; to act is to live; the poem is evidence of existence; poetry is its absolute source and only essence. The very act of creation establishes value in human and cosmic terms—not the result, but the act itself.

Hence, the dice may indeed be viewed as words on the page, forming different patterns for the reader with each turning of the page and with each rereading of the text. Only the layout of *Un Coup de dés* permits the possibilities of acting for the reader; he figuratively faces a game board and rolls the dice. Just as the human condition is unalterable, so is the game board, but the circumstances can perhaps be modified—varied. The reader "bets" with dice (words) on the layout (paginal space) in order to "jouer . . . la partie"; he accepts the challenge: "veillant doutant roulant brillant et méditant avant de s'arrêter à quelque point dernier." It does not matter what turns up, only that the reader act, create ways to deal with the board before him, and, in the process, play the game.

One of the interesting elements of the Mallarmé text is that nowhere does he identify the number of dice involved, only that there is more than one ("dés"). Traditionally, it is assumed that a pair of dice is involved.[8] However, several board games involve more than two dice. For example, the English dice game, Hazard, which was in vogue during Mallarmé's visits to England, may be played with three dice. It may well be that Mallarmé borrows this game for his text. The penchant for linguistic word games certainly surfaces throughout the lexicon of *Un Coup de dés* in the multivalent nature of the vocabulary and its syntactical distortions. *Un Coup de dés* could be based on a dice game, which has an arbitrary fixed layout, on which the betting takes place, and which is based on odds that are favorable to the house (author), while demanding at the same time a skillful player; the reader is, then, the metaphorical player, who actively accepts the challenge of reading, all the while aware that the contextual structure, the layout, cannot be changed; only the inner space of the board is free from constraints and dictated procedures. On this point, there is a discernible relationship between *Un Coup de dés* and the Mallarmé fan poems; the words and elements of the print form the rods, which are enclosed by two definite terminal slats, the dice which begin and end the text. The flat and static plane of the page is transformed by the reading throw of the dice into a mobile circle of activity. A rhythm of folding and unfolding is reinforced by a vocabulary of motion, yet there remains an immovable quality to the text, just as dice themselves have only so many points and combinations of points. The form of the cube controls the figures, just as the rods of a fan continually retract to their terminal slats and each page is arranged with prescribed verbal pivots. The balance between stasis and dynamism affirms the fiction as one of conjunction, not disjunction, neither contracted nor expanded, formed nor unformed, but suggestive of all form, as the idea of a constellation—thought—is transformed into an object—dice or words. The image of the dice which opens and closes the text is both visual and verbal. Dice must be seen (form) in order to be read and interpreted (content); in addition, the throwing of dice is an act or gesture, while its pattern is always grasped as a whole and a whole which emerges without a logical, preordained cause or explanation. A throw of the dice begins and ends in chance. Hence, *Un Coup de dés* affirms the necessity of chance in verbal creation, expressed earlier by Mallarmé in "Le Démon de l'analogie." Just how important chance is in Mallarmé's esthetics occurs in his selection of dice as the initial and final image in *Un Coup de dés*.

Every reader sees the "coup de dés" as gaming dice and an affair in which chance has a role. However, the word *dé* is by no means limited to the cube in games. *Dé* is the word applied to the rectangular domino ("dés des étendus"), which contains white points on a black surface—the very opposite of the traditional black points on a white surface which characterize gaming dice. *Dé* is also a marine term, referring to the plaque which "exécute la couture des voiles," and it is a printing term, die, the piece which holds the actual piece of type and by extension anything that holds something else, such as a vise. Moreover, Mallarmé uses the verb *lancer* not *jeter*, which is the correct verb to describe the act of throwing dice. The expression "jeter les dés" evokes the element of choice; one risks removing some constituent elements in opting for others. On the other hand, the proverb "le dé en est jeté" (the die is cast) denotes the impossibility of transformation. Still, another use of *dé* occurs in the phrase "un coup de hasard," which is a variation of "un coup de dés"; while "un coup de dés" refers to the throw of the dice and the inherent role of chance in that throw, "un coup de hasard" evokes the number of points which turn up in the throw. From this point of view, Mallarmé's title, *Un coup de Dés jamais n'abolira le Hasard*, in which only "*Dés*" and "*Hasard*" are capitalized, is read quickly as "*Un coup de Hasard*" since the two capitalized nouns are typographically related and visually call attention to their thematic importance. Only when one grasps the relationships of *"Dés"* and *"Hasard"* on the title page does the use of the verb *lancer* receive meaning. *Lancer* denotes release rather than the actual throwing, tossing, or hurling of an object; second, there is a direct semantic agreement between *lancer* and *émettre*; both are verbs of projection and connote the beginning or start of something. In the beginning pages of *Un Coup de dés*, the throw of the dice is released into the circumstances of the space of the page (or board or intervals of the fronds of a fan); on the last page of the text, the dice are sent forth again, reinforcing the circular structure of the text but also offering up an abridged reading of the text. Instead of rereading from the title page and from the first page of the text, the reader begins on recto 2, a procedure which now validates the complete emptiness of verso 2, and the text is read: "Toute Pensée émet un Coup de Dés [qui] **JAMAIS QUAND BIEN MÊME LANCÉ DANS DES CIRCONSTANCES ÉTERNELLES.**" The type visually expands the emission of the thought into the concrete object of dice, space is crossed and filled, presence replaces absence, contact is established, and the reading activity is the experience of creation, in which the text emerges as both object (fixed points or words and their arrangement) and subject: a perpetual coming into being. Like a circle, there is no beginning, middle, or end; there is only circulation in its inner space. *"Un coup de Dés"* is *"un coup de Hasard,"* launched over and over again in every act of reading. Endemically anti-linear, space expands experience; it does not record it. Hence, Mallarmé's structure of a contrived, highly artificial layout annuls relationships in order to affirm the absence of stratification. The text does not reproduce the familiar and the known, and it does not imitate appearance; rather, *Un Coup de dés* initiates experience (*"le vierge indice"*), as origin or source is result or outcome. There are no designated directions, just as a circle has no fixed order or procedure; the top is the bottom, the doublet pages negate left and right sides, contraction is expansion. The text enters the space of the reader for whom *"un coup de Dés"* is the poem and *"un coup de Hasard"* is the reading; the text is the event and the place of the communication. Order is established.

The establishment of an ordering is not chance, *"un coup de Dés,"* but a mark of *"un coup de Hasard,"* the certainty of meaning in the chaos of the a-logical, asymmetrical features of the layout. Not only is there always a result with dice, regardless of its referents, but other images in the text also express identity and definition: the fixed stars of the constellation, the print on each page, the mode of presentation (groupings), the standard vocabulary. Language itself is an ordering. The very layout of the text denies chance and authenticates textual unity of the fiction. Chance, then, is an act of faith which expresses belief in the value of creation, if not a divination of creation "qui le sacre." The lack of an argument to persuade the reader, such as that which characterizes *Igitur*, moves the text from being a work of the imagination to the realm of pure assembly through the intelligence, into synthesis, harmony, the reader's creation of explanation, meaning, even myth. The reader "reads" what is not said and the opposite of what is said, for the message is neither the medium nor the dice, but "**LE HASARD**," as the reader undertakes the text and responds to it. The print will never abolish chance in the range of meanings or interpretations: *"plume solitaire éperdue / sauf / que la rencontre ou l'effleure . . . / et immobilise / . . . cette blancheur rigide."* Reality is dissolved ("toute réalité se dissout") into space, into the Absolute of formlessness.

The dice image is not, however, limited to gaming and other mimetic and teleological possibilities. Rock formations jut chaotically along the coast of Brittany, formed by the chance activity of the elements, especially water and wind. Northwestern Brittany in particular is characterized by violent currents, frequent heavy fog and mist, choppy waves, rocks, lighthouses (as in the "feux" of *Un Coup de dés*), alarm systems ("sirène"), and two-masted boats; in addition, the typical Breton costume is a severe one of black velvet, with a head-covering, not unlike the "toque" of the text.

Much of the vocabulary of *Un Coup de dés* can be directly related to Mallarmé's stay in Brittany, first at Douarnenez and then at Le Conquet in August 1873—in fact, it was at Le Conquet that he wrote his "Toast funèbre" for Théophile Gautier.

Visiting Brittany was very popular in the latter half of the nineteenth century; Hugo, Flaubert, Barrès, Villiers de l'Isle-Adam, Gautier, Lecomte de Lisle, Corbière, Littré, Hérédia, various painters, etc., vacationed in Brittany, and Mallarmé's *La Dernière Mode* advocated visits to the Breton coast in the summer months. The traditional vocabulary used to describe the Breton coast, especially the area known as la Corniche bretonne runs through the vocabulary adopted by Mallarmé for *Un Coup de dés*: *flots, étale, gouffre, vague, naufrage, roc, manoir, sirène, brume, écume, cime, écueil, scintille* (to describe water), as well as the fact that Brittany is famed for its legends, myths, and superstitions. Off the Coz-Porz beach at Trégastel, there is a rock named "Le Dé," which is a perfect cube in appearance, and opposite "Le Dé" is "Le Gouffre," a rocky cavity accessible only at low tide. Hence, the very geography of *Un Coup de dés* has a base in the physical world and in the poet's personal experience. Resembling the serrated, jagged appearance of the coastline of Brittany, the layout of *Un Coup de dés* is one of displacement, loss of equilibrium, abrupt obstacles, and an uneven rising and falling motion. Like the captain of a fishing boat, the reader is pitched and tossed amid small islands, the density of fog distorts the scene before him, even the expanse of the sea is broken by rock formations which cannot be predicted in either place of appearance or shape. Navigation is indeed perilous, even for the most skillful mariner, for the unexpected is a daily circumstance.

The dice also relate to numbers, and numbers offer one of the more standard readings by space: the points on the dice, the stars of the constellation, and the repetition in the text of the word *nombre*. After all, Mallarmé did admire Descartes (851), for whom the science of mathematics is a language. The most commonly proposed number is seven because it brings together the points on the dice and the seven stars which form the Little Dipper. All points or dots on opposite dice faces add up to seven (1 + 6, 2 + 5, 3 + 4), and one wins a dice game with either the number 7 or 11—11 being also the traditionally stated number of doublet pages of the text. And, in numerology, seven is the number which symbolizes perfect order, as well as the number of the planets, the gods, cardinal sins, sorrows, and

Assembly by Space 127

virtues, the musical scale, even space (six dimensions plus the center). However, nowhere does Mallarmé show interest in numerology, and the number seven is, in dice, a losing number if it is the first combination of points thrown. The number 21 also comes into play because each di adds up to 21, the number of total synthesis in which there is no conflict, the Tarot card for The World and the senses (again synthesis), and there are a total of 21 printed pages for Mallarmé's text. Still other readers use the number 12, the midnight of *Igitur*, because they see, first, so many affinities between the two works and, second, because the "toque" of *Un Coup de dés* is described as *"une toque de minuit."* However, *"minuit"* is not restricted to a temporal frame; it also has use in coloration, describing the deepest hue or effect possible. Ronat's argument, based on the number 12 (and 24), rests, for example, on two erroneous premises; first, a misunderstanding of the use of signature sheets, and, second, there is no mathematical system which is built on the number 12.

The "unique Nombre" and *"LE NOMBRE"* are no more than the text says they are: products of the mind ("Esprit"), used by man to create order in the chaos of his human situation. Man invents numbers and then uses them as a tool for identifying his world and acting in the circumstances of his condition. Number in *Un Coup de dés* has to do with probability and possibility, based in turn on calculation. Any number is a "somme" and any number can be deciphered and can be enlightening according to its application. The "unique Nombre"—and it must be remembered that this phrase was modified by Mallarmé twice (first the capital letter N, second the initial position of the adjective "unique")—is the number which is applicable in the event, the chance one takes to act. There is no predictability, only the place is certain, and there is a final stopping point. Optimistically, chance is the only certitude; hence, *"LE NOMBRE"* and "LE HASARD" appear on the same page, but "LE HASARD" is in 22-point bold, the dominant (victorious) element.

If there is a number in *Un Coup de dés*, it can only be the number zero, a number which is neither differential nor representative of essential definition—the only purely undifferential number possible, for it neither designates nor describes. And, indeed, the text is one of circular structure.

The number four also appears to some as a means of reading the text because the title is dispersed in four segments: **UN COUP DE DÉS, JAMAIS, N'ABOLIRA, LE HASARD**. These four segments then offer four formal divisions to the text and four themes. Four is also a traditional number for the movements of a musical symphony, and there is a vocabulary of music in the text, as well as musical references in the "Préface" and throughout Mallarmé's commentaries on poetry. For Mallarmé, music is the multi-scenic or "extra-scénique" (349), that is, non-descriptive and not narrated, and he equates musicality with dispersion (653). But Mallarmé did not really know music[9] and did not understand it technically. Moreover, *Un Coup de dés* has no resonance, no formal rime or meter; it is not an orchestration, but a fully integrated work, whose circular structure denies identification of direction, progression, sequence. Music is a metaphor, just as theater, dance (especially ballet), mime, and the church are metaphors.

Certainly, *Un Coup de dés* is not written in the manner of a musical symphony or opera. It cannot be read aloud, cannot be performed, cannot be enacted. Yet, it is true that Mallarmé enjoyed ballet, especially Dégas's painting and sketches of dancers ("Polichinelle"), had a special fondness for theater (his own summer productions and performances at Valvins, as well as his *Crayonné au théâtre*), and he greatly admired Wagner. In fact, it is more than tenable to see in *Un Coup de dés* a parallel with Wagner's *Le Vaisseau fantôme*, for Mallarmé's captain is in the midst of a "naufrage . . . sans nef," the text is built around the effort to control destiny ("un destin et les vents"), and the shipwreck itself is human: "naufrage cela / direct de l'homme." In addition to a thematic relationship with Wagner's opera, it should be noted that Wagner had a preference for using a mythology of black and white: black is time, the period which permits germination, while white represents timelessness when crystallization is possible. Black and white are then similar to the young science of photography, a positive and negative viewing of the same event, rather than colors. In fact, black and white are not formally part of the color spectrum, but instead permit the rise of color. Indeed, Mallarmé's *Un Coup de dés* is a colorless text,[10] and the black print in all its variations does evoke a sense of sequence (even though there is no actual ordering) and implies temporality through the many adverbs of time and verb tenses, while the vast amount of space erases sequence, temporality, formation (germination) and may indeed be described as the place of crystallization or integration, the end of separation and division.

Black is inferior to white and represents limitation, constraints, division, and contradiction, while white is pure, absolute, free, and indivisible. It should also be noted that one of the major aspects which separates Edouard Manet from the Impressionists is his use of black. The Impressionists refused to admit black on their palettes because it delineated substance and solidity. While Manet exhibited with the Impressionists, he never considered himself a part of them, an esthetic distinction which the Impressionists also recognized. Yet, Manet did achieve the art of suggestion or impression in his paintings with the use of black, just as Mallarmé was able to practice the art of the "nuance" through the interplay of black and white.

The use of black was more of an issue in the late nineteenth century than is usually suspected. The color spectrum itself was debated and color systems were developed. Among Mallarmé's "Mardistes," René Ghil, for example, tried to expand Rimbaud's "Voyelles" by assigning a color to every letter of the alphabet in his 1886 *Traité du verbe*.[11] But the widening interest in photography and the camera, including the birth of cinematic film, as well as the development of the popular press and interest in poster art all contributed to a general artistic fascination with the use of black and white, as well as to greater preoccupation with perspective, optics, and space. Mallarmé's close friendships and his own pantheon of admired figures (Poe, Wagner), as well as his personal interests (poster art, Japanese woodcuts and fans, printing technicalities), come together in the black-white concerns of his time. Even music, which figuratively presents black notes and lines on white, shares this sphere of activity, as in his title, *La Musique et les lettres*. Hence, ballet is "sidéral" (303) and a "forme théâtrale de Poésie" (308). In one very real sense of the word, Mallarmé's prose commentaries evoke the black-white interplay that preoccupied the artists, scientists, and technicians of his day: reaction to discoveries and the importance of the visual in those discoveries.[12] The perspective shifts on all fronts: from the intellect to the intuition, the philosophical to the psychological, content to its appearance, and then from the author to the reader-viewer, even from the divine to the human, time to space, noumen to phenomenon, and theme to construct or structure. Perhaps the structure of the Eiffel Tower captures best the spirit of the times.

One of the criticisms frequently aimed at Mallarmé is that he placed his faith in language and not in man, in the mysteries of the word and not in those of life. Yet, an impersonal text such as *Un Coup de dés* is anything but a non-man-centered poem, for it is written to be read and reconstructed by its reader: "Résultats de l'accointance de l'idée de Science et de l'idée de Langage. . . . Résultats pour l'Esprit, Fiction. Moyen. Résultats pour les Sciences. Enfin, avenir ouvert à l'étude de l'Homme" (853). Its very impersonality demands a personal response; the ambiguous and multivalent terms require intense and precise interpretations, the lack of a message does not mean there is no communication, the absence of tonality is perfect harmony, the elimination of punctuation eliminates conformity and subordination, and the incomplete quality of the text as printed entity (its circularity) testifies to a text of maximum reader circulation and initiative. Reader response replaces authorial decision. Like a Manet canvas, the first reading-viewing impression of *Un Coup de dés* is its synthetic appearance—its conjunction of extremes, and its invitation to share an inquiry into the text as text, into the text as poem, and, ultimately, into Poetry itself. Instead of closing the text, Mallarmé opens up the mysteries of Poetry in giving it the value of reader response, what he calls "la lecture salvatrice" (262). It is not a question of a story or legend; it does not matter if the dice have been thrown or not, if the shipwreck occurs or not, if the captain goes down with his ship or not; rather, it is a question of textual production. It may well be that Mallarmé's interest in Descartes is not the Cartesian notion that language is a form of mathematics, but that the glory of man is that he can think. Hence, Mallarmé constructs a text which is, first, to be seen as a synthetic whole and, second, to be appreciated analytically by reader-viewer concentration on the assembly of those parts. The reader is a viewer and a thinker—he is Rodin's contemplative figure, not free to determine the order, not free to create, but free to interpret what his eyes see and what his mind establishes as significant.

Indeed, the primary question which reading by space engenders is just what does the viewer behold? What does he see? What does he think about the spectacle before him? The norms of perspective have been jettisoned, the reading grids confused, the referents obfuscated, logical sequence repudiated, and word reconciliation and groupings impeded by the syntax and vocabulary. So many responses are stimulated that no decision can be made with any measure of confidence. The definite ordering of the layout distorts reader experience and destroys every point of contact. The minimal structure confers maximal freedom upon the reader. Separation and absence are synonyms of integration and presence, negatives are positives, the atonal is harmonious, and detaching—structuring by fragments—establishes contact, agreement, and unity. The text is tentative.

The lexical debate offered by the vocabulary is not based on logic. In a long poem, 21 pages, there are surprisingly only 700 words.[13] The basically sparse use of words deverbalizes the text; they are not tools of textual entry, instruments which usually provide logical access into a text: "il faut pressentir l'ensemble sublime du poëme impliqué en peu de mots" (241). The words are terms which seem to have been deliberately pulled from a dictionary and are therefore based on dictionary arguments, not experience ("le dictionnaire me suffirait," 854). For example, the word *barre* belongs to a nautical lexicon (tiller), as well as to a musical one (bar) and a printing one (matrix); *LE MAÎTRE* can be a ship captain, a master artisan, or "Everyman," anyone who is not subordinate to someone else, a poet, even Mallarmé himself, who was affectionately called both "Maître" and "Capitaine" by his friends and followers; *manœuvre* is both a nautical and a gaming term, while the expression *jouer la partie*, which cannot be used to convey a role or function, includes both games and music. *Toque* is a cap, a head covering, but while it is the sort of cap usually worn on the stage by an actor portraying Hamlet, a "toque" is also typical of French Renaissance dress, is popular in seventeenth-century French literature (La Fontaine, for example), regional costumes, and even today refers to the cap worn by professors, who are also "maîtres."

On dictionary readings alone, *Un Coup de dés* may be read as a board game, a nautical event, the printing process, a musical work, a mathematical maze, armchair theater (monodrama or ballet), a myth, an architectural parallelepiped, even a dialectic between prose and free verse. It may also be viewed as a psychological street plan,[14] the figuration of a human thought, especially in terms of generative grammar, and the "historical" birth of "mécriture."[15] Other interpretations may include various philosophical concepts: existential anguish, the death of God to its reverse as in Rodolof Hinostroza's "death of Nietzsche" through the white space or "Axe vide" (18-19), Bonnefoy's negative theology, Pascalian wagering, the tragedy of human existence in general, the separation of conscience from matter, a neo-Platonic demonstration of the Non-Being of being.

Still other readings may detect a Promethean poet who survives his words and so gains immortality through his work (rebirth follows destruction), the conquest of chance through words or the defeat by chance since thought comes from chance and returns to it, or a fragment of Mallarmé's unfinished *Livre* which was to have contained the "explication orphique de la Terre" (663) and reconciled all contradictions as well as all the arts (chance would become Infinity as proposed in *Igitur* and the yawning abyss and constellation of *Un Coup de dés* would be conjoined in a supreme order which would include a synthesis of *plume* and *écume, nombre* and *ombre*, alpha and omega). These and other "readings" are spatially based on the linguistic differentiation of the vocabulary, the interference of the deliberate arrangement of the lexical elements, and the intertextual nature of Mallarmé's writing.

Assembly by Space 133

In a very real sense, Mallarmé rewrites himself; the vocabulary is typical of his themes, textual structures, and visual arrangements on the page: type variations ("L'Après-midi d'un faune"), circular structure ("L'Azur" and "Mes bouquins refermés sur le nom de Paphos"), object signs ("Le Démon de l'analogie" and "Ses purs ongles très haut dédiant leur onyx"), dispersion (form in "A la nue accablante tu" and theme in "Prose [pour des Esseintes]"), elimination of coloration ("Le Vierge, le vivace et le bel aujourd'hui"), black-white interplay ("Ses purs ongles . . ."), presence through absence ("Une dentelle s'abolit"), dissolution of substance in a reconciliation of subject and object ("Toute l'âme résumée"). The foam of "Salut" is a variant of the lace of "Une dentelle s'abolit" which is the reworked smoke ring of "Toute l'âme résumée." Text is associated with text, just as within *Un Coup de dés* the dice are associated with "LE HASARD" (subject), the circumstances of the shipwreck (situation), the agony of the master (agent), and the resulting formation of a constellation (act).

Each printed grouping recalls a previous text, as well as at least one other grouping within the text itself. However, working along the pattern of word clusters, based on word repetition, the reader discovers that even dictionary arguments are not reliable. For each discovery of lexical certainty, there is an accompanying expansive grammatology which undermines semantic stability. Using the 12 substantives repeated in the text, the following groupings emerge into view:

coup de dés: chance, jeter, raillant, probabilité, hasard
ombre: fantôme, silence, mystère, ombrage, ténébreuse, brumes, secret, voile, gouffre, abîme, menace, illusion
nombre: calculs, résume, âge, une, chiffrât, somme, résultat, Septentrion, constellation, énumère, compte total, dernier, unique, division, exigüment, ultimes, minuit, probabilité, chance
aïeul: cadavre, chenu, homme, ancestralement, legs, vieillard, issu, âge
mer: bord, flots, vague, écueil, sirène, squames, écumes, clapotis, gouffre

lieu: mer, nef, profondeur, roc, manoir, borne, vague, réalité, surface, point, conjonction, endroit, bâtiment
plume: aile, toque, velours, coiffe, aigrette, vol
naufrage: inclinaison, voile, envergure, coque, bâtiment, barre, nef, foudre, vertige, torsion, sinistre, délire, crise, perdition, tempête, barbe, sombre, feux, heurt, lancé
profondeur: fond, ciel, stature, cime, élévation, altitude, Nord, sursauta, inclinaison, debout
au-delà: infini, éternelles, horizon, suprême, stellaire, supérieure, sacre, destin
hors: à l'intérieur, coque, plane.

As word clusters based on lexical repetition emerge and begin to take on meaning and definition in the reader's mind, a pattern of interaction from cluster to cluster also emerges. For example, *gouffre* is strictly a term used with water, while *abîme* is one which applies to an opening in the earth only; however, the two are used synonymously, a word usage which negates their formal application and links the opposites of earth and sea; in turn, they semantically recall the clusters of *ombre, naufrage*, and *profondeur*, which are in turn absorbed by the cluster *au-delà*. Each cluster ceases to be an identifiable block, as the groupings regroup lexically and each term per cluster moves from its dictionary meaning into the reading experience: *tempête-tourbillon-vertige-torsion, folie-délire-hantise-maniaque-oubliée, ambiguvoile d'illusion-inférant-insinuation, maître-chef-homme-vieillard-prince-seigneuriale*. Synonyms and antonyms appear: *puérile-pubère-vierge, solitaire-unique-supérieur, immémorial-mémorable-oubliée-oubli, altitude-élévation-profondeur; borne-point-bord, circonstances-évènement-chance-hasard-résultat*. The list is endless.

Word doubles further contribute to a loss of verbal identification: *le vol* (flight, theft), *la barre* (bar, rail, tiller, matrix), *les ais* (planks, press bars or boards), *la plume* (feather, pen), *sinistre* (disastrous, left-handed), *la coque* (shell, hull), *nef* (ship, nave). The crisis is lexical and semantic; common words are suspected, devalued, and reassessed. *Division* may be a simple division or the organization used in naval military maneuvers, the double bar in music, the hyphen in the printing world—or all three at the same time. While *ouvrir* may refer to the nautical unfolding of sails, *barbe* could well be the double marine anchor, the burr in typesetting, the double edge of the page. *Couler* may be read as to flow or it may in some way link up with *naufrage*, as in the expression "couler un naufrage" (to sink). Even *direct* may indicate straight, right out of, an adjective, or it may be an allusion to the noun for the printing-out of paper. Even a term which is most likely stable, such as *naufrage*, becomes suspect; originally, a shipwreck is a term of destruction and loss and it usually conjures up a picture of an undesired and unfortunate event; however, to the inhabitants of small islands, off the coast of Brittany for example, a shipwreck was at one time a desired event, a gain not a loss, a benefit materially and psychologically.

The marine vocabulary may be figurative only, an extended metaphor which when placed in counterbalance with the musical allusions and printer's lexicon loses its predetermined and historical significance in order to become a sign of linguistic neutrality in which matter is vaporized ("toute réalité se disout") and something else is "en formation." Is the vocabulary to be taken at face value, one of "illusion," "hantise," "hallucination," "folie," "mensonge"—is *délire* to be associated with *folie* or with a lexical un-reading? Can the words be read? Or are they shipwrecked by their very selection, "en foudre"? The tumult of the ocean could actually be a mental activity, while the "tempête" stirred up by a storm which joins the elements of wind and air may be a creative term because it combines more than one element and incarnates energy. If the storm is creative in its destruction, then so is the "conflagration" which transforms one element into another and assimilates different parts into one entity. To destroy is to create, to end is to begin, to disperse is to assimilate, to abolish is to establish: unity between all disparates—sea and sky, heaven and earth, loss and salvation, even the sexes (the male prince and the female siren)—surges forth. Semantic limits are annihilated, and the words testify to verbal—human—liberation. All logical categories of differentiation are abolished. Words themselves are let loose to assemble and reassemble by similarity, contrast, homographically, homophonically. The destruction of verbal connotation and denotation is also the destruction of verbal derivation. The word is truly initial, creative, and generative.

The lexical shipwreck is reinforced by syntactical ambiguities. For example, *étale* can be an adjective, slack (tide) or steady (breeze), or a verb with several possible frameworks: to spread out (sails or paper) or to display, or to ride out as to weather a gale. *Plane* may be an adjective, level, or a form of the verb to hover over, to look down upon, to contemplate, while *sombre* may be the adjective dark or the verb to founder and sink. *Rencontre* can be either a noun or a verb, and *blanchi* and its noun *blancheur* may refer to sea spray, a manuscript and its revision, or typographic spacing. Even *retombée* loses its identity, for it is either a falling back down again (relapse) or a coming around again, just as *bercer*, to rock (as in a lulling, swaying motion) may also mean to delude.

The crisis of semantic stability finds its counterpart in an anxiety of syntactical arrangement. But syntactical ambivalence is not limited to wordplay, the elimination of punctuation, or even the dislocated positioning of the verbal units, for the groupings are based on grammatical laws. For example, in the phrase "à n'ouvrir pas la main," the positioning of *pas* after the infinitive results in a negation of the agent of the action, *main*, and not the verb, *ouvrir*. The exact same disruption occurs in the title, where the adverb *jamais* is placed before the conjugated verb, *abolira*. Word positioning affects the meaning of the words themselves. Science replaces logic: "La Science ayant dans le Langage trouvé une confirmation d'elle-même, doit . . . devenir une CONFIRMATION du Langage" (852).

The discontinuous emerges as the principle of cohesion: conjunction lies in "obliquité" and "déclivité." Hence, *plane* and *sombre* share a verbal relationship when they are read as verbs and not as adjectives, and the sonorous link between *sombre, ombre,* and *nombre* is jeopardized; the clusters change, as neither form nor meaning of the word is trustworthy: "Dans le 'Langage' expliquer le Langage, dans son jeu par rapport à l'Esprit, le *démontrer* sans tirer de conclusions absolues (de l'Esprit)" (853).

Every lexical, semantic, and syntactical fragment of *Un Coup de dés* demonstrates creative energy. The vocabulary in general is one of motion: activity in both the human and cosmic spheres. As a result, the text is one of change—nothing is what it seems to be, for what comes into view and is apparent is evidence only of something else. The reticent and held-in-check adjective *clos* recalls "silence," "secret," and "mystère," but the very impenetrability also suggested by *clos* conjures up *somme* (mass) and its opposites: *éparse-profusion-disperser-ouvrir*. In fact, *Un Coup de dés* begins and ends on a term of enclosure, *dés*, and the text itself is noticeably marked by terms of containment and restraint (*roc, manoir, voile, coque, os, ais, nef, bâtiment, bord, constellation, poing, écueil, stature, ensevelir, endroit*), as well as terms which indicate measurement and limitation (*inclinaison, jaillissements, bond, penché, horizon, division, imposa, élévation, ordinaire, surface, arrêter*). Both groups of words, those which connote enclosure and those which refer to measured limits, are accompanied by the vocabulary of motion, physical activity and emotional stress: *lancé, furieux, désespérément, retombée, vol, surgi, s'agite et mêle, vents, tempête, tourbillon, flots, vague, rejailli, précipité, hurlé, choit, vertige, sursauta, folie, délire, disperser, roulant*. Basically, the vocabulary is human; not only are parts of the body (*main, pieds, poing, cadavre, front*, etc.) enumerated along with terms of emotivity, but the very title of the work and final line are man-centered: "Coup de Dés" and "Pensée." The general outline of the event depicted is a human drama: the master and the shipwreck; the use of number and a constellation are man-made figures for imposing logic on the world and for establishing directions.

Calibration of the layout of the printed elements and the vocabulary of enclosure and measurement reinforce the poem as one of finiteness, bounds, unalterable order, which impedes logical procedure, sequential development, and termination. Still, the text itself is so enclosed in its circular structure that there is no mode of reader entry into it and the poem cannot be enacted, performed, "read." It can only be seen, admired, appreciated—not fully grasped, understood, deciphered, decoded; it invites reaction. Hence, every page is different; individual versos, rectos, doublets begin and end on dissimilar lines. The variations in type, indentation, capitalization, interval spacing, number of lines, length and arrangement of groupings prevent and forego debate on reader procedure. There is no pattern, confirmed by a very human vocabulary of constraint, limitation, gesticular motion, emotionalism, mental agitation, risk. The obstacles to success for the Master are captured in the vocabulary and its disposition, obstacles to success for the reader. Chance is concretized in the rolling dice, the turning of the pages, but the element of chance does not guarantee success, only that there will be points on the dice and words on the page, and this will continue because the whole venture—that of the Master and that of the reader—is no more than a throw of the dice, a gamble.

However, study of the layout shows that the actual structure of *Un Coup de dés* is one of space, and the varying amount and use of space per page dramatically affects the black printed elements, frees them from their lexical and semantic moorings, cuts them loose to be read either top to bottom, left to right, or across the center gutter, permits the reader to circulate freely within the text. The vocabulary of activity supports the dynamism of the white space of the text, as change emerges as the predominant motif of both the print and the surrounding white space.

Change is, of course, a principle of chance, non-stasis, and permits transformation. The multiplicitousness of the vocabulary and multilinearity of the arrangement confirm the text as fiction. Reader awareness of the possibilities of recreating the text and transforming it into meaning establishes the authenticity of the text as its own process and procedure, a conjunction between the finite and the abstract, the "Hasard" of reading and the "coup de Dés" of Poem. The text itself is the event; there is no subject and no theme in formal terms. The text comes into being each time it is read. The printed elements do not change, but their relationships one to the other undergo metamorphosis. It is as though Mallarmé has structured his entire poem under the aegis of a pattern or dialectic of opposites; the thesis is the surrounding whiteness and the antithesis is the print. Consequently, the actual synthesis of the text—aside from its initial organic or synthetic impression of unity—must take place in the reading experience, on the surface of the text. The element of change or counteraction rests in its space. By opposing print to the unprinted, Mallarmé composes a poem, but in their opposition (minimal use of print and maximal use of space), he enables a third image to emerge into view: Poetry. Mallarmé renders creativity or poetry visible within the configuration of a thought: "Toute Pensée émet un Coup de Dés": "**POÈME.**" The throw of the dice is the act or event of the text—the concrete poem— but the reading is the response to the challenge to penetrate its form, discover its process and production, recreate it by undertaking its layout, and thereby enact not the poem, "Un Coup de dés," but the act of creation itself: "Pensée" is Poetry.

Just as the pole star is the unchanging element in the Little Dipper and represents in the text the one constant, so Mallarmé's authorial pole star is Poetry, unique source, unchanging idea of order. And just as the rotation of the axis of the earth may alter the viewer's perspective of the Little Dipper and bring into view other constellations and formations, so the reader uncovers different figures, myths, conjunctions, and points of agreement, but only if he *sees* that one immutable point of orientation in order to read (navigate) the text before him. The text, as Gide said, is the vessel in which the reader sets out on a voyage of discovery (1582), accepts the challenge to conjoin on the plane of the page the fragments or traces of poetic creation. Because there is no authorial address and no exchange between the author and his reader, the initiative passes from the author to the words and then to the reader. The author—Mallarmé—has set relationships in the print, in the space, and in the opposition of the print to the space; he has literally deformed poetry by devaluating reading codes in order that the reader may pursue his own system, destructure and restructure meanings through the groupings, and recreate his own text. The mutations in and by paginal space permit Mallarmé to construct the tentative text, which is the only text which the reader may make his own. The text must be circular in order to negate the concept of a single literary or philosophical system in order to include all systems (all readings). The circularity of *Un Coup de dés* enables the text to remain incomplete; it has no forward progression and no retrogressive sequence, it is, instead, a structure of re-beginning: self-generative in its own destructive construction, what René Char develops later as the "poème pulvérisé" and the matinal text: "Mallarmé est à la fois unique et conditionnel."[16]

The conditional quality of Mallarmé's *Un Coup de dés* is dramatically captured by the dispersed first line, which is a repetition of the title of the work. Taken by itself, the title expresses a general truth; in the form of a proverb or axiomatic statement, *Un Coup de Dés jamais n'abolira le Hasard* confers authority upon the text and implies a trustworthy order within the text; the title contains valuable information, functions as an atmospheric-settting device, giving the overall idea of the text and the relationships within the poem *"Dés"-"Hasard."* The title is synthetic, organic, complete, and precise. Contemplative in nature, the title suggests the solid structure of human thought. The future tense of the verb suggests indivisibility, continuity, and singleness of the affirmation. The title forecloses debate in its credibility and evocation of an unalterable discovery. However, the first few pages distort the stability of the truth declared in the title by splitting it into four separate parts which are placed at four differing and irregular positions in the text. While the title retains its quality as a setting device in both its typography and topography, being the only line which appears in 22-point bold upper-case letters, the largest and most visually dramatic display type face in the poem, the position of the four segments of the title draws attention to the divisibility of the relationships which the title originally affirms.

By breaking up the authoritative axiomatic statement of the title, Mallarmé shows how elements are actually unrelated, how matter or phenomena are limited, how discontinuity is the actual ordering, how the mind forges agreements and disagreements, numbers and constellations. By enlarging single elements of thought by space, "**UN COUP DE DÉS**" / "**JAMAIS**" / "**N'A-BOLIRA**" / "**LE HASARD**," he distorts the original premise of unity and logical argumentation; he destabilizes the dependability and trustworthiness of his own text. Instead of a text which demonstrates the cohesiveness of its design and universal application, the dispersement of the axiom which is the title turns against itself by its own spatial display and array. The event is arrested, isolated, no longer useful. Yet, the information contained in the title and dispensed by it exists because of reader memory.

The reader can never read the text without recalling the completeness of the titular phrase and its inherent authority. While the dispersed title may pose at first an element of surprise and disorientation for the reader, he, nonetheless, reads within the experience of the title. Divergence and discontinuity—the fragments of the title in the poem—emerge into the sign of the co-referentiality of the text; each titular fragment offers an expansion of the figure of relationships set by the title itself. The reader experiences creative correlation by orienting his reading around the simultaneous appearance of the previously read title and its segmented appearance on different pages of the text. Significantly more emphatic by its disjunction than by its initial conjunctive, constative, proverbial nature, the title is unique in the authorial information it contains, but its dispersion renders it conditional in the eye of the reader.

The text becomes no more than a demonstration of the energy of human thought and faith in the unlimited potentiality of human creativity. Moreover, the final segment of the title, "**LE HASARD**," does not end the text; the text continues for four and one-half pages after the appearance of this segment, beyond chance as a visual topographic obstacle which interrupts the flow of the reading experience on recto 9, into chance as the unique mode of entry and access. The title is dispersed only to a point, for the text continues beyond the limitations of the title itself. The abstract negation of the "**JAMAIS N'**" is negated by the textuality of the pages which follow the segment, "**LE HASARD.**" Although the poem is constructed in controlled segments and appears as an act of divergence, reinforced by the discontinuity of the titular phrase, the very concision of the arrangement—an arrangement which goes beyond its own authority—frees the text from experience and opens it to a new synthesis, expressed by the final declaration on the last page:

"Toute Pensée émet un Coup de Dés." Hence, chance is the positive circumstance thought to discover integration, harmony, formation, and order: "L'art a lieu par chance" (578).[17]

As the final line of the text returns the reader to the title and the first page, the poem takes on the quality of all-inclusiveness of its last line. Place—the space of the page—is actualized and concretized, just as the first reading occurs always under the aegis of its constative title. How the reader reads may never be determined, but that he will respond to the conditional quality of the text is assured: "RIEN N'AURA EU LIEU QUE LE LIEU." Beginning and ending with aphorisms, *Un Coup de dés* neither denotes nor connotes a falsity; it only conjoins the reader's outer space (reading) with his inner space (setting relationships or rewriting). The "fil conducteur" is reader arbitration, as the absences—the non-verbalized of the non-printed—are transformed into presence. The moment of reading experience coincides with the moment of reader expression. The poet's objective and impersonal text of minimal structure becomes the reader's maximal discovery of Poetry. By space, *Un Coup de dés* reverses dispersion into fullness and the real into the ideal, word into Idea, poem into Poetry. The text is pure, beyond all attitudes, even beyond the confines of its own printed words and paginal placement. It is supreme in its unlimitedness, self-generative, and uniquely immune from external compulsion and dictation: "Virginité qui solitairement, devant une transparence du regard adéquat, elle-même s'est comme divisée en ses fragments de candeur, l'un et l'autre, preuves nuptiales de l'Idée" (387).

Chance is indeed conquered word by word (387), as the reader establishes points of agreement and contact—meaning—in that act. Exchanging his identity as reader for that of viewer, player, and thinker, he confers value upon poetic creation. His thoughts about the visual display before him send forth *a* poem, his throw of the dice, and its figure sets relations, forms a constellation: "rien de fortuit, là . . . par la lecture . . . la signification" (380). As the reader organizes the fragments before him and determines their relationships—a procedure possible only because of the structure of flexible paginal space in opposition with fixed printed words—he assigns to the text a character or quality which is exalted, sacred, and supreme. Life and Art conjoin in the reader's act upon the space of the page.

Chapter V

TEXT AS SPACE

Space is the only authoritative frame in *Un Coup de dés*. The amount and variety of white space in the text and on every page of the text (interval, pause, break, finality) control groupings and multiply combinations of those groupings. Space is the structural element of the poem and the primary field of reader encounter and activity. But, as space affirms the design, it denies reader expectations, destroys referents, distorts language, betrays relationships, and confirms loss of contact with the printed words, which space alone validates, makes legible, and organizes into disciplined patterns of meaning. On the one hand, space confers different values on the language and its arrangement. It fixes words in fragments and in clusters. On the other hand, it sets those same fragments and clusters in flux by eliminating all familiar principles of stratification. The use of space to replace punctuation not only frees the text from form and sound (intonation), but also imbues the work with an unfinished quality.[1]

As the word "**POÈME**" overpowers the other three lines of the title page, so the element of the unprinted overpowers the printed elements of the text. It is so overwhelming by amount and by variety that it alters the very groupings it establishes and sets them in opposition with each other. Meanings of words change by matter of their positioning in space on each page and within the text as a whole. The 12 repeated words, for example, are not reliable in connotation nor in denotation, for each repetition negates previous insights and offers different ones. In the last lexical analysis, every word in the text may be grouped into one of the 12 clusters based on repeated usage, yet these clusters themselves so interrelate that all distinctions between them are blurred. Word clusters based on association ("Abîme"-"*gouffre*"), capitalization ("RIEN N'AURA EU LIEU QUE LE LIEU EXCEPTÉ PEUT-ÊTRE UNE CONSTELLATON"), repetition ("l'unique Nombre"-"*LE NOMBRE*"), and juxtaposition ("DU FOND"-"au-delà") are not based on logic. Rather, they are carefully selected and placed on the page and in the text for their multiple meanings: "les mots ont plusieurs sens, sinon on s'entendrait toujours—nous en profitons—et pour leur sens principal nous cherchons quel effet ils nous produiraient" (852). The impersonal, dispassionate "instrumentation" of the various pieces and parts testifies only to an author who is aware that he is maneuvering and manipulating his reader, not to an author who has a definite message to impart. Mallarmé complicates the reader's access to his text in order not to be decoded and decomplicated; and his esthetic structure of complication is achieved in space, by space, and through space. Space is the place of encounter, the eternal circumstances of the reading.

"CIRCONSTANCES ÉTERNELLES" is the complication rendered by the layout. The reader is shipwrecked by the deliberately contrived arrangement before him. The print does not serve as a navigational guide; on the contrary, the waves and the foam are the white space which directs him and frees him to read. The double play in *Un Coup de dés* between "la vague" and "le vague" captures the deception of the construction before the reader and encapsulates the structure of approximation. The layout is so visibly and visually dramatic against a panoramic spectacle of space that it is unquestionably artificial, made up, and illogical. It is not a "mémorable crise" for the "Lecteur habile." The reader knows from the outset that the print is untrustworthy as the unit of value and significance.

The words are ambiguous in selection and in placement, which combine literal and figurative meanings without regard to context. Syntactical problems, homophones, and homographs disrupt and destroy lexical and semantic references; they dissolve reader reality. Mallarmé's word choice is studiously drawn from the realm of objective knowledge, which suggests the familiar

Text as Space 147

and therefore appeals to the reader's intellect and to his experiences. But, by drawing on the literal and figurative simultaneously in his word usage, Mallarmé creates new and previously unsuspected and undetected word associations in space with a vocabulary of space: *abîme, gouffre, infini, lieu, neutralité, simple, vierge, blanchi, vide, silence, rien*. Words of space are placed in space in order to negate the anecdotal lexicons of music, nautical world, printing industry, numerology, gaming, etc.: "un endroit fusionne avec au-delà." The Mallarmé variations on *langage-tantage-lançage* which characterize all of his poetry and written commentaries is transformed from theme to form in *Un Coup de dés*, as space becomes the text for reader confrontation. The reality of *Un Coup de dés* is spatial and not historical. The many adverbs of time and the use of all verbal tenses and moods contribute greatly to the eradication of chronology in the work. In addition, time is further effaced through the construct of a circle, which has no sequence of events, as well as through the internal ordering of the work in which the order of appearance is not related to the order of occurrence (the dispersed title, for example).

The destruction of time, which is, after all, a human invention for imposing order on man's situation and condition, does not, however, carry with it the destruction of the reader's sense of time. Rather, the reader discovers that the obliteration of chronology and sequence in the text—the shipwrecked disorder of temporality—provokes an aspiration to remember what has been seen and read, the complete form of the axiomatic title, for example. The appeal to reader desire for order, logical occurrence and appearance, and integration of the pieces—a reconstruction of the "bâtiment" and creation of a "nef"—is a creative act of encounter. While the space of the page does not preserve reader memory, it does condense it by permitting all fragments, the flotsam of the shipwrecked text, to come together regardless of textual occurrence. Memory persists; both psychological and sensorial memory as well as intellectual recall conjoin in the neutral whiteness of the text. Hence, the deliberate elimination of historical reality does not signify a loss of reality itself; on the contrary, it signals a sense of form below the disordered, chaotic appearance. The disquieting nature of the language, the lack of sustained metaphorical codes, and the dislocated syntactical groupings devalue normal codes of reading in order to establish different values by generating an artistic reality which gains its meaning from the reading process. As a result, the reader crosses and crisscrosses space (type face to type face, word cluster to word cluster), as the lexical, semantic, and syntactical signs trigger within a sense of form. In the space of the text, the reader's memory persists in making various associations among the printed elements and creating previously hidden relationships among those items. The very freeing of the form of the text—its dispersal in space—offers the possibilities of reader restructuration and the detection of form.

The form of *Un Coup de dés* could indeed be the hull of what has been torn apart—Mallarmé's "bande du vaisseau" reported by Gide. Certainly, every reader to date has detected a ship image in a text which clearly states that there is no ship. Reader response values to the "NAUFRAGE" limits the setting of the text although the subsequent conjunction of nautical and musical terms, for example, do not provide confident reader access to a consistent and authoritative meaning of the text. Instead, they offer too many reading codes by their virtual and historical interrelationships. Logic is tentative, reading the black type reinforces the separation of the parts and recovers only some of the pieces. The text is not governed by a system of rational order, for *"sa petite raison virile* [est]*en foudre,"* but it is lucid and readable because of the numerous signs which trigger reader memory and generate a sense of form in the spaces between and around the black print.

By esthetic exigency, the surface appearance of *Un Coup de dés* is not straight; it is "penché" and positioned in an antilinear, asymmetrical manner: "signalé en général selon telle obliquité par telle déclivité . . . vers." *Vers* is the primary direction in the text. Every printed unit and every blank or unprinted unit is a sign of incompletion, becomingness, emergence: "ce doit être" is, at best, evocative of the Little Dipper but by no means limited to the formation of that or any other constellation. *Vers* suggests that form follows the function of space, not that of language, for the function of language has been demonstrated in the layout to be non-rational, a-logical, and non-reliable. Only the space is coherent, line to line, page to page, and only the space is the plane or place for reader differentiation. The intertext of the printed is replaced by the extratext of the unprinted, as space emerges in the interreferential totalization of the reading activity. In the space, the reader performs his act of reading; the flexibility of the whiteness of each page enables him to make associations, not comparisons, to circulate without metaphorical interference and without a referential reading method. He does not observe the words or print; on the contrary, he acts out the space around each word and grouping, making lucid but not rational coherence arise from the chaos of the surface appearance of the layout. The mind, "Pensée," sends forth its own reality, "Un Coup de Dés."

Because *Un Coup de dés* is a text of expansion and incompletion, a tentative text ("vers ce doit être"), it is marked by an interplay between terms of non-fixity and those of conjunction (but not fusion). The ambiguous vocabulary and syntax, as well as the elimination of chronology and time, find expression in the dominance of the present (all time or a-temporality) and in the parenthetical reading clues: *"sauf," "COMME SI,"* "EXCEPTÉ," "PEUT-ÊTRE," *"quelque,"* "ombre," *"brumes," "délire," "mystère," "gouffre,"* "Abîme," "**HASARD**," "vers." The tentative nature of the lexicon and syntax shipwreck every piece recovered by the reader and suspend referential frames of logical procedure. In contrast, however, are those terms which propose conjunction of the fragments and the structuration of a new frame, form or hull: "Fiançailles," "hantise," *"insinuation," "ironie,"* "clos," "profusion," "mensonge," *"lucide,"* "illusion," "adapter," "inférant," "CONSTELLATION," "endroit," "Nombre," "compte total." Juxtaposing non-fixity, that which is "roulant," with the possibility of result through the contemplation of significance, that which is "brillant et méditant avant de s'arrêter," engenders an exchange of creative energy between the author and his reader, as the reader undertakes his act of textual reform. The author completely disappears: "L'œuvre pur implique par la disparition élocutoire du poète" (366). The reader ceases to be concerned with authorship, as he begins to produce his own *Coup de dés*.

And, indeed, *Un Coup de dés* takes on the structure of the self-generative text—it is on and about its own structure through its meta-linguistic discourse and absence of codes of communication; there is no address, no access, no internal intermediary of systemic metaphors and referentiality, no analogue, no philosophy, no described or prescribed communicated order. In fact, *Un Coup de dés* is immune from the limits of experience, the principles of logical and instrumental function, all external dictates and compulsions, even generic classification. Being its own structure and procedure, *Un Coup de dés* is about itself, a self-governing text which originates from within, determines its own restraints, and is ultimate within its own sphere. Basically abstract in that it evokes a situation and event which do not occur, the word dispenses with commentary, denies temporal progression and spatial direction, and stubbornly resists decoding into a system.

Patterned along the fundamentals of inversion, *Un Coup de dés* is to be seen before it is read, grasped in its fullness before its incompleteness is recognized, independent in its layout until its calibration is identified, stratified until its undeniable categorical perfection of harmony is sensed, and sensorially phenomenal until its projection of thought, emotion, and desire into the realm of objective mental processes is grasped. Elusive, yet substantial, the lexical, semantic, and syntactical components contradict each other in order to demonstrate their compatibility; hence, the vocabulary is multiplicitous and the syntax is duplicitous. The combination of letters and sounds does not limit each printed unit by its existence in identifiable words and groupings of words; on the contrary, the external characteristics of the words are expanded from recognition as conceptual modes into the actualized accord of expression; isolation is integration, absence is presence, silence is communication, the closed is open, the fixed is mobile, factuality suggests effectualness, and the subjective is objective, as the poem self-destructs into its own source, Poetry. The reader undertakes the layout not to reconstruct the poem but to experience poetry. The act of composition is an act of living which creates a work of art. Life and art conjoin, as the reader inquires into the nature of poetry through his rearrangement of the poem. Each reading is different because the text coheres fixed points within a circular procedure of becomingness. Reader response is a reaction of investigation. By adjusting the print into relationships of form and function, he discovers the substance of poetry, not the meaning of the poem. In point of fact, his reaction is necessarily one which unstructures the formal poem.[2] Only the space of the unprinted permits the reader to impose order on the objects before him, dissemble them and reassemble them in a cataphorical pursuit of meaning.

Unity is attained by the possibilities of reader points of agreement and disagreement. Hence, the text has an unfinished quality, a non-linear layout, and significantly more space than print. The exchange between the reader and author remains incomplete and the place of revelation is always on the page, not in the author and not in the reader. Only in the space of the text do art and life come together, overlap, and renew each other. Each act of reading demands another and accordingly generates another poem; all readings testify to poetry, which in the long run is Mallarmé's only subject and only object, for every page of his work, including his newspaper articles and correspondence, is a variation on the nature of poetry and everything for him is poetic: bottles of Calvados, the London expositions, English philology, clothing styles and fashion, graphology: "La Poésie résume tous les arts" (P144). For Mallarmé, Poetry is the coherent principle of the universe and the individual poem is its evidence: "une relique" ("Don du poëme"), Poetry is "de lis multiples la tige" ("Prose [pour des Esseintes]").[3]

Being a text which is on its own structure and procedure, *Un Coup de dés* must then be seen as a composition which expands experience through space as the element of design. Space is the undeniable constant in the text and the self-sufficient plane of organization for the reader's particular set of circumstances (his existence, his optic, his experience, and his investigative skill). Space makes his readings possible because it controls the possible combinations to be read by grouping elements, dispersing them, isolating them—multiplying them. Space determines the images seen and grasped. Space is place and it is chance—the act, or throw of the dice. The text depends on the reader's reading of space, where he determines that an image begins, stops, or reappears: "Le papier intervient chaque fois qu'une image, d'elle-même, cesse ou rentre, acceptant la succession d'autres et, comme il ne s'agit pas, ainsi que toujours, de traits sonores réguliers ou vers" ("Préface," 455).

Mallarmé's "Préface" to *Un Coup de dés* is primarily addressed to space and spatiality—expansion of the fixed words beyond the page—of Poetry. Second, the "Préface" is on the reading of the spaces and the space. He openly admits that the text gains meaning through the reader's ability to penetrate the white and the black elements at the same time. Although he did not wish his "Note" to *Un Coup de dés* read but preferred to have it forgotten, the commentary does serve the reader in alerting him to "le tout sans nouveauté qu'un espacement de la lecture." The "Préface" actually sets out the reading process required in the text—which Mallarmé's protest against its publication recognizes. It must be recalled that he wrote the "Préface" for the first printing in the magazine *Cosmopolis* and knew from the outset that its printed appearance in periodical form would not preserve the integrity of the amount of space; instead, it reduces it, compacts it, and accordingly decreases its importance in the composition. Hence, he carefully calls attention to the fact that the printed element "occupe, au milieu, le tiers environ du feuillet." He insists that the reader realize the role of "les 'blancs,'" that two thirds of the work consists of the unprinted, and that the text is to be seen mentally, not emotionally, read in its separation of the groupings: the "places variables" (the different type faces) depend on spatial intervals for their effects. Key terms in the "Préface" are clusters around reading as viewing and the substantive use of space in the layout: "regard," "disposés," "espacement," "'blancs,'" "disperse," "papier," "subdivisions prismatiques," "mise en scène spirituelle exacte," "sépare," "vision simultanée," "à nu," "l'état élémentaire," "pagination spéciale," "présentation," "ouvrir les yeux." The reading will be rapid ("vite") because of the "arrêts fragmentaires"; nothing will occur ("Tout se passe, par raccourci, en hypothèse") and the "fil conducteur" is that which is not obvious, but "latent."

At no point does Mallarmé suggest that the dispersed title is the organizing thread of his work; rather, this "phrase capitale" demonstrates the "mobilité de l'écrit," its multiplicity. The "Page" replaces "Vers" as the unit of unity, an arrangement which the dispersed title demonstrates, but, while the title is the "motif prépondérant" among the printed elements, the fact remains in the "Préface" that the "fil conducteur," that which organizes the text, is its space: "c'est à des places variables, près ou loin du fil conducteur latent, en raison de la vraisemblance, que s'impose le texte. L'avantage . . . littéraire, de cette distance copiée qui mentalement sépare des groupes de mots ou les mots entre eux . . . selon une vision simultanée de la Page: celle-ci prise pour unité comme l'est autre part le Vers. . . ." There is nothing "latent" about the title phrase, which is visually and technically printed in the most spectacularly displayed type face and placed in the most dramatic positions. In fact, the appearance (face and place) of the title page in the text calls attention to itself at every turn; moreover, because it is the title, already read and absorbed by the reader before he begins to read the text itself, the line is all the more seized upon as the unifying element of print and therefore of the fiction before the reader. However, the line ends well before the text itself reaches its final page. Moreover, the four segments of the title are not unexpected after the turning of the first page; on the contrary, the remaining two segments, after "**JAMAIS**" on 2r, are expected, even anticipated, by the reader. In addition, Mallarmé discusses the "fil conducteur latent" early in his "Préface," while his comment on "la phrase capitale," which he identifies as the title, appears only after he has stressed the importance of the space ("'blancs,'" "papier," etc.) in the text. There is no linking by Mallarmé of the titular phrase with the "fil conducteur," and the "fil conducteur" certainly cannot be one of anecdote or analogy since he carefully points out that "on évite le récit." It is in the print that he traces his "Poème" and in the space that he demonstrates "que ne reste aucune raison d'exclure de la Poésie—unique source." Writing in November 1896 about his *Divagations*, Mallarmé anticipates his *Coup de dés* in contemplating space as a signal factor in composition: ". . . malgré le désarroi, premier, causé par la disposition typographique. . . . Raison des intervalles, ou blancs. . . . Les cassures du texte, on se tranquillisera, observent de concorder, avec sens et n'inscrivent d'espace nu" (1576).

Describing his reaction to seeing *Un Coup de dés* for the first time, Valéry unerringly grasped the significance of the reader and space: "il me semble de voir la figure d'une pensée, pour la première fois placée dans *notre espace*" (1582, my emphasis); and, again, in recounting the last time he saw Mallarmé, which followed his seeing the "magnifiques feuilles d'épreuves de la grande édition," Valéry describes the poet as "pris dans le texte même de l'univers silencieux . . ." (1582). Gide later reported that Mallarmé had written to him that the layout of space constituted the primary effect of the text: "Le poème s'imprime, en ce moment, tel que je l'ai conçu quant à la pagination, où est tout l'effet. Tel mot en gros caractères a lui seul demandé toute une page de blanc, et je crois être sûr de l'effet" (1582). "Salut," the text which Mallarmé chose to place at the beginning of his *Poésies*, spells out his esthetic of space: "Rien, cette écume, vierge vers / . . . / Le blanc souci de notre toile" (27). Space is the "legs" of the text, the testament to future reading and readings which will take place; moreover, it is "legs en la disparition," vanishing as the poem receives form from its reader, becoming a subject-object—occupying space and filling in space. The poet's legacy is eternal, but it is also a gift which transcends time, as the future of its disposition emerges into the present and presence of poetry on every page of the reader's layout.

The reader cannot avoid reconstructing the text before him because the work is both self-generative and reader-conscious. The reader is free to pursue meaning and meanings, to make of the poetic testament whatever he chooses. The destruction of linearity and sequential order contribute to reader freedom to proceed in any reading direction whatsoever. Reminiscent of Mallarmé's fan poems and the Easter egg texts, the reader may approach *Un Coup de dés* in any order; after all, the text has no single system of procedure, being multiplicitous and duplicitous at the same time. It has certainly been well established that Mallarmé had considerable knowledge of and interest in the printing process and his esthetics are in great part based upon his mastery of the industry. Just as many readers attempt to recover the meaning of the work through grouping together the type faces, a reading which denies the arrangement of the double page layout and omits the space of each page, singlet or doublet, so may a reader read in other directions.

For example, it is possible to lay out the text page by page, in either a vertical position or horizontal one. Creating a single sweep vertically or horizontally emphasizes the Impressionist techniques at work in the visual appearance of the poem. In fact, such a layout recalls vividly Mallarmé's prose poem, "Le Nénuphar blanc," and his personal enjoyment of sailing in his "yole." The text resembles physically the problems of navigating a small boat down a stream in which water lilies grow in abundance, the print evoking the verdure of the plants and the white space taking the role of the water on which the skipper (or captain) must sail. The flowers then become interval spaces which attract by contrast with the deep green (nearly black) stretches of the vines and leaves. Water lilies grow both above and below the surface of water; encountering them in a small skiff such as a "yole" can pose unseen and unexpected obstacles, for the vines beneath the surface can indeed cause a small boat to capsize—shipwreck. In fact, Mallarmé never named his skiff: "Je laisse cette grande page blanche."[4] Such a strictly visual approach to *Un Coup de dés* recalls Monet's pond of water lilies at Giverny, a place visited and admired by Mallarmé. Just as Monet's man-made pond offered him endless possibilities of pictorial subjects to paint, so Mallarmé's pastime of sailing at Valvins and his friendships with many Impressionists may well have provided him with a respect for and admiration of the varying moods and textures within the world of nature, especially when nature is assisted by man.[5] Certainly, Mallarmé's text draws upon the world of nature (sea, storm, fog, reef, to name only a few). And the ever-changing quality of nature as glimpsed, for example, in the man-made garden was important to his inner circle of painter friends, who also frequently painted along the banks of the Seine and along the coasts of Normandy and Brittany.

In his "Préface" to *Un Coup de dés*, Mallarmé announces that he is offering the reader a "réunion" between "le vers libre et le poëme en prose" and that this poetic form combines a "chant personnel," while it keeps "intact l'antique vers." This is, of course, the very principle at work in the Impressionist canvas, which is carefully assembled and intellectually designed in order to free the subject from its defined substance. Describing Monet's lily pool, John Rewald writes that it offers

> an unending variety of compositional arrangements. . . . Indeed, the water-lily pond was built especially to provide Monet with an endless series of subjects . . . everything at first sight seems formless, for a shifting light plays over the scene, the eye no longer distinguishes between what is solid and what is reflection. Be it water, mirrored sky, or floating leaves, the subject appears unsubstantial. Not a single brushstroke stoops to the task of defining an object. . . . But as the viewer steps back, the process is reversed: what Monet knew was there but had chosen to reduce to flickering spots of pigments coagulates at a given distance into distinct features, into the subject that had been the artist's point of departure.[6]

Disorganized organization characterizes both Monet's manmade pond and Mallarmé's *Un Coup de dés*. The very first verb in Mallarmé's text is *abolir*, which means to make something non-existent in human terms, not in physical or natural terms. To abolish is to negate distinctive traits of identification in order to establish or send forth (*émettre*) the other possibilities of its passage. In both "Une dentelle s'abolit . . ." and "A la nue accablante tu," Mallarmé uses the verb *abolir* as one of creation, not as one of nullification. And, in both texts, the verb is used in a human context only. In "Une dentelle s'abolit . . . ," Mallarmé evokes a freeing of the piece of lace from the confines of precision in meaning, situation, and application (". . . vers quelque fenêtre / . . . / on aurait pu naître"), while in "A la nue accablante tu," the white foam testifies to the destruction of the ship's mast and its subsequent sinking or disappearance into the depths of the sea. Hence, for Mallarmé, *abolir* is a verb of presence; used in the future tense, "**ABOLIRA**," it points directly to the final verb, which appears in the present tense, "émet." The legacy of the captain is in the chance ("**LE HASARD**") of life ("**UN COUP DE DÉS**") which will never abolish the sending forth of human thought.

Like the verb *abolir*, "**UN COUP DE DÉS**," which is the initial and final phrase of the text, is a human term; certainly, "Pensée" indisputably refers to man. Indeed, the entire drama of the text—the captain, the shipwreck at sea, even the identification of number and constellation—refer strictly to the human world of existence. Even if the text is based on theater, music, graphomatics, numerology, etc., all are man-made categories and all receive meaning only within a human context. Moreover, all are interpretive manipulations of nature, just like Monet's lily pond and the Impressionist canvas. Because the human mind imposes coherence on the chaos of the external world, it develops explanations through a reading of the signs in nature: throwing dice makes risk and possible loss acceptable; stars, particularly the pole star of the Little Dipper, offer navigational aids, and numbers order variables into systems, and so on, but no system is definitive, for each has its own limits and particular set of circumstances. Yet, every system, including myth and legend, serves man to some degree historically and artistically. For Mallarmé, the supreme text—"**POÈME**"—must be one which abolishes the notion of system and replaces it by the presence of systems, what he calls Poetry. Hence, every reading of *Un Coup de dés* calls forth a rereading, which in turn demands further rereading and rereadings. But, the problem in any reading and rereading of *Un Coup de dés* is to read it in its unending variations, strata, and systems. Since the text has been shown to be one of disorganized organization, a text of space more so than of print, the challenge is then to read that space as text and the print as space.

In order to grasp the text as space, the reader's reconstructed layout must take into account not only the amount of space per page, but also the spatial esthetics at the basis of the text. When Valéry first saw *Un Coup de dés*, he noted with surprise that Mallarmé had set out his poem on graph paper ("feuilles quadrillées"). The use of graph paper is a specified way of writing to illustrate pictorial or symbolic representation, not verbal reproduction. Using a diagram to show coordinates among variables, Mallarmé approached the construct of *Un Coup de dés* as an intellectual exercise to demonstrate the one subject which obsessed him throughout his literary career: Poetry. Mallarmé does not write for personal satisfaction; rather, his work is aimed at the reader, who must organize the text before him, seize relationships, and confer meaning upon it (363, 380, 381, 870); reading is "salvatrice" (262). As early as 1864, in "Symphonie littéraire," he sets out the problem which he addresses several decades later in *Un Coup de dés*: how to write about "la fête du poëte" (265). In *Un Coup de dés*, the thematic problem of "L'Azur" is resolved in the form of space which testifies to the existence of Poetry. Hence, his "Préface" to the text emphasizes the role of the "blancs" and not that of the print, and his original pages, seen by Valéry, are carefully laid out on graph paper, a means of capturing not verbal units, but the poetic field of space.

Understanding the technical aspects of printing, Mallarmé calibrates the space of his text in graph form. The reader who undertakes a layout on graph paper is struck by the tediousness of counting not words but spaces; in fact, it is not overly difficult to write out or chart the 220 lines of the printed text, but the 570 lines of space and the many interval spaces are exceedingly complex. However, writing on graph paper shows just how space provides the continuum page to page. In addition, it must be noted that Mallarmé wanted *Un Coup de dés* published in folio form, that is not stitched along the seams—bound—but in six signatures of four pages each. The folio, reproduced only by the Ronat edition, is basically mobile. The text can, indeed, be read by signatures, and from signature to signature: six groups of four pages each. Such an organization would result in the following arrangement of the pages:

1. Title page, printer space page, 11r (the last page), printer space page (Pléiade 453, 454, 477, 478)
2. 1r, 2v, 10r, 11v (Pléiade 457, 458, 475, 476)
3. 2r, 3v, 9r, 10v (Pléiade 459, 460, 473, 474)
4. 3r, 4v, 8r, 9v (Pléiade 461, 462, 471, 472)

5. 4r, 5v, 7r, 8v (Pléiade 463, 464, 469, 470)
6. 5r, 6v, 6r, 7v (Pléiade 465, 466, 467, 468).

In such a layout, the title is only a "phrase capitale" and by no means a "fil conducteur"; the title page remains the initial reading frame, but it changes in the text from *"Un coup de Dés jamais n'abolira le Hasard"* to **"UN COUP DE DÉS JAMAIS LE HASARD N'ABOLIRA."** *"Hasard"* receives the greatest emphasis and moves from object of the verb to its subject; chance will never abolish a throw of the dice. The title page leads directly across space to the final page: "fusionne avec au-delà . . . signalé . . . de feux . . . vers . . . UNE CONSTELLATION . . . avant de s'arrêter . . . Toute Pensée émet un Coup de Dés." "Fusionne" is now an imperative verb form, as the title, *"Un coup de Dés jamais n'abolira le Hasard,"* is resumed ("à l'intérieur") into a consecrated value: "Toute Pensée émet un Coup de Dés." The circle is established from the outset in the circumstances of paginal space; the printed elements are neutralized (*"la neutralité identique du gouffre"*), the print is literally shipwrecked, as the dispersion of the groupings by and in space emerges as a more important element of structure than the groupings of the printed units. Space dictates and controls the reading, as *"le Hasard"* becomes the major subject and object of the poem.

Continuing to read by six signatures, the reader discovers that the throw of the dice has been "accompli" by dispersing "l'acte vide"; the act is empty because it has occurred, empty in that its potential (to act) has been exhausted (result of the activity): "toute réalité se dissout." Matter, the print, has indeed been absorbed by its surrounding space. A rapid glance at the remaining signatures reaffirms relationships by space. The construct of the printed double page is destroyed, as only "LE LIEU" of reader encounter in the space of each page remains as a coordinate among the printed variables. Type size and face no longer strike the reader, as he grapples with the artistic reality of spatial esthetics. The sixth or final signature sheet ends with the very simple page: *"plume solitaire éperdue . . . sauf."* The *"plume"* takes on the rather definite dimension of pen, not feather, and the text ends in suspension: *"sauf."* But, the first signature has already established the unending circularity of the text; the second signature has drawn attention to "EXCEPTÉ . . . PEUT-ÊTRE . . . un endroit," which directly refers to "LE LIEU." The solitary pen is bewildered, if not desperate or mad (mad as in a loss of sanity or mad as in wild with joy), but not because there is an exception to the situation, but because it is subject to the circumstances of Poem, the reader's text which springs from Poetry, the only source of coherence, meaning, and value: "à quelque point dernier qui le sacre."

Reading by signatures alters word connotations and their groupings because of the spatial graphics at work. New and previously undetected relationships are seen; even new crossover lines are discovered. In destroying one order—the paginal sequence of a bound edition—different doublets are created. But, what is singularly fascinating is how the doublets created by reading in signatures convey a sense of logical probability and artistic procedure. The new doublets are: 2v-10r, 3v-9r, 4v-8r, 5v-7r, 6v-6r, and each can be "read" as a single paginal unit.[7] For example, the "par" of 3v now leads to ***"LE NOMBRE"*** of 9r, while the juxtaposition of 4v and 8r reveals how the medium print of 4v ("LE MAÎTRE") refers to the external physical situation of the captain, while the italics of 8r (*"rire"*) describe his internal emotions and reactions. The curved position of *"rire /que/SI"* is pictorially more dramatic psychologically when it is read as part of the master's internal dilemma, just as the placement of 5v opposite 7r and the italics of *"soucieux/expiatoire et pubère/muet"* elucidate being "hors d'anciens calculs." In addition to the doublets established by the signatures, there are other doublets created in reading from signature to signature: 11v-2r, 10v-3r, 9v-4r, 8v-5r, and all may be read logically.[8] The reading approach by signatures even maintains the integrity of the page of printer space, for the title page is followed by such a page, and it safeguards the written page of space (2v); however, it creates an additional page of space by forming a doublet with 10r.[9]

Nevertheless, using an approach of reading by signatures gains validity through the appearance of the notes and fragments of

Text as Space   161

Le Livre, published in 1957 by Jacques Scherer.[10] Throughout his edition, Scherer studiously calls attention to the double structure proposed by Mallarmé. For Scherer, Mallarmé is interested in the investigation of words and the discovery of a hidden order of meaning. Reproducing the notes by an A and B system, Scherer accurately pinpoints the role of the reader and how each reading is different, indeed is supposed to be different. Scherer does not recognize, however, the topographic blockings and directions of the numbers, signs, and notations used by Mallarmé, and, in fact, these markings are standard signs in the printing world, just as the pattern of doubling is regular in the first set of signatures, which are flat, not folded. For example, when folded, Signature 2 consists of 1r, 2v, 10r, 11v and its only doublet is 2v-10r; when flat, Signature 2 consists of two doublets, A and B: A consists of 1r-11v, B of 2v-10r. The issue of juxtaposition is then one of technical layout, which increases reading possibilities, but it is not one of verbal representation; the space brings about verbal changes and alterations. The published fragments titled *Le Livre* are concerned with spatial arrangements, not lexical and semantic explorations, and they relate more to signature sheets than to verbal composition. Mallarmé's notes reveal that the interpretation of the text requires ten different reading approaches: "le même avec 10 Lect. —cela 10 fois = le même" (L111A). Certainly, reading by flat and by folded signatures, a predominant subject in *Le Livre*, is a viable approach.

Is, then, *Un Coup de dés* a mobile text? Most readers are convinced that it is not mobile, that it does not resemble the elasticity inherent in a Mallarmé fan poem, that the pages cannot be substituted one for the other. Certainly, every printed text is manufactured in signatures and so from that point of view is mobile, but very few writers are learned in the production process. Mallarmé is the first poet of stature to understand the process and draw upon it in his esthetics. Hence, it is reasonable to assert that the mobility of the signatures is a component of the structure of *Un Coup de dés* and, accordingly, plays a role in Mallarmé's construction and in the reader's reconstruction of the text. However, construction by signatures does not determine a text as having a fan structure; certainly, such does not come into play in Mallarmé's fan poems. On the other hand, reading by folded signatures does present a fan structure in reverse; rather than opening the fronds—the usual reading procedure in the fan poems—*Un Coup de dés* contracts: "RIEN / de la mémorable crise ou se fût l'évènement / très à l'intérieur résume." The text literally and figuratively closes upon itself within a circle of space, while the print units increase in their tentativeness. The only anchor or pivot is space, which contracts and expands at the same time. The printed units of instability gain in their impact, as reader memory blocks of "**COUP DE DÉS**," "**NAUFRAGE**," "**MAÎTRE**," "**CONSTELLATION**" are replaced by "*SOIT*," "*SI*," "*EXCEPTÉ*," "*PEUT-ÊTRE*," "*COMME SI*," and verbs in the imperfect subjunctive and conditional moods. The pen is indeed *"le vierge indice,"* subject only to "**POÈME**." The historical past, indicated by past participles and the passé simple tense, is absorbed into the present eternalness of the circumstances of space, as the "prince amer" is no more than one of the master's ancestors ("aïeul") and the future is evoked as a repetition of that past, absorbed by human thought and fused into the creativeness of textual space, the original Orphic explanation of the universe. Hence, *Un Coup de dés* is mobile in that it permits, in fact insists upon by its structured arrangement, differing and different readings, multiple approaches in its organization, and reader investigations into its unprinted, not just its printed, possibilities of meaning: "La lecture, enfin, a trait à un . . . Texte. Ouvrage" (L112A).

Reading by signature sheets sets space in even greater relief than the paginal layout of a bound sequential order indicates and also deemphasizes the function of varying type faces and sizes. The "busiest" page of the bound edition is 9r, on which five type faces are mixed. However, when 9r is read with 3v (Signature 3), it ceases to be typographically and topographically confusing and becomes instead a lucid demonstration of the "Abîme blanchi," and the "aile" of 3v is spatially rendered by the falling pen (*"Choit la plume"*), which leaves its trace through "**LE HASARD**." The text is created through chance, not inspired by a specific idea, just like the discovery of the "phrase absurde" of "Le Démon de l'analogie" as an "aile" which appears suddenly, detached and suspended in space:

> La Pénultième
> Est morte.

The source of these "paroles inconnues" cannot be identified; they are simply there, in their artistic reality and poetic magic. The actual moment of arrival cannot be established; only "son délire" is known, "vivant de sa personnalité" (273).

Similarly, arrangement in signatures offers a more vivid description of the impending disaster for "LE MAÎTRE" by juxtaposing 4v and 8r ("naufrage cela"/*"une borne à l'infini"*) while 5v and 7r together suggest that the "conjonction suprême avec la probabilité" is *"la rencontre,"* a merging of past and present ("l'aïeul contre la mer"/*"en opposition au ciel"*). Haunted by the mythic call of heroism, the gesture is logical only in terms of human memory, not in terms of the absurdity of the effort to impose logic upon such acts: "folie." Yet, the *"blancheur rigide"* of the page and the churning sea of endless white crests challenge both the Master and his spectator-viewer-witness. The struggle on 5v-7r and 4v-8r takes place in the interplay of space; the space of the page threatens to engulf the lines of print, just as the waves threaten to swallow the master. Because of an arrangement by signature sheets, space emerges as subject as well as object, structure and procedure at the same time.

Since it is possible to read *Un Coup de dés* coherently by signature sheets and accordingly discover how form follows function in the text, it is then equally possible to read it by versos and by rectos. After all, the signature sheets destroy the standard editorial theory that "il n'existe pas de page recto ou verso, mais que la lecture se fait sur les deux pages à la fois, en tenant compte simplement de la descente ordinaire des lignes" (456). The lines follow "ordinary" descending patterns only on versos and rectos, as the layout of each page demonstrates, and there are very few crossover lines verso to recto. Actually, more crossover lines are established in a signature sheet arrangement although the text remains structurally and artistically tentative.

Because the design of space prevents reader determination of all points of contact, the problem of reading cannot be based on logic, but rather on what Mallarmé terms in *Igitur* as "Folie utile . . . le hasard infini des conjonctions" (434-35).

Reading by rectos, and one begins by rectos because the first page of a text is always, in the printing world, a recto, the reader first discovers that the rectos are more heavily weighted in terms of the amount of information imparted. The dispersed title appears only on the rectos, and the final page ("le dernier point") is also a recto. The rectos are pages of formation, construction, description, and limits. Moreover, they are not affected by the versos; they can be read independently, for only on the rectos does the reader sense the preservation of form.

Beginning with the initial setting of the text, the throw of the dice and the shipwreck (1r and 2r), 3r describes the pitching ship ("la coque d'un bâtiment penché");[11] "vol" and "envergure" are linked with "voile" and seen as parts of the ship itself in a struggle to maintain balance, as space frames the substance of the structure, the "bâtiment." Page 3r is visually a material mass identified by its enclosure of space; the print is compacted, yet in a descending (sinking) display; the hull is visually and spatially breaking up. Interestingly, it is 3r which calls attention to 3v, especially the phrase "cette voile alternative," a phrase which also furnishes transition from 3r to 4r. On 4r, the space activates the irregularly placed lines; the page is active and indeed activity is the main subject of the print, grasped, first, by the use of space to expand the printed message and, second, by the central positions of "Esprit" and "la tempête." A decision needs to be made—both by the agent in the text, "il," and by the reader; the textual actor must set a course. Former approaches ("jadis") must be discarded for a different one ("un autre"); just as the actor or agent, "le chef," must confront his destiny, so must "l'homme sans nef," the reader. The imposing appearance of "**N'ABOLIRA**" on 5r affirms the will to respond and persist; it is a page of freedom to reform the emptiness (the "horizon unanime") and confer meaning. Page 5r breaks dramatically and drastically with the preceding pages, an attitudinal shift by space which is captured on 6r.

On 6r, space asserts control and effectively neutralizes the threat of destruction on 3r and the chaotic turbulence of 4r. Page 6r offers the hypothesis (*"COMME SI"*) of working with space, not against it: *"et en berce le vierge indice."* The pure sign of space is *"simple,"* in its stabilizing function. The vocabulary of the printed elements is one of intense activity: *"précipité," "hurlé," "tourbillon," "joncher," "fuir," "gouffre."* Yet, the space so controls the upheaval that the page appears to be one of calm and the tone one of confidence; one is merely *"autour du gouffre,"* and there is safety in having abolished former approaches and in adopting new techniques—attitudes— to the spectacle in view and at hand. Page 7r, also a visually stable page, demonstrates the theories posed by 6r. Space (*"cette blancheur rigide"*) permits the emergence of form (*"rencontre"*) and the identification of particularities among formations (*"prince amer de l'écueil"*). Space attracts the eye (*"effleure"*) and contracts the vastness of the spectacle (*"irrésistible mais contenu"*) so that relationships may be grasped (*"immobilise"*) in their similarities and differences (*"raison... en foudre"*). Space is limitlessness in the possibilities of creation, while at the same time it determines the recognition of patterns. Space confers value on form. Yet, the print fragments of 8r disrupt the serenity of 6r and 7r in an attempt to define more clearly space as the controlling agent. Where closure is posed as a possibility on 6r and 7r, it is dissolved on 8r; there is no termination to the drama of space, which quickly dissolves directions (*"de vertige," "évaporé en brumes... une borne"*). The rock is a *"faux manoir,"* not the end of the journey nor even the ultimate place of destruction. Page 8r is dizzying in its layout; the *"SI"* appears as a sign of hypothetical direction, but it is quickly dispersed as the page turns against the reader; the *"SI"* is an illusion of interruption, as the text is opened by space and aspires to disappear into space.

The function of space is undeniably one of formation, the *"écumes originelles"* of 9r. Page 9r reveals that space has the function of destroying print codes; the fixed *"**NOMBRE**"* is not real, even its very existence is suspect. The imperfect subjunctive verb forms are reinforced by their spatial suspension, literally set aside, having no analogue. "LE HASARD" looms out of the surrounding space, denying validity to deductive and inductive calculations. "LE HASARD" is where the pen then falls in order to receive at least equal weight with the dispersed printed fragments. Page 9r, the one page of *Un Coup de dés* which is the most striking by its typography and topography and the most occupied by print, is interestingly the "whitest" page, for the lexicon is one of non-coloration: "*NOMBRE*," "hallucination," "agonie," "profusion," "rareté," "HASARD," "*sinistre*," "*écumes*," "*délire*," "*cime*," "*neutralité*," "*gouffre*." Even the one object which should contain maximum material identity, "*plume*," is suspect; feather, pen, or trace. Indeed, material reality is visually dissolved in the space of the text; even five type sizes and the mixture of type weights and faces (bold, medium, italic) are impotent. It is not a product (*"NOMBRE,"* "CONSTELLATION") which draws attention, but the process.

Hence, 10r confirms the authority of space, "accompli en vue," and the actual subject moves from that of a storm-tossed ship at sea and the struggles of its Master in the throes of impending destruction to that of the reader. The key lies in the dissolution of the material message ("dans ces parages/du vague"). The presence of space ("verse l'absence") establishes the occurrence of authentic place: "N'AURA EU LIEU . . . QUE LE LIEU."

As the reader reaches the last recto, 11r, he discovers that he has not navigated through choppy, threatening seas, but "sur quelque surface vacante et supérieure." Every thought about the display before him triggers a response, a throw of the dice, the chance to diverge from established patterns ("selon telle obliquité par telle déclivité"). The text itself is an impersonal signal, a poet's constellation, but its meaning lies not in its materiality ("pas tant qu'elle n'énumère"), but in the reader's reality on the page. The text is a fiction; it cannot be experienced or enacted, only its reading is reality, which determines the points of the dice and confers upon them form, meaning, consecrated artistic value. The initiative passes to the reader to reread and undertake the poem: "compte total en formation."

Text as Space 167

The rectos are, then, about the role of the reader and the process of the poem; they are pages for reformation and reconstruction, as evidenced by the fact that the title is dispersed solely on these pages and the text reaches its final axiomatic sentence on a recto, which invites reader circulation in the space of his own thought-out throw of the dice, his own experience of life and art. By contrast, the versos, which contain a minimum of print and a maximum of space, relate to poetic deformation and deconstruction. The first verso is completely empty, a page of space,[12] establishing space as the primary field for poetic design and creation, reinforced by the "Abîme" (space) of 3v. Moving from left to right through space, 3v indicates that the space is to be read neither vertically nor horizontally, but "sous une inclinaison." Changing the angle of reading is indeed what 3r does to 3v:; the angle of the ship is "penché," as the outer frame of the shipwreck drama clarifies the inner frame of the artistic spectacle. Page 3v does not alter 3r, but 3r does affect the reader's reading of 3v; 3v is now seen at an angle and it is clearly "cette voile alternative," the other page. In fact, the versos do not generally affect the rectos, but the rectos consistently affect the versos, as this inner-outer structuring frame emerges as a constant in the art-life, poet-reader counterplay in the space of the text.

The appearance of "LE MAÎTRE" on 4v threatens the space established by the preceding versos ("surgi / inférant . . . menace naufrage"), as he considers the problem of filling space. He is hesitant in his approach—to work from an idea ("Nombre") or to let the words lead him of their own accord. The first course is one of traditional poetic creation, while the other is unorthodox ("en maniaque") and risky ("une chance oiseuse"). Page 5v is clearly a break with the past in the decision to write for an unknown reader ("legs . . . à quelqu'un"). Abandoning standard practice, especially analogy, the Master Poet is free ("ayant / de contrées nulles / induit / le vieillard"). Placing his faith in language and imbuing his act with the freshness of innocence ("son ombre puérile"), he establishes his own poetic maneuvers: a union ("Fiançailles") between the author and the reader in the suggestivity of space: "conjonction suprême avec la probabilité /

. . . le voile d'illusion rejailli leur hantise / . . . le fantôme d'un geste." Madness ("folie") is only in the hope of succeeding extratextually, as the hypothetical tone of 6v emphasizes in its juxtaposition of "*insinuation*" and "*silence*," which are united in the mobility ("*voltige*") of poetic gesture.

Hence, the "*plume*" of 7v is the tool for his act of lucid distortion; anticipatory yet somewhat youthful in the originality of his attitude, he works not in binaries but in antithetical alternatives: "*expiatoire et pubère*," "*lucide et seigneuriale*," "*scintille*"-"*ombrage*," "*stature*"-"*torsion*," "*muet*"-"*impatientes*," "*aigrette*"-"*squames*," "*lucide*"-"*ténébreuse*," "*pubère*"-"*seigneuriale*," "*invisible*"-"*scintille*"; illogical but lucid associations are wrought by two patterns of alliteration: "*s*oucieux-*s*eigneuriale-*s*cintille-*s*tature-*s*irène-*s*quames" and "expia*t*oire-aigre*tt*e-s*t*ature-*t*énébreuse-*t*orsion-impatien*t*es-ul*t*imes." Page 7v is a demonstration of the poet's method, his esthetics in practice. Even the form of the page mirrors the "réunion" of the free verse and prose poem genres announced in the "Préface," for the first three lines are laid out like a free verse text, while the remaining lines, although in free verse appearance, are more akin to the structuration by paragraph of the prose poem. Mallarmé, as a critical poet ("poète-critique") is perhaps the first to recognize that the free verse poem, inaugurated by Gustave Kahn in 1886, actually has its base in the prose poem developed throughout the nineteenth century; both poetic genres are characterized by a freedom of rhythm; the elimination of regular cadence and preestablished stanza organization is replaced by coherence through visual groupings; unity is created not by verse but by the whole page, as each unit has multiple effects and the unsaid is a unit of meaning.[13]

Structuration through space and antithetical alternatives is captured by the large amount of space on 9v. Setting the imperfect tense against the conditional mood, Mallarmé graphically demonstrates how the text emerges from the display of the words on the page; a traditional or "official" poem used to be an emanation from an idea ("*issu stellaire*"), and would continue to be so, but the actual creative process of the poem—the "crise . . . évènement" of 10v—is not the essence of Poetry.

Poetry is found on 11v above the line, "à l'altitude," in the space, which alone testifies to its existence as the coherent principle of the universe (328).

A reading by versos is, however, not as satisfactory as a reading strictly by rectos, for the eye is continually pulled to the right. And, indeed, each recto does offer insight into its verso. However, the rectos, which may be read as independent units, also express what the spatial areas of the versos suggest: the *"rythmique suspens du sinistre."* The initiative passes from the words displayed on the recto into the space of the verso, as the text emerges from the *"neutralité"* of the page. Hence, the rectos may be said to evoke the reader's activity, while the versos treat the poet's art—a poet who gradually disappears from his text, leaving only a visual display for the reader to undertake. Art (the poet in his versos) and Life (the reader in the rectos) overlap; the poet's dispersion and deformation of the page are countered by the reader's reformation.

Readings by paginal rearrangement (signatures, versos, rectos) are of value in that they demonstrate the integrity of each page of the text and reveal the demands placed upon the reader by the poet in the space of the text. Such exercises also show that there are certain constraints placed upon reading procedures; one can read by signatures and by rectos and versos, just as one can read by sequential doublets; however, the pages themselves are not interchangeable, a printing restraint which Mallarmé draws upon in constructing his text: "mobile, mais . . . stable" (1050). On the other hand, *Un Coup de dés* is irrefutably circular in its structure, regardless of the reading approach adopted and investigated.

Being circular in that the final line refers back to the title and the opening phrase and the final line is one of incompleteness, the text can then be read beginning at any point, beginning on any page. The text has no verbal center, only a spatial one, hence it has no pivotal axis for reader orientation. The text has no sustained narrative, being composed in a multiplicitous lexicon and duplicitous syntax; further, it is irregular in line length and semantic groupings, and it has no marks of punctuation to designate performative functions and inflexion. The vocabulary is rather ordinary, elevated only by its polyvalent character and its separation, word from word, grouping from grouping, by space. Reconstruction of the text as a prose poem, using each page as a paragraph and ignoring the artifice of capitalization,[14] offers a somewhat banal text, fascinating only in its destruction of chronological sequence and temporal logic. However, even such a layout is an interpretive undertaking by the reader, for he finds himself creating short, medium, and long units of meaning and of possible performance. Despite himself, he punctuates the text, imposing established conventions on the words before him. While certain rhythmic patterns may appear in some patterns (the 19 traditional metric patterns noted by Ronat, for example), the text still remains tentative as a piece of prose; it calls for space, and, accordingly, the reader of *Un Coup de dés* in prose format imposes space upon the lines. Hence, a layout which eliminates space as a component element of design testifies to the esthetic exigencies of space in any reading of the text.

Un Coup de dés is a text constructed in, by, and with space. No matter the reading approach, space is the only consistent element of the structure and procedure. The unconventional display of space makes the somewhat ordinary lexicon melodic and the internal irregularly grouped phrases rhythmic. Space turns the written text into Poem. The diaeresis on the word *poëme* is no longer necessary. Space draws attention to the importance of the composition and adds to the word a dimension previously achieved through orthography. *Poème* is sacralized by its spatial construct: a combination of words in a performative display which becomes its own sign: Poetry.

Being both the signifier and what is signified, *Un Coup de dés* is its own medium and message. Structured on itself, it invites reader inquiry into its self-generative source, Poetry; every human thought triggers a poem because Poetry exists; "L'art a lieu par hasard" (578) and "se limite à l'infini" (580).

Thought alone grasps the coherent principle of Poetry, which manifests itself in Poem: "ma Pensée s'est pensée et est arrivée à une Conception Pure" (P87). Thought, then, must be the reader's point of departure. While the word "Pensée" does not appear in the text until the last line, Mallarmé forewarns his reader that the dispersion of the first words of the Poem lead to the last ones because of the "espacement" of the text ("Préface," 455). Hence, the last line recalls the title and the opening words of the text; once the reader arrives on the last page, he is never again free from reading the text under the aegis of either the title or this last line. Thought, pure idea which is free from ideology and attitude, emerges as the cosmic sign of Poetry, captured by the calibrated layout of *Un Coup de dés*.

Beginning by the end—by the experience of the whole text— is in keeping with most readings of Mallarmé's poetry: "Commencer par fin."[15] One need only recall Jean-Pierre Richard's discussion of an early text, "Las de l'amer repos . . ."; [16] the last six lines of the text establish the material reference of the poet: a painted porcelain cup; once the reader grasps the object which intellectually triggers the sensation expressed, he reads back through the text and discovers reading clues which hint throughout the poem at the identity of the cup: "paysage," "tasses," "peindre," "Chinois," etc. Indeed, writing from the end enters Mallarmé's esthetics early, for in his 1864 correspondence, he takes up the notion of beginning by the general effect of the text, the primary idea which places the last word first. He candidly admits that this technique is in opposition to the approach to composition practiced by Emmanuel Des Essarts, who writes quickly; instead of following Des Essarts, Mallarmé turns to Edgar Allan Poe, who, in creating the American detective story, determined that it had to be begun from its ending. From "Las de l'amer repos . . ." on, Mallarmé's texts increasingly demand readings in reverse: the circularity of "L'Azur," the final question mark of "Don du poëme," the identification of Saint Cecilia in "Sainte," and the basic structures of "Quand l'ombre menaça de la fatale loi," "Ses purs ongles très haut dédiant leur onyx," "Une dentelle s'abolit," "Mes bouquins refermés sur le nom de Paphos," as well as the syntactic experiment of "A la nue accablante tu." Even internally, the Mallarmé text is read in reverse; for example, the sonnet "Ses purs ongles très haut dédiant leur onyx" not only evokes inversion thematically (the mirror which encloses the Big Dipper and then returns the image from the interior of the room to the sky), but also structurally, as the last line, "De scintillations sitôt le septuor," refers to the preceding one, "fermé par le cadre, se fixe," which recalls its preceding one, "le miroir," which then returns to the end term "septuor," by sonority and by thought. Each word emits a thought, and each thought a pattern of inverse association and meaning: "objet" recalls "nul ptyx," "le septuor" the "croisée au nord vacante," "cadre" the "décor," and "scintillations" the "or." Absence is not emptiness but presence, as the text has no real beginning or end and is composed "non de mots mais d'intentions" and depends on its layout or arrangement.[17]

In *Un Coup de dés*, Mallarmé brings together all of his investigations into Poetry. Even the vocabulary of the poem is one which permeates his critical commentaries. The text is on its own structure and every word testifies by its spatial positioning to the existence of Poetry in which art and life coincide and renew each other through the spectacle of the Poem. Hence, the Mallarmé text is one which poeticizes life ("poétiser par l'art plastique," 536). But, to read *Un Coup de dés* in reverse does not undermine the basic circular structure of the text; rather, it confirms its eternal circumstances because the reader has already "read" it in a manner of forward progression; hence, reversing the reading direction is not retrograded in a formal sense, but retroactive in response to the poet's invitation to share his inquiry into the text itself—its composition, not its words. The composition is, then, the procedure of the throw of the dice and its structure is thought. The last line initiates reader circulation into the space of the page and provides access into the poetic encounter. Reading becomes the creative act, as the reader dissembles the assembly of the first forward reading, then reassembles it in his response. The reader imposes order, adjusts the printed blocks, and discovers, in his translation, a unity of interaction among the possible agreements and disagreements. Even the relationships annulled by the space of each page multiply points of contact, for authority is found only in the freedom of space. The encounter affirms the all-inclusiveness of the design, the layout, as the reader pursues meaning in his rereading—the concurrence of analysis and synthesis is "l'idée mise en jeu" (400), a retroactive totalization of the creative process, which is "un compte . . . en formation."

Beginning with the last line, "un Coup de Dés," recalls both "UNE CONSTELLATION" and the process of reading beyond the fixity of the printed words. There is no product, only the page "vacante et supérieure" for a possible "compte total." The text is not a result of comparisons among the units, for a comparison depends on logical and/or familiar associations; hence, there is no intertext among the elements and no differentiation between the word groupings. On the contrary, there is only expansion of the words in the extratext of space.

The image of the dice is read first, regardless if the reader begins on the first or last page, and it visually dominates the text. However, the number of dice, much less the number of points on the dice when they cease to roll, is not identified; it is not the result (message) which is of interest, but their rolling and the roller's reflection on their possible outcome ("méditant") which occupies the reader. The reader's act is in the space of the page, "surface vacante," and it takes place in a multiple ("n'énumère") process of "le heurt" brought about by different reading signals ("feux" or type sizes, changes, and mixtures) used by the impersonal author whose text ("vers") "fusionne avec au-delà," in the area above the print.

The reading process in reverse also affirms how Mallarmé's construction by space provides points of intersection and how the rectos alter the versos. As a reading of the rectos by themselves demonstrates they may be read independently, offering insight into the versos, but the versos do not alter the rectos. The weight of the text in its occupation of space is predominantly on the rectos and the rectos invariably draw the attention of the reader's eye before the versos, regardless of the reading approach adopted. In order to grasp the "endroit" or "au-delà" in its unicity, the print must dissolve as the primary reading network and become complimentary to the space ("dans ces parages du vague"). Otherwise, there is only loss, error, and absence; print fills space but does not control it; the text is to be seen, "en vue," through the authority of the writing-reading process. The printed text is fiction; the place of that fiction,

"LE LIEU," is performative space. The author's impersonal style demands a personal response, as reader space and activity replace authorial assembly; "LIEU" effaces reader awareness of the author as creator ("RIEN").

And, indeed, all authorial codes are destroyed *"par la neutralité identique du gouffre."* Space has at the very least equal importance with the print, if not more impact, *"cime,"* and is to be "read" (*"délire"*) as the original source. The writing instrument captures these "écumes originelles" in the undetermined happenstance of space: **"LE HASARD"** gives birth to art, no more no less. Writing by inspiration and from a preestablished idea is attitudinal and sentimental, descriptive and derivative; it imposes meaning upon the reader and prevents him from being actively involved in the process of the text. Deciphering fixed themes, messages, and forms—what the traditional poem reflects (*"C'ÉTAIT / issu stellaire"*)—is "évidence de la somme pour peu," "nié et clos," "hallucination éparse d'agonie." Argumentative in its point of view, personal if not overtly didactic, conventional poetry is production, not process, dictation not invitation, separation not integration. In order to create meaning from the page before the reader, preconceived concepts of stratification, hierarchy, and a personal referential method—authorial creation—must be replaced by reader activity. The fixity of words and their groupings into lexical, semantic, and syntactical units must be distorted so that the richness of their differences, contradictions, and deviations provokes the reader to respond. The text must be its own subject and object, not the preservation of a given form, function, message.

Limits, mainly those of prescribed definition and usage, are dissolved; the closed quality of the intertext of established referentials is opened by a paginal design of creative enthusiasm (*"vertige . . . rire"*), as the non-conceptual quality of space generates an anxiety of form for the reader. Separation from fixity creates a desire for unity and signification, an inquiry into the nature of form itself, and deliberate provocation of the reader to react to the text in order to discover its meaningfulness. Dispersal of the printed elements (*"en foudre . . . raison . . . héroïque"*) is the author's technique, *"pour ne pas mar-*

quer," in order to elicit reader response, not in the stars, *"en opposition au ciel,"* but on the page before him: *"cette blancheur rigide"* in which the black type sinks (*"sombre"*). No longer immobile and static, the page is vibrant, as the print suggests encounter (*"la toque de minuit effleure la rencontre"*) in space, interrupted only by the quill. The pen is free, just as if there are no traces at all for the reader to glimpse and follow; *"le vierge indice"* controls and harmonizes the summons to the reader.

As the writing separates the units, the reading unites them (**"N'ABOLIRA"**); "folie"—creative enthusiasm generated by the unconventinonal layout—remains, as the reader forges links by reading memory blocks in a conjunction ("Fiançailles") with the poet. The reader does not replace the author, but he does share the challenge of the communication in his quest for contact and in his perception of the poetic experience. Free from debate on lexical and logical grounds, the text annuls relationships between verbal qualities and in their place invites active participation by the reader. "Sans nef . . . direct de l'homme," he pits his own creative faculty onto "l'horizon unanime" of the page, confronts the Master Poet's destruction of codes ("naufrage") and from the debris reads his own "**COUP DE DÉS.**"

Deformation triggers an intimate sharing of the poetic adventure, as the response by the reader asserts the value of the poet's composition. The calibrated, highly disciplined layout of the text calls into being creation itself. Reader encounter with the poet in the space of the page affirms contact between art and life, and each in turn renews the other. In the spatial configuration of *Un Coup de dés*, Mallarmé bestows upon his reader the experience of poetic creation and offers visual, concrete, material evidence of the presence of Poetry as the ultimate sign of human value, dignity, and salvation. In the dynamics of space, in the "Salut" to "Rien . . . vierge vers . . . qui valut / Le blanc souci de notre toile," Mallarmé authenticates the text: "Toute Pensée émet un Coup de Dés," Poem.

NOTES

Introduction

1. Stéphane Mallarmé, "Préface," *Un Coup de dés*, in *Oeuvres complètes* (Paris: Gallimard, 1945). References to this edition appear in the text.
2. Yves Bonnefoy, "L'Acte et le lieu de la poésie," *Du mouvement et de l'immobilité de Douve* (Paris: Gallimard, 1970), 191-202.

Chapter I

1. For further discussion on the elastic intertextuality of the fan structure, see my "Mallarmé and the Elasticity of the Text," *Sou'wester* 6 (1978), 1-12; also see Jean-Pierre Richard, *L'Univers imaginaire de Mallarmé* (Paris: Seuil, 1961) 19, 28, 79, 122, 177-79, 285, and Robert Greer Cohn, *Toward the Poems of Mallarmé* (Berkeley: U of California P, 1965 and 1980).
2. In *Mallarmé vivant* (Paris: Nizet, 1956) 8, Robert Goffin is one of the first critics to describe "A la nue accablante tu" as an elastic text.
3. Ibid. 278. The bath was a popular subject for Impressionist painters, especially for Edgar Degas ("Le Tub") and Edouard Manet, whose "Le Déjeuner sur l'herbe" was originally entitled "Le Bain." Robert Goffin even raises the possibility that Mallarmé's "M'introduire dans ton histoire" is based on a bidet (253-57) and points out that "Petit Air" was first entitled "Bain" (151).
4. For a more detailed study of how Mallarmé's poetic practice is anchored in word games (plastic circumstances and verbal challenges), see my "Mallarmé and the Plastic Circumstances of the Text," in *Pre-Text/Text/Context. Essays on Nineteenth-Century French Literature*, ed. Robert L. Mitchell (Columbus: Ohio State UP, 1978), 173-83.
5. In *Toward the Poems of Mallarmé*, Cohn shows how Mallarmé's "Hommage" (72) to Puvis de Chavannes is faithfully constructed along the lines of a Chavannes painting (186-88).
6. The quatrains of the "Oeufs de Pâques" (139-41) are so structured that the lines of verse may be rearranged and exchanged at will. According to Mallarmé, "chaque vers était écrit à l'encre d'or sur un œuf rouge et précédé d'un numéro de manière à reconstituer le quatrain. —Une seule fois, le numérotage put être omis, et, en invertissant les œufs, l'ensemble lu ainsi plusieurs fois de façon différente" (139). It is interesting to note that Manet exhibited painted Easter eggs in 1880 and one of them was decorated with Polichinelle.
7. J.-K. Huysmans, *A rebours* (Paris: Fasquelle, 1955), 240-46. In turn, Malmé acknowledged "le livre exceptionnel d'Huÿsmans" (392).

8. Art historians have debated the label "Impressionist" for well over a century. However, it is generally accepted as a term to describe a generation of artists born between 1830 and 1840-41 who exposed their work as "Indépendants" in 1874. The term is based on an 1874 painting by Claude Monet, "Impression, Soleil levant." The Impressionist movement is usually dated from 1865 to 1906, Paul Cézanne's death. While perhaps not a member of the Impressionist movement, Manet was nonetheless part of the group and participated in their exhibitions and is therefore listed as an Impressionist more often than not. "Post- or neo-Impressionism" is the effort to rationalize or "geometricize" Impressionism around 1885 by such artists as Geroges-Pierre Seurat and Paul Signac. Jean-Pierre Richard attributes the mobility of the Mallarmé poem to his association with the Impressionists: "c'est l'*intervalle* qui, dans les toiles impressionistes, devient l'agent essentiel de motricité" (*L'Univers imaginaire de Mallarmé* 472).

9. Mallarmé's attitude toward Hugo is ambivalent; at times, he praises Hugo (259-60), while at other times he tends to ridicule him (360-61, 866). For Cohn (*Poems of Mallarmé*), Mallarmé was always a great admirer of Hugo. On the other hand, Jacques Roubaud equates Igitur with Hugo and interprets *Un Coup de dés* as the death of Hugolian verse ("official" poetry, formalism) and the birth of the modern poem; see his "n'abolira Lazare," in Stéphane Mallarmé, *Un coup de Dés jamais n'abolira le Hasard*, ed. Mitsou Ronat (Paris: Change/Errant/d'Atelier, 1980), 10-11, and his *La Vieillesse d'Alexandre* (Paris: Maspéro, 1978).

10. Roland Barthes, *Mythologies* (Paris: Seuil, 1957) 251.

11. Carol Clark in *Colloque Mallarmé en l'honneur d'Austin Gill* (Paris: Nizet, 1975), 86-87.

12. Michael Riffaterre, "On Deciphering Mallarmé," *Georgia Review* 29 (1975), 75-91.

13. For an analysis of Mallarmé's use of a standard and limited vocabulary, see Robert Greer Cohn, *L'Oeuvre de Mallarmé: Un Coup de dés* (Paris: Librairie des Lettres, 1951).

14. Stéphane Mallarmé in Jacques Scherer, *"Le Livre" de Mallarmé* (Paris: Gallimard, 1957). References to this edition appear in the text and are prefaced by the letter L.

15. For a study of Mallarmé's poetics as a dialogue between the poet and his reader, see my "Mallarmé: 'Je dis: une fleur!'" *Nineteenth-Century French Studies* 10 (1981), 96-106.

16. Just as Mallarmé plasticizes written expression, his friends among the Impressionist painters poeticize the plastic; even Claude Monet changed the title of his "Nénuphars" to "Les Nymphéas." In *Manet and the Modern Tradition* (New Haven: Yale UP, 1979) 42, Anne Coffin Hanson credits Mallarmé with the "new view of the role of painting as a kind of visual poetry."

17. For an informative description of the role of space in the reading of literature (how the eye and the mind move), see W.J.T. Mitchell, "Spatial Form in Literature," in his *The Language of Images* (Chicago: U of Chicago P, 1980), 271-99.

18. For a discussion of language as maximum sign, see my "Mallarmé's *Livre*: The Graphomatics of the Text," *Symposium* 34 (1980), 249-59.

19. Jacques Damase, *Révolution typographique* (Geneva: Galerie Motte, 1966), ix-xii.

20. Claude Minère, "Le Risque picaresque," in Ronat ed. 17.

21. In his "Crise de vers," Mallarmé observes that the "exquise crise, fondamentale" in literature is also a preoccupation of the printing industry (360). "Quant au Livre" (369-87) centers on a one-word paragraph, "Publie" (372), and treats together the problems of the press, bookstores and book sales, the writer, and the formal appearance of the writer's work: "Ton acte toujours s'applique à du papier" (369). At one point, Mallarmé observes that the publication process is approaching "d'un rite la composition typographique" (380). According to Littré and other dictionaries, the primary meaning of "Livre" is "l'imprimé," "le papier imprimé," "ce qui est imprimé."

22. Throughout *Mallarmé lycéen* (Paris: Gallimard, 1954), Henri Mondor uneasily attempts to excuse the biting satire in so many of Mallarmé's youthful texts in *Entre quatre murs* as a form adopted to exorcize the past. With regard to the three notebooks, *Glanes*, Mondor notes that Mallarmé's taste in the 8,000 lines of poems by others which he faithfully copied in 1858 as a means to learn and master poetic methodology is rather unorthodox. In *Les Clés de Mallarmé* (Aubier: Montaigne, 1954) 57, Charles Chassé dismisses these early poems as Parnassian calembours. The texts of *Entre quatre murs* have been republished and thoroughly documented by Carl Paul Barbier and Charles Gordon Millan in vol. 1 of Stéphane Mallarmé, *Oeuvres complètes* (Paris: Flammarion, 1983). The Barbier-Millan notes include a complete description of Mallarmé's attention to paginal arrangement; as early as 1858, he uses a cross to indicate the space between the stanzas (9, 14, 35, 49, 56, 69, 75, 87, etc.). Every topographic and typographic detail preoccupies him in the publication of *Poésies* and *Vers de circonstance* (734-59).

23. Ursula Franklin, *An Anatomy of Poésis . . . The Prose Poems of Stéphane Mallarmé* (Chapel Hill: U of North Carolina P, 1976).

24. Mallarmé's poems frequently rely on the use of parentheses to indicate a plastic sign of form and identity. Parentheses appear in the title of "Prose (pour des Esseintes)," several times in the text of "Hérodiade," and throughout his prose poems and written commentaries. One section of *Crayonné au théâtre* even bears the title, "Parenthèse" (322-24), while the only marks of punctuation in "A la nue accablante tu" appear in the second stanza between parentheses. In the "Scolies" to *Les Poëmes d'Edgar Poe*, Mallarmé notes that parentheses avoid repetition and increase visual demands on the reader: "Force m'a été de transcrire ces séries de répétitions seulement parmi des parenthèses; et comme des indications que le lecteur ne lira que des yeux, plutôt que des mots réels ajoutant leur vertu au texte français" (240). For Jean-Paul Sartre in his "Préface," *Mallarmé*, Coll. Poésie (Paris: Gallimard, 1967) 5, Mallarmé's refusal to dirty his hands in a protest against the world leads him to put the world between parentheses, while in the introduction to Ernest Fraenkel's *Les Dessins trans-conscients de Stéphane Mallarmé* (Paris: Nizet, 1960) 8, Etienne Souriau finds that Mallarmé places meaning between parentheses. Certainly, a fan is a concrete parenthetical structure.

25. Roland Barthes, *Roland Barthes* (Paris: Seuil, 1975) 145. In *The Aesthetics of Stéphane Mallarmé in Relation to His Public* (Cranbury, NJ: Fairleigh Dickinson P, 1976), 201-18, Paula Gilbert Lewis finds that Mallarmé evolves from a "snobbish" writer to a poet who has "faith in . . . the instinctive intelligence of the people," as he discovers that all aspects of reality are valid objects of poetry and their transformation on paper is a form of thought transference. For Charles Chassé, it is Mallarmé's sense of humor (laughter and gamesmanship) which creates complicity between the poet and his reader (*Les Clés de Mallarmé* 201-18).

26. Mallarmé's lexical, semantic, and syntactical gamesmanship, his love of words, and his use of structures which replace rhetorical devices by visual effects and reader reaction led André Breton to list him in the 1924 Surrealist pantheon of ancestors: "Mallarmé est surréaliste dans la confidence." "Premier Manifeste du Surréalisme," *Manifestes du Surréalisme* (Paris: Pauvert, 1962) 39. For Breton and the Surrealists, Mallarmé is confident of his reader's untapped ability to play the artistic game and experience the absolute through the creative process. Ironically, it is this very point that leads Sartre to argue that Mallarmé lacks confidence, demonstrated by his parenthetical approach to poetry, for "il sait bien que son art est une imposture. Mais il a aussi l'air de dire: *C'eût été la vérité*" ("Préface," 15). In his *Mallarmé: La Lucidité et sa face d'ombre* (Paris: Gallimard, 1986) 159, Sartre finds an existentialist Mallarmé whose work is marked at every turn by "lucide désespoir" and a form of "suicide poétique [qui] entraîne la destruction du langage." Yves Bonnefoy, who edited *Un Coup de dés*, Coll. Poésie (Paris: Gallimard, 1976) and consistently defends Mallarmé against a materialistic and nihilistic view, is, nonetheless, convinced that modern poetry should return to the optimism of Baudelaire and not continue to follow the pessimism of Mallarmé ("L'Acte et le lieu de la poésie," 191-202).

27. Jean-Paul Sartre, "Qu'est-ce que la littérature?" in *Situations* (Paris: Gallimard, 1948) 2: 109.

Chapter II

1. A type style refers to the design or characteristic mode of typographic display, such as Didot, Elzevir, Garamond. Hence, a type style is consistent in a printed work; in the nineteenth century, the selection of the type style often determined the choice of the printing firm. Mallarmé's correspondence with printing firms and publishers and his frequent changing of firms are due to his quest for a type style which would capture in print his esthetic sense of the typographic art. On the other hand, once he settles on a particular printing firm, his notations on proofs and correspondence about proofs concern only type sizes, weights, and faces.

2. Robert Greer Cohn, *Mallarmé's Masterwork: New Findings* (The Hague: Mouton, 1966), 89-111.

3. The planned Flammarion edition will not be able to reproduce the size and folio form that Mallarmé desired.

4. Danielle Mihram, "The Abortive Didot-Vollard Edition of 'Un coup de Dés,'" *French Studies* 33 (1979) 47-48.

5. Other editions, such as the 1976 Gallimard Coll. Poésie volume by Yves Bonnefoy and the one reproduced by Julia Kristeva in her *La Révolution du langage poétique* (Paris: Seuil, 1974), also greatly reduce the amount of space and do not provide adequate, much less accurate presentations of the text for critical study.

6. Mitsou Ronat, "Cette Architecture spontanée et magique," in her ed. 1.

7. Because the Pléiade edition is the most accessible one to readers, the following table of equivalents may be useful:

folio page		Pléiade page
title page	=	453
1r = recto 1	=	457

2v =	verso 2	=	458
2r =	recto 2	=	459
3v =	verso 3	=	460
3r =	recto 3	=	461
4v =	verso 4	=	462
4r =	recto 4	=	463
5v =	verso 5	=	464
5r =	recto 5	=	465
6v =	verso 6	=	466
6r =	recto 6	=	467
7v =	verso 7	=	468
7r =	recto 7	=	469
8v =	verso 8	=	470
8r =	recto 8	=	471
9v =	verso 9	=	472
9r =	recto 9	=	473
10v =	verso 10	=	474
10r =	recto 10	=	475
11v =	verso 11	=	476
11r =	recto 11	=	477

doublets via folio		Pléiade pages
two	=	458-459
three	=	460-461
four	=	462-463
five	=	464-465
six	=	466-467
seven	=	468-469
eight	=	470-471
nine	=	472-473
ten	=	474-475
eleven	=	476-477

The numbering of the doublet pages (there is no doublet number one) is consistent with and corresponds to the numbering of the individual versos and rectos.

8. Mitsou Ronat bases her edition and commentary on the number 24, which she then divides for the double pages of the text and comes up with the "architectural" number 12. While ingenious, Ronat misunderstands that a signature always consists of an even number of pages, usually four, and therefore that the printer had to use 24 pages or six signatures in order to accommodate a 21-page text. As a result, Ronat misreads the text through her intellectual play with the number 12. Hence, the importance of understanding certain technical details of the printing process is fundamental to a reading of *Un Coup de dés*. Most of Ronat's descriptions of the text are subsequently erroneous because she insists on basing her argument on 24 pages and the number 12. However, she does accurately reproduce the page size and in general her placement of the words on each page is correct, as well as her reproduction of the Didot type style.

9. The figure, 224 lines of print, includes the four lines of the title page.

10. Throughout this study, I have used the standard abbreviations: v=verso,

r=recto. Mallarmé used these same abbreviations in his proofreading and in his instructions to printers. There is no doubt that Mallarmé thoroughly investigated the exigencies of typographic and topographic composition. His instructions concern interval spacing, margins, blank pages, what is to be on a verso and what is to be on a recto; for an excellent example, see the notes on Mallarmé's instructions to Edmond Deman in 1894, in the Barbier-Millan edition of the *Oeuvres complètes* 1: 749.

11. Malcolm Bowie, *Mallarmé and the Art of Being Difficult* (Cambridge: Cambridge UP, 1979) 177n8: central margins are "properly 'semantic' spaces."

12. In order to discuss the distribution and relationship of typography and space, one must first establish the physical dimensions of the text. In *Un Coup de dés*, the amount of space required to encompass the greatest spread and placement of characters from left to right and top to bottom coincides with dimensional specifications adopted by the printer, that is, printer margins. Typography may be distributed within these margins so as to suit the poet, but it may not exceed them. In order to measure the line-length available within the allotted space of *Un Coup de dés* I have adopted 8-point type as my unit of measurement. As a result, the maximum measurement of any one line in this size may not exceed 72.6 characters and the total number of lines available is 38 (8-point type on 10 leading), hence a page size of 22 x 31 picas. No matter the number and kinds of variations in type size within the page, the proportional increase (a line set in 3-point, for example, will accommodate more characters) or decrease in the number of characters and lines throughout the allotted space are measured as a function of the agreed upon format. My text, for instance, set in 11-point type (in Theme style) with a line-length of 25 picas, can print a maximum of 62.5 characters per line, while the maximum number of characters per line for this footnote, set in 8-point, is 82.5 characters. Throughout this study, due to technological considerations, all quotations from the poem are uniformly presented in 11-point, the size elected for the composition of my text. Only variations in type face and weight are indicated in the quotations. In establishing the space of *Un Coup de dés*, a reader may adopt any point size as his base for analysis and measurement, as long as he takes into account the spatial dimensions and variations required by Mallarmé in the construct of his poem.

13. On this point, it is of interest to note that only Ronat's edition places the *Cosmopolis* "Préface" at the end of the various commentaries on the text; she thus interprets it correctly as a postscript text and not as an introduction to the text.

14. Mitsou Ronat, "Cette Architecture spontanée et magique," 3.

15. Gardner Davies, *Vers une explication rationnelle du 'Coup de Dés'* (Paris: Corti, 1953) 204.

16. In the Didot type style selected by Mallarmé, the letter f has only one kern, an ascending one. In the Firmin-Didot style, f has a descending kern; see, for example, the 1976 Gallimard Coll. Poésie edition.

17. Davies views the last line as "une proposition indépendante," 206.

18. Jean-Paul Sartre, "Préface," *Mallarmé* 10.

Chapter III

1. Many Dada experiments are aimed at denying the communication of meaning by an illogical arrangement of the print; computer and word processor products also negate traditional printing codes, as well as the art of typography.

2. Marshall McLuhan, "Joyce, Mallarmé, and the Press," in *The Interior Landscape: The Literary Criticism of Marshall McLuhan 1943-62*, ed. Eugene McNamara (New York: McGraw-Hill, 1969), 5-21.

3. Robert Greer Cohn, *Mallarmé's Masterwork* 51; *Towards the Poems of Mallarmé* 4; and *L'Oeuvre de Mallarmé: Un Coup de Dés* 80n15.

4. In *La Dissémination* (Paris: Seuil, 1972) 283, Jacques Derrida states that Mallarmé structures the empirical object on empty space, what Jean-Pierre Richard terms "l'agent essentiel de motricité" (472) and Sartre describes as "une logique négative" ("Préface," 11). For Maurice Blanchot, *Le Livre à venir* (Paris: Gallimard, 1959) 287, space gives depth to the Mallarmé text, while Malcolm Bowie views it as the basis for Mallarmé's "world of alternative logics" (128). Julia Kristeva also finds that space for Mallarmé has constructive properties: "La vérité que le texte signifie [est] plurielle" (289).

5. Paul Valéry, *Ecrits divers sur Stéphane Mallarmé* (Paris: NRF, 1950) 17 and 18.

6. Teodor de Wyzewa, *Mallarmé* (Paris: La Vogue, 1886) 28. It is especially interesting to note that one of Mallarmé's close friends was aware of the poet's deep interest in the visual aspects of a verbal communication a full decade before the writing of *Un Coup de dés*; for Wyzewa, Mallarmé is both a logician and an artist, for whom "l'art est un travail" (10-11).

7. Tibor Papp, "'qui mentalement sépare,'" in Ronat ed. 24.

8. Rodolfo Hinostroza, "Le Dieu de la page blanche," in Ronat ed. 18-19.

9. Stéphane Mallarmé, *Propos sur la poésie* (Monaco: Rocher, 1953). References to this work appear in the text, preceded by the letter P.

10. Mallarmé's letter to Edmund Gosse in 1893, quoted in Henri Mondor, *Autres Précisions sur Mallarmé et inédits* (Paris: Gallimard, 1961) 115.

11. On this point, it is interesting to note that Auguste Rodin's "Le Penseur" was unveiled in 1880 and that his original name for the sculpture was "Le Poète," presumably Dante. Rodin and Mallarmé knew each other; in fact, Rodin was asked to contribute a sketch to a planned edition of Mallarmé's *Poésies*.

12. For a discussion of Poe's use of space as a "philosophy of composition," see Joshua C. Taylor, "Two Visual Excursions," in *The Language of Images*, 25-36.

13. Claude Roulet, *Elucidation du poème de Stéphane Mallarmé* (Neuchâtel: Ides et Calendes, 1943).

14. Other changes in the extant proofs have been well documented and described by Danielle Mihram.

15. According to various "Mardistes," Wagner was a popular subject of discussion for Mallarmé, whose interest was in Wagnerian composition (structure), not in his music in a formal sense or even in a performative sense. In fact, Mallarmé repeatedly told the "Mardistes" that he did not understand music well enough to appreciate it during a performance. For Mallarmé on Wagner, see his "Richard Wagner: Rêverie d'un poëte français" (541-46). In addition, Mallarmé fully understood the printing industry's use of signatures, and the notations compiled by Jacques Scherer in *Le "Livre" de Mallarmé* are mainly those which concern layout and proofreading. For a discussion of Mallarmé's equation of "Le Livre" with "La Presse," see Marshall McLuhan's "Joyce, Mallarmé, and the Press," Mitsou Ronat's introduction to her edition, "Cette Architecture spontanée et magique," 1-7, and my "Mallarmé's *Livre*: The Graphomatics of the Text."

16. The saga behind the publication of *Poésies*, for example, is one of visual presentation (topographic and typographic); for a succinct summary, see the Pléiade *Oeuvres complètes de Stéphane Mallarmé*, 1394-1406, and the Barbier-Millan edition.

17. *Jeu* is also a musical term for style or technique.

18. For more detailed discussion, see my "Mallarmé and the Plastic Circumstances of the Text."

19. Mallarmé greatly admired Poe's "pur jeu intellectuel" (229).

20. Mitsou Ronat 4-5. For a highly creative reading of *Un Coup de dés* as the announcement of the death of the alexandrine verse and advent of free verse, see Jacques Roubaud's "n'abolira Lazare"; the shipwreck is that of classical verse and "Le Maître" going down with his ship is Hugo; also see Ronat's elaboration of this theory in which tradition is the print (the visible constraints of classical versification) and innovation is the space of the page (the invisible) (2).

21. "Toast à Emile Verhaeren," found after Mallarmé's death, is the only extant Mallarmé text which could possibly be described as a free verse poem. Mallarmé was always ambivalent on the subject of the free verse poem, which his followers, especially Laforgue, Kahn, and Vielé-Griffin embraced so enthusiastically.

22. Rimbaud's "Marine" and "Mouvement" were not published until 1895 and so were unknown to Mallarmé's followers who thought they were "inventing" free verse.

23. While some critics maintain that "Hérodiade" is Mallarmé's last work, it remained an on-going, unfinished project, begun in 1864. *Un Coup de dés* is his last "completed" text.

24. For a complete presentation of Valéry's views on and reminiscences of Mallarmé, see his *Variété* (Paris: Gallimard, 1929) 2: 161-202.

25. Malcolm Bowie states that "no subsequent work provides even a remotely useful explanatory model for this one" (118), and he includes Apollinaire, Pound, Queneau, and Roubaud as poets who do not even come close in this century to the creation of a text which has such a "multifarious semantic texture" (123).

26. Mallarmé points directly towards Pierre Reverdy, who was a proofreader and book designer. While Reverdy was influenced by cubism and rejected the notion of relationship between theme and layout (ideogrammatic arrangements as practiced by Apollinaire), he finds that a poem is less attractive when it is not in a set (visual) pattern on the page although the Reverdy arrangement is for effect only and not an attempt to suggest visual images within the text. Hence, his free verse texts are offset for purely visual effects usually achieved through juxtaposition, while his prose poems are based on a pattern of discontinuity which in turn suggests an esthetic structure of the whole beyond the distillation of its parts. Reverdy may continue the evolution of Mallarmé's hybrid "poème" in a metapoetic vein, but Francis Ponge turns it into a pre-iconic form in his term "proême," which fuses the traditional terms "prose" and "poème." In fact, it is increasingly difficult to name a single important twentieth-century French writer who is in some major way not influenced by Mallarmé: Apollinaire, the Surrealists, Sartre, Char, new novelists (especially Robbe-Grillet), even the Tel Quel and post-Tel Quel writers, including the deconstructionists. Ponge, however, stands out in such a list because of the four (to date) "discoveries" of his work; first by the Surrealists, then in turn by the Existentialists, the Tel Quel-istes, and the Deconstructionists. While each group has been drawn to a different aspect in Ponge's work, all four have unerringly (albeit not admittedly) been attracted to a Mallarmé esthetic and practice in the Pongian text. In a very real sense,

Mallarmé's *Un Coup de dés* serves as a "fil conducteur" for the literature of this century. It may also be true that because Mallarmé so towers over this century, it is through twentieth-century perspective and practices that his work is at last "readable."

27. See Malcolm Bowie's skillful analysis of "Prose (pour des Esseintes)" as a means of working out Mallarmé's difficult and broken poetic textures (22-89). See also Marshall C. Olds, *Desire Seeking Expression: Mallarmé's "Prose pour des Esseintes,"* French Forum Monographs 42 (Lexington, KY: French Forum, 1983).

28. Mallarmé did not even want the reader to decode *Un Coup de dés*. He did not want the "Préface" republished, he asked that all of his notes be destroyed, and he pointedly abandoned *Igitur*, just as he only published "Scène," the second of the four parts of "Hérodiade." Unfortunately, most critical readings of *Un Coup de dés* rely considerably on the very texts and notes that Mallarmé rejected as unfinished or as not meeting his own esthetic theories and standards. Sartre is critically astute to base his essay on the poem "Salut," which Mallarmé chose to place at the beginning of *Poésies*. "Salut" is all too frequently overlooked, yet it serves as an esthetic statement in verse form. Certainly, Mallarmé's posthumously published rough drafts and notes are helpful as supporting evidence; the problem lies in the amount of authority placed on them.

Chapter IV

1. "Avant-propos" by Etienne Souriau, in Ernest Fraenkel, *Les Dessins transconscients de Stéphane Mallarmé* 38. "Presentative art" is a form of abstract art, "une transposition édiétique," based on "le silhouettage et le mouvement de 'lecture,'" 40-41.

2. The individual characters are fixed, just as the dice and the constellation have fixed points, but the figure which emerges arises only from a chance encounter. Hence, the medium of print is not the message and does not contain a message. Comprehension is in the "blanc," what Mallarmé describes as "espace où se trouve l'armature intellectuelle" (P207): the "poëme dégage . . . du scribe" (304); the line is recast by Mallarmé when he responds to an inquiry about Poe: "L'armature intellectuelle du poëme se dissimule et tient—a lieu—dans l'espace qui isole les strophes et parmi le blanc du papier" (872).

3. For further discussion, see my "Mallarmé's *Livre*: The Graphomatics of the Text"; see also Jacques Scherer, *Le "Livre" de Mallarmé*; Jean-Pierre Richard, *L'Univers imaginaire de Mallarmé*; various commentaries by the "Mardistes" and Henri Mondor, as well as studies by Gardner Davies and Robert Greer Cohn.

4. For a detailed discussion, see Stéphane Mallarmé, *Pour un tombeau d'Anatole*, introd. by Jean-Pierre Richard (Paris: Seuil, 1961); see also Gardner Davies, *Les "Tombeaux" de Mallarmé* (Paris: Corti, 1950), and Robert Greer Cohn, *Mallarmé's Masterwork: New Findings*, 28-37.

5. "Préface" to *Igitur* by Mallarmé's son-in-law, Edmond Bonniot, *Oeuvres complètes*, 423-32. The Pléiade arrangement of Mallarmé's work unfortunately places Bonniot's commentary and the text of *Igitur* immediately before *Un Coup de dés*, an ordering which further forces critical and psychological links between the two texts. In the 1976 Gallimard Coll. Poésie edition, Bonnefoy cleverly places *Igitur* first and

Un Coup de dés last, separated by *Divagations*, an arrangement which indicates an evolution in Mallarmé's work from *Igitur* to *Un Coup de dés*.

6. For a judicious assessment and analysis of para-Christian elements in Mallarmé's work, see John Porter Houston, *Patterns of Thought in Rimbaud and Mallarmé*, French Forum Monographs 63 (Lexington, KY: French Forum, 1986), 108-30. Houston also points out how the notion of play (music, games, and theater) coincides with Mallarmé's notion of ritual and interest in a theology of ritual, and parallels a Hegelian salvational dialectic: "esthetic, Hegelian, and para-Christian concepts overlay one another in Mallarmé's thought" (129).

7. Again, one is reminded of Gide's Lafcadio, "un être en formation."

8. Redon's illustration clearly depicts a pair of dice; it is reproduced by Robert Greer Cohn in *Mallarmé's Masterwork: New Findings* 83.

9. For a detailed study of Mallarmé's lack of musical knowledge, see Henri Peyre's excellent study, "Poets against Music in the Age of Symbolism," in *Symbolism and Modern Literature: Studies in Honor of Wallace Fowlie*, ed. Marcel Tetel (Durham, NC: Duke UP, 1978), 179-92.

10. The only possible colors in the text are red or green: the "feux," which probably refers to the marine lights such as those used by lighthouses, and the "conflagration." On the other hand, these two words may be seen as emotional terms and their actual color is unimportant; both elements imply energy, just as music itself shows how energy behaves.

11. In *Les Mots anglais*, Mallarmé takes up how the form and meaning of a word are frequently interchangeable; see also his *Crise de vers*. However, René Ghil's invention of a philosophical system, his "verbal instrumentation," led to a break with Mallarmé in 1888. Mallarmé was not a Symbolist in the historically formal sense of the term: "J'abomine les écoles . . . et tout ce qui y ressemble" (869).

12. "Ses purs ongles très haut dédiant leur onyx" is, for example, structured around a black-white tension. He also describes writing as a black and white watercolor (98). It is more than possible that his interest in "une vision simultanée" refers not to double pages, but to a black-white interplay: "l'art se limite à l'infini" (580).

13. The word count of 700 is approximate; any tabulation depends on the inclusion or omission of articles and auxiliary verb forms, as well as on a decision to count a repeated word as one or two words, etc. The point is that there are approximately 700 words, a figure which is far less than the number of words per Mallarmé prose poem and not dramatically more than the typical Mallarmé sonnet, which runs about 100 words. *Un Coup de dés* is not even twice as long as his "Toast funèbre." However, the number of words is not important in and of itself; what is significant is reader recognition of just how very few words there are in such a long poem. In the Pléiade edition, *Poésies* occupies 49 pages and *Poèmes en prose* another 20; the 21 pages of *Un Coup de dés* equal paginally almost one third of Mallarmé's total "formal" poetic production.

14. For a graphic presentation of Mallarmé's text as an urban street plan, see Tibor Papp's "Déville," in Ronat ed., 8-9.

15. Bruno Montels, "Convoquer le peu," in Ronat ed., 12-13.

16. René Char, *Oeuvres complètes* (Paris: Gallimard, 1983) 711.

17. For Yves Bonnefoy, in "L'Acte et le lieu de la poésie," 211, "Le vrai lieu est donné par le hasard, mais au vrai lieu le hasard perdra son caractère d'énigme"; see also his "La Poétique de Mallarmé," the preface to *Stéphane Mallarmé: Igitur, Divagations, Un coup de dés*, Coll. Poésie (Paris: Gallimard, 1976), 7-40.

Chapter V

1. "M'introduire dans ton histoire" is Mallarmé's first unpunctuated text. In a letter to Gustave Kahn in 1886, he emphasizes his deletion of punctuation in the construct of the sonnet: "vous remarquerez l'absence de toute ponctuation, c'est à dessein" (Barbier-Millan ed. 321). Unfortunately, printing practice usually adds a final period.

2. See Sartre's reading of Mallarmé in his "Préface" to Mallarmé's *Poésies*: "Puisque l'homme ne peut créer, mais qu'il lui reste la ressource de détruire, puisqu'il s'affirme par l'acte même qui l'anéantit, le poème sera donc un travail de destruction" (10).

3. On this point, Mallarmé is not only a precursor to the Surrealist emphasis on creative activity and marriage between the dream/subconscience and real/conscious planes of existence, but also the forerunner of certain twentieth-century iconic poets, such as Denis Roche. Writing in *Eros énergumène* (Paris: Seuil, 1965) 14, Roche attempts to place Mallarmé on a shelf by declaring that the only modern interest in *Un Coup de dés* is in its reading. However, Roche's statement, "la poésie est inadmissible, d'ailleurs elle n'existe pas," is a translation of Mallarmé's esthetic investigation into Poetry. For Mallarmé, Poetry is all-inclusive, unlimited in agreements and disagreements, and it is demonstrated in its interactive components rather than by its generic relationships. Furthermore, poetry is not rational, derivative, nor descriptive; it is non-generic. Despite himself, Roche shares this esthetic view; his refusal to admit the existence of poetry may be a repudiation of Molière's bourgeois gentleman who discovers that he has been speaking prose all his life, but for Mallarmé, as well as for Ponge and the Surrealists after him and before Roche, there is no distinction between poetry and all other forms of spoken or written expression. Poetry is not a separate genre; all traces of expression are poetic. Hence, poetry as a separate subject or object does not exist, a view which Mallarmé initiates.

4. *Documents Stéphane Mallarmé*, ed. Carl Paul Barbier (Paris: Nizet, 1968) 1: 573.

5. At the risk of "reducing" Mallarmé's text on a storm at sea to a microscopic view which has him sailing a skiff down a stream full of water lilies, it must be remembered that Mallarmé often expanded a small personal object or scene into a vast panorama, as in "Toute âme résumée" and "Las d'amer repos." Second, the one Rimbaud text which we know Mallarmé read and admired as a masterpiece is "Le Bateau ivre," in which Rimbaud artistically creates the experience of the ocean through a "flashe." Mallarmé even quotes five stanzas of this text in his portrait of Rimbaud (512-19).

6. John Rewald, "Introduction" to *The Gardens at Giverny: A View of Monet's World*, by Stephen Shore (Millerton, NY: Aperture, 1983) 13 and 10. One of Mallarmé's *Vers de circonstance* is on Monet at Giverny (88).

7. In the Pléiade edition, the five double pages formed by the folded signatures are:

2v-10r	=	Pléiade 458 & 475
3v-9r	=	Pléiade 460 & 473
4v-8r	=	Pléiade 462 & 471
5v-7r	=	Pléiade 464 & 469
6v-6r	=	Pléiade 466 & 467

8. The doublets formed from signature sheet to signature sheet are:
11v-2r = Pléiade 476 & 459
10v-3r = Pléiade 474 & 461
9v-4r = Pléiade 472 & 463
8v-5r = Pléiade 470 & 465

9. The doublet 2v-10r corresponds to Pléiade pages 458 and 475.

10. Jacques Scherer, Le "Livre" de Mallarmé.

11. For the correlation of rectos and versos with the Pléiade edition, see ch. II, 180-81n7.

12. Page 1v does not exist, being printer space; the first verso to be read is 2v.

13. It may well be that one of the lessons learned from Mallarmé by Gide is the use of space—sense units of silence to evoke emotion and to provide the text with rhythmic organization. Gide incorporates into his prose spatial intervals which actually supply meaning; for example, the ending of Les Caves du Vatican is found only in a reading of the non-spoken. The prose of Fargue and Valéry also reveals the practice of the esthetic of silence as an organizing textual component.

14. In "Solitude," Mallarmé describes typography as artificial and admits a preference for the non-punctuated text (407).

15. Stéphane Mallarmé, Correspondance (1862-71), ed. Henri Mondor and Jean-Pierre Richard (Paris: Gallimard, 1959) 1: 103.

16. Jean-Pierre Richard, L'Univers imaginaire de Mallarmé 69.

17. Correspondance 1: 103-04, 137, and 155.

SELECTED BIBLIOGRAPHY

Barbier, Carl Paul. *Documents Stéphane Mallarmé.* Vol. 1. Paris: Nizet, 1968.
Barthes, Roland. *L'Empire des signes.* Geneva: Skira, 1970.
———. *Mythologies.* Paris: Seuil, 1957.
———. *Roland Barthes.* Paris: Seuil, 1975.
Blanchot, Maurice. *L'Espace littéraire.* Paris: Gallimard, 1955.
———. *Le Livre à venir.* Paris: Gallimard, 1959.
Bonnefoy, Yves. "L'Acte et le lieu de la poésie." In *Du mouvement et de l'immobilité de Douve.* Coll. Poésie. Paris: Gallimard, 1970, 185-214.
———. "La Poétique de Mallarmé." In *Stéphane Mallarmé: Igitur, Divagations, Un coup de dés.* Coll. Poésie. Paris: Gallimard, 1976, 7-40.
Bowie, Malcolm. *Mallarmé and the Art of Being Difficult.* Cambridge: Cambridge UP, 1978.
Char, René. *Oeuvres complètes.* Paris: Gallimard, 1983.
Chassé, Charles. *Les Clés de Mallarmé.* Aubier: Montaigne, 1954.
Chisholm, A.R. *Mallarmé's "Grand Oeuvre."* Manchester: Manchester UP, 1962.
Cohn, Robert Greer. *Mallarmé's Masterwork: New Findings.* The Hague: Mouton, 1966.
———. *Mallarmé's "Un Coup de Dés."* New Haven: Yale UP, 1949.
———. *L'Oeuvre de Mallarmé: Un Coup de Dés.* Paris: Librairie Les Lettres, 1951.
———. *Toward the Poems of Mallarmé.* Berkeley and Los Angeles: U of California P, 1965 and 1980.
Colloque Mallarmé en l'honneur de Austin Gill. Ed. Carl Paul Barbier. Paris: Nizet, 1975.
Damase, Jacques. *Révolution typographique.* Geneva: Galerie Motte, 1966.
Davies, Gardner. *Mallarmé et le drame solaire.* Paris: Corti, 1959.
———. *Les "Tombeaux" de Mallarmé.* Paris: Corti, 1950.
———. *Vers une explication rationnelle du "Coup de Dés."* Paris: Corti, 1953.
Derrida, Jacques. *La Dissémination.* Paris: Seuil, 1972.
Elsen, Albert. *Rodin's "Thinker" and the Dilemmas of Modern Public Sculpture.* New Haven: Yale UP, 1985.
Faye, Jean-Pierre. "L'Entre croisement." In Ronat edition, 14-16.

Fraenkel, Ernest. *Les Dessins trans-conscients de Stéphane Mallarmé.* Introd. Etienne Souriau. Paris: Nizet, 1960.
Franklin, Ursula. *An Anatomy of Poésis . . . The Prose Poems of Stéphane Mallarmé.* Chapel Hill: U of North Carolina P, 1976.
Goffin, Robert. *Mallarmé vivant.* Paris: Nizet, 1956.
Hanson, Anne Coffin. *Manet and the Modern Tradition.* New Haven: Yale UP, 1977.
Hinostroza, Rodolfo. "Le Dieu de la page blanche." In Ronat edition, 18-19.
Houston, John Porter. *Patterns of Thought in Rimbaud and Mallarmé.* French Forum Monographs 63. Lexington, KY: French Forum, 1986.
Huysmans, J.-K. *A rebours.* Paris: Fasquelle, 1955.
Kahn, Gustave. *Symbolistes et décadents.* Paris: Vanier, 1902.
Kravis, Judy. *The Prose of Mallarmé.* Cambridge: Cambridge UP, 1976.
Kristeva, Julia. *La Révolution du langage poétique.* Paris: Seuil, 1974.
La Charité, Virginia A. "Mallarmé and the Elasticity of the Text." *Sou'wester* 6 (1978), 1-12.
———. "Mallarmé: 'Je dis: une fleur!'" *Nineteenth-Century French Studies* 10 (1981), 96-106.
———. "Mallarmé's *Livre*: The Graphomatics of the Text." *Symposium* 34 (1980), 249-59.
———. "Mallarmé and the Plastic Circumstances of the Text." In *Pre-Text/Text/Context. Essays on Nineteenth-Century French Literature.* Ed. Robert L. Mitchell. Columbus: Ohio State UP, 1978, 173-83.
Lewis, Paula Gilbert. *The Aesthetics of Stéphane Mallarmé in Relation to His Public.* Cranbury, NJ: Fairleigh Dickinson P, 1976.
Mallarmé, Stéphane. *Correspondance.* Ed. Henri Mondor and Jean-Pierre Richard. Vol. 1. Paris: Gallimard, 1959. Vol. 2, 1965. Ed. Henri Mondor and Lloyd James Austin. Vol. 3, 1969. Vol. 5, 1973.
———. *Un Coup de Dés.* Trans. Daisy Aldan. Tiber Press, 1956.
———. *Un coup de Dés jamais n'abolira le Hasard.* Ed. Mitsou Ronat. Paris: Change/Errant/d'Atelier, 1980.
———. *Igitur, Divagations, Un coup de dés.* Ed. Yves Bonnefoy. Coll. Poésie. Paris: Gallimard, 1976.
———. *Oeuvres complètes.* Ed. Henri Mondor and G. Jean Aubry. Paris: Gallimard, 1945 and 1965.
———. *Oeuvres complètes.* Ed. Carl Paul Barbier and Charles Gordon Millan. Vol. 1. Paris: Flammarion, 1983.
———. *Pour un tombeau d'Anatole.* Introd. Jean-Pierre Richard. Paris: Seuil, 1961.
———. *Propos sur la poésie.* Monaco: Rocher, 1953.

Mauron, Charles. *Introduction à la psychanalyse de Mallarmé*. Neuchâtel: La Baconnière, 1968.
———. *Mallarmé l'obscur*. Paris: Denoël, 1941.
McLuhan, Marshall. "Joyce, Mallarmé and the Press." In *The Interior Landscape: The Literary Criticism of Marshall McLuhan, 1943-62*. Ed. Eugene McNamara. New York: McGraw-Hill, 1969, 5-21.
Mihram, Danielle. "The Abortive Didot-Vollard Edition of 'Un Coup de Dés.'" *French Studies* 33 (1979), 39-56.
Mitchell, W.J.T. "Spatial Form in Literature: Toward a General Theory." In *The Language of Images*. Ed. W.J.T. Mitchell. Chicago: U of Chicago P, 1980, 271-99.
Mondor, Henri. *Autres Précisions sur Mallarmé et inédits*. Paris: Gallimard, 1961.
———. *Mallarmé lycéen*. Paris: Gallimard, 1954.
———. *Mallarmé plus intime*. Paris: Gallimard, 1944.
———. *Vie de Mallarmé*. 2 vols. Paris: Gallimard, 1940-42.
Montels, Bruno. "Convoquer un peu." In Ronat edition, 12-13.
Mossop, Daniel J. *Pure Poetry. Studies in French Poetic Theory and Practice, 1746-1945*. Oxford: Clarendon, 1971.
Olds, Marshall. *Desire Seeking Expression: Mallarmé's "Prose pour des Esseintes."* French Forum Monographs 42. Lexington, KY: French Forum, 1983.
Papp, Tibor. "Déville." In Ronat edition, 8-9.
———. "'qui mentalement sépare.'" In Ronat edition, 24-27.
Peyre, Henri. "Poets Against Music in the Age of Symbolism." In *Symbolism and Modern Literature: Studies in Honor of Wallace Fowlie*. Ed. Marcel Tetel. Durham, NC: Duke UP, 1978, 179-92.
Poulet, Georges. *La Distance intérieure*. Paris: Plon, 1952.
Rewald, John. "Introduction" to *The Gardens at Giverny: A View of Monet's World*, by Stephen Shore. Millerton, NY: Aperture, 1983, 5-13.
Richard, Jean-Pierre. *L'Univers imaginaire de Mallarmé*. Paris: Seuil, 1961.
Richardson, John. *Manet*. Oxford: Phaidon, 1982.
Riffaterre, Michael. "On Deciphering Mallarmé." *Georgia Review* 29 (1975), 75-91.
Roche, Denis. *Eros énergumène*. Paris: Seuil, 1968.
Ronat, Mitsou. "Cette Architecture spontanée et magique." In Ronat edition, 1-7.
———. "Le 'Coup de Dés': Forme fixe?" *CAIEF* 32 (1980), 141-47.
Roubaud, Jacques. "n'abolira Lazare." In Ronat edition, 10-11.
———. *La Vieillesse d'Alexandre*. Paris: Maspéro, 1978.

Roulet, Claude. *Eléments de poétique mallarméenne d'après le poëme "Un coup de dés jamais n'abolira le hasard."* Neuchâtel: Griffon, 1947.

———. *Elucidation du poëme de Stéphane Mallarmé.* Neuchâtel: Ides et Calendes, 1943.

Sartre, Jean-Paul. *Mallarmé: La Lucidité et sa face d'ombre.* Ed. Arlette Elkaïm-Sartre. Paris: Gallimard, 1986.

———. "Préface." *Mallarmé: Poèmes.* Coll. Poésie. Paris: Gallimard, 1967, 5-15.

———. "Qu'est-ce que la littérature?" In *Situations.* Vol. 2. Paris: Gallimard, 1948.

Scherer, Jacques. *Le "Livre" de Mallarmé.* Paris: Gallimard, 1957.

Soula, Camille. *La Poésie et la pensée de Stéphane Mallarmé.* Paris: Champion, 1931.

Taylor, Joshua C. "Two Visual Excursions." In *The Language of Images.* Ed. W.J.T. Mitchell. Chicago: U of Chicago P, 1980, 25-36.

Valéry, Paul. *Ecrits divers sur Stéphane Mallarmé.* Paris: NRF, 1950.

———. *Variété.* Vol. 2. Paris: Gallimard, 1929, 161-202.

Wyzewa, Teodor de. *Mallarmé.* Paris: La Vogue, 1886.